OMINOUS WELCOME

A streak of lightning lit up the room and outlined a dark, hulking figure filling the doorway. I drew a breath. He lumbered into the room, and the floor shook with his heavy steps. I smelled the dampness that enveloped him, saw the droplets of rain glistening on his black cape.

"Who are you?" he bellowed, moving closer to me.

My cheeks began to burn beneath his bold stare. His eyes, black and as cold as marble, surveyed me. His chiseled features were sharpened more so in the glow of the fire, and the power in his expression nearly left me breathless.

"I could ask you the same thing, sir," I said with a rush of bravado that surprised me. "I am a friend of the Blackwells."

His eyes widened and his features twisted into a maddening leer. "Well, if you're a guest of the Blackwells, then you're a guest of mine as well, I'm afraid."

SUZANNE HOOS

WHISPERS IN THE NIGHT

For Helen, Donna, Marie, Johnnie, and Kaye, who knew I could. . .

For my husband, Gary, who said I could. .

Book Margins, Inc.

A BMI Edition

Published by special arrangement with Dorchester Publishing Co., Inc.

Printed in the United States of America.

WHISPERS IN THE NIGHT

Chapter One

"You must come to Raven Manor." The hurried scratchings blurred before my eyes. These were desperate words. Compelling, ominous words that made me gasp inwardly as I read them over and over.

The message had arrived just days ago. There was no signature, and I did not recognize the handwriting. I could only assume that the frantic plea for help was from Margaret Tuttle, the housekeeper at Raven Manor.

For as long as I had known her, she had never been the nervous sort. Steady and sure was Margaret. That was why this message intrigued me so. Worried me. I was positive that it had something to do with the death of my dear friend, Sorcha Blackwell.

That tragic news had arrived in another letter from Margaret. One that came a month too late for me to attend Sorcha's funeral. Feeling helpless and heartbroken, I could do nothing but mourn her untimely passing alone and in my own way. But Margaret's claim that Sorcha had taken her own life had angered more than saddened me.

That just couldn't be, I told myself many times. There was no one more in love with life than Sorcha. No one more spirited or unpredictable. But she was not so impulsive as to end her life so violently. No. I could not accept it. I would never believe she could have done such a thing.

Clearly disturbed about Sorcha's supposed suicide, I had thought many times about leaving New York City and returning upstate to Raven Manor. I knew that Margaret would be pleased to see me. I was sure that we could comfort each other. Still, I had wondered if she would be residing at the Blackwell house. After all, Sorcha's parents had died in a carriage accident last April. With Sorcha gone, too, I had assumed Margaret would seek employment elsewhere.

That was why I was completely taken aback upon receiving Margaret's latest message. She had remained at Raven Manor and she was desperate for my help.

When I had spoken to Mrs. Hemsley, the head mistress at the Brynwood Academy in the city, where I was completing my studies to be a teacher, she had frowned upon my leaving school to embark on this quest.

"Are you sure this is what you want to do, Britanny?" she had asked, peering at me from above the rimless spectacles sitting on the edge of her thin nose.

Her resolute tone had not dissuaded me. "Mrs. Hemsley, please understand. Sorcha Blackwell and I were friends since childhood. We spent wonderful summers together at Raven Manor. She was like a sister to me. We were so close that at times we knew what the other was thinking." A veil of skepticism had clouded her face. Nevertheless, I had continued, "Now, for whatever reason, Margaret, the Blackwells' housekeeper, has asked for my help."

"And you believe that her request involves this friend?"

I had nodded. "It's more than a request. Margaret's letter sounds so urgent. This is something I must do." I had taken a deep breath and exhaled. "Even if it means forgoing my education."

Small, ice-blue eyes had studied me, making me uneasy. Maybe guilty was a better word. A questioning sigh had followed. I knew that she wasn't at all pleased with my decision.

"You're a bright, young woman, Britanny.

9

You have a rare combination of intelligence and common sense. The teaching profession would be at a loss without someone like you. Perhaps this housekeeper is overreacting." Her stone face had softened. "Please reconsider."

But I had not relented. My determination must have been evident in my expression, my posture, for Mrs. Hemsley had breathed a surrendering sigh.

"How long would you be gone, Britanny?"

"A few weeks. A month at the most."

She had nodded. "You do understand that you will be behind in your studies. When you return, you will have to work very hard if you still wish to graduate with your class."

"Yes, Mrs. Hemsley. Thank you." Though I had remained calm, my heart had leaped in my chest. She had understood and I was grateful.

Now, as the carriage bumped over the rocky terrain, my mind whirled with anticipation. The blood coursed through my veins like ice-cold needles. I questioned my motives. My brain was boggled with so many theories. Right or wrong, though, I had chosen this path. Something was wrong at Raven Manor, and I had to find out what it was.

I peered out the window. Twilight was embracing the early evening and the dim light within the carriage was quickly fading. I folded the letter into a tight rectangle. The words felt as though they were burning my fingers as I stuffed the paper into my draw-string purse.

Wide-trunked trees, their bare branches scratching eerily against the gig, seemed to be trying to hold me back, warning me to stay away. A cold wind blew and I heard a faint boom of thunder in the distance. A storm was coming, leaving me with a feeling of dread. Never had I felt so alone.

I tried to conjure up other thoughts, hoping that my overactive imagination would settle down with pleasant reveries. And as I did, my childhood came to mind.

My parents were hard-working people, proprietors of a fruit-and-vegetable stand in New York City that had become their whole life. Through no fault of their own other than having the will to survive, the attention they gave me was minimal. Often, I would entertain myself with imaginary friends and inventive games. I learned to enjoy being in my own company, preferring to be alone than with children my own age. When I began my schooling, I found socializing with the rest of my classmates somewhat of a bothersome thing, and I looked forward to the end of the day when I could be by myself with my thoughts and dreams.

When my mother died, though, my father was left to raise a nine-year-old daughter he had hardly known. Yet, if the truth be told, I would have been able to take care of myself.

11

But because of my father's guilt, he had other plans. Consequently, I was sent upstate to live with his sister, my Aunt Elizabeth, who was kind and caring. As she lavished her attentions on me, I came to realize that being alone was not the best thing for a child. For anyone. Though I had my independent nature to thank my parents for, my way of thinking was slowly changing, as was the quality of my life. But the real change came that fateful day when I first met Sorcha Blackwell.

Acres and acres of woods separated Raven Manor from my aunt's house. I remembered it was dusk and I was busying myself with catching fireflies and putting them into an empty glass flask. I was not being cruel, just satisfying a child's natural curiosity about these odd, mystifying insects.

"They should be free."

The soft, yet determined voice had interrupted my scientific investigation and I turned, not expecting another little girl about the same age as I, to be reprimanding me. She was a wisp of a thing, her long black hair cascading in fluid curls that reached her waist. My own red-golden hair, which I hated at the time, was always severely pulled back from my face. Aunt Elizabeth knew how I loved to play outdoors, and so I would not suffer the painful consequences of unknotting my thick tresses later, she devised her own way of styling my hair.

"I was going to free them," I said, mesmerized by the girl's silver-blue eyes and heart-
shaped face. "I wanted to study them first."

She tilted her head. "Why?"

"I want to know what makes them light up
the way they do." I peered into the container,
then offered her a look. She stepped back as if
frightened.

"No. You're killing them. Can't you see
they're dying?" An odd mix of terror and compassion filled her pale face.

I wanted to scoff at her remark, but when I
took another look at my captives, I realized
she was right. The tiny lights at the ends of
their bodies were faltering, flickering in a dance
of impending doom.

"Please. Let them go," she begged.

Pity rushing over me, I did as she said. I
uncapped the lid, shook the flask, and we both
watched as the fireflies happily escaped their
glass prison.

"Thank you," she said quietly and her ra-
diant smile lit up the twilight that was slowly
descending around us.

I smiled to myself recalling that time. It was
interesting to me now that our initial conversation had dealt with death. She seemed so
afraid of it then, so unwilling to allow the life
of the tiniest of creatures to be snuffed out because of a child's whim.

That was why, in my heart of hearts, I truly
believed that Sorcha Blackwell could not have

died at her own hands. She had an uncommon respect for life even as a child, and as we grew into womanhood that ideal never wavered. So much so that news of death, even a stranger's, brought tears to her eyes and left her heartbroken for many days.

No. Something else must have happened. Something that until Margaret's letter, I had kept hidden in the back of my mind. I dared not even think about what had been gnawing at my common sense since I had heard of Sorcha's death. But now, slowly approaching Raven Manor, the thought was overpowering and I couldn't stop its evil from seeping into my mind. For somehow I knew that Sorcha Blackwell had been murdered.

"Whooaa..." The deep voice of the driver wavered above the rumble of thunder. The carriage stopped abruptly. The horses' restless whinnies jarred me out of my frightening pensiveness. I bolted to the edge of the hard leather seat and pressed my nose against the window. A jagged bolt of lightning cut the sky, illuminating Raven Manor. Thunder again boomed over the carriage, bringing with it torrents of rain that slashed against the windows like lances. Nervously, I twisted my gloved fingers.

Raven Manor was the Blackwells' summer home. I had been here many times before as a little girl and guest of the family. No, more than a guest. I had always been treated like another daughter, fussed over in a way my own parents could never find the time to do. I had many wonderful memories of this place. I only wished now that I had returned under happier circumstances.

The carriage door opened suddenly, making me jump.

"Raven Manor, miss." The driver, a short, rounded man tipped his hat, then offered his hand. The rain had soaked his coat and face, making him look forlorn.

As I stepped into the biting rain, the wind rudely billowed my navy skirt and almost blew the wine-colored cloak off my shoulders. I managed to cover my head with the ample hood, holding it securely under my chin with my free hand. Was it the strong gusts that made me shiver, I wondered, or was it sheer dread that caused my heart to pound?

Raven Manor, as I remembered, was a wonderfully romantic place. Its white fluted columns and immense picture windows added to that sense of childhood fantasies. But, sadly, I was no longer a child and in the rain-soaked darkness, Raven Manor was now an ominous, almost foreboding thing. Its splendor quickly ebbed before me now, its life force already a fleeting memory.

I stumbled up the stairs, my soft-soled shoes squishing on the planks. Out of the driving rain now, my heart quieted. I stopped for a moment. The wide veranda, spanning the full length of the mansion, caused a rush of recollections. With a heavy heart, I welcomed them, hoping they would change the discouraged way I felt at the moment.

In the oppressive heat of the summer, Sorcha and I had played and dreamed here. The shade from the oak trees had protected us and the frosty lemonade that Sorcha's mother made had quenched our parched palates. I could almost taste the sweet tartness sliding down my throat like liquid gold. I smiled, content in my reminiscing.

Another crack of thunder jolted me back into the present. The driver had retrieved my trunk. The slick handles slipped from his grasp and it fell onto the porch with a resounding thud. I fumbled with the drawstrings of my purse.

After my father's death, I had sold the business in the city, making a sizable amount of money from the sale. Even though most of it had been deposited in the bank for my education, I was not without resources. I was glad now that I had had the foresight to put aside some funds for my personal use.

He accepted payment readily and appreciatively, and I watched as he and the carriage soon disappeared into a slash of darkness.

A nervous expectation overcame me. I knocked several times on the heavy oak door only to have my rapping obliterated by an explosion of thunder. Poised to knock a second time, my hand now fell into thin air as the door opened wide. A lantern was thrust close to my face.

"Who's there?" A wary voice which I immediately recognized warmed me.

"It's me, Margaret. Britanny. Britanny St. James." The wavering yellow light blurred my vision and I was unable to see her face.

There was a pause, a guarded one at first.

"My stars! Britanny! Is it really you?"

I was amused at the way her elation chipped through her skepticism. "Yes, Margaret, it's really me," I confirmed.

Strong arms pulled me into the shadowy foyer and crushed me against the softness of a familiar bosom. "Oh, Britanny, how wonderful to see you again!"

"Margaret," I heard myself whisper. The sound of her name was a comfort to me and I found myself saying it several more times. My first impulse was to remain wrapped tightly in her arms but my sodden state made me wrestle away from her. "Oh, Margaret, I'm getting you all wet."

She laughed and shook her head, holding onto my hand with her own plump one. With the other, she raised the lantern. "Look at you. So grown up. And so beautiful, too."

I smiled, studying her in the flickering light. It had been two years since I had seen her. Quite amazingly, she looked the same except for some creases around her pale blue eyes and thin mouth. Her hair, streaked with more silver than I could recall, was piled neatly on top of her head and fashioned into a small bun. The seams of her severe gray dress bulged slightly.

"How long has it been, my sweet thing?"

"Too long, I'm afraid," I said. "Much too long."

She made a clicking noise with her tongue. "My, my. Here I am going on and on, and you're standing there soaked to the skin. Let me have your cloak." She whisked the drenched material off my shoulders and draped it over her arm. I also handed her my gloves and purse. "There's a fire in the hearth in the parlor. Go. Warm yourself by it. I'll make tea and then we can talk." She was breathless, almost anxious, and sincerely happy to see me. Yet there was something odd about this brief reunion. She never once alluded to the letter she had sent me or to her desperate need for help. I wanted to bring up the subject but she didn't give me a chance. She shooed me toward the parlor and disappeared into the shadows. With a heavy sigh, I decided that she would discuss the matter once we settled down to talk.

I glanced curiously around the foyer. Since my visit two years ago, I hadn't seen Raven Manor, and yet, it almost seemed as if I had been hurled back into my past. Candles, burning in sconces around the wall, vaguely illuminated the pink-tinted marble floor, the gold brocade wall covering, and the ornate scrolls along the ceiling. Everything was the same. The recognition felt comforting and I was glad I had come.

I felt a draft of cold air flow over me as I crossed the threshold into the parlor. A glowing fire burned intensely in the black marble fireplace. I closed the doors behind me. A blast of warmth filled the room and the light softened the austere furnishings. The velvet sofas, walnut bookcases, and the polished spinet that Sorcha and I used to play were wonderfully familiar. There was a sense of classic splendor that made me feel at home.

I neared the fireplace, intent on drying my hair and clothing. Instead, my gaze rose over the mantel where a large portrait caught my attention. I had never seen it before. It was a painting of Sorcha. Possibly a very recent one for she looked older than I remembered. She sat, her hands crossed in the lap of a red velvet dress. Her silver-blue eyes, darker than usual, were almost piercing. Her heart-shaped face was soft and alluring. Captured in the vibrant oils, she looked so alive, so beautiful that tears sprang to my eyes. I blinked them away. It was still so difficult to accept the fact that she was gone.

Lightning flashed against the window, its brightness streaking across the portrait. A clap of thunder shook the room and the pelting rain persisted unmercifully.

The disquieting noise drew me back to Sorcha's picture. My heart jumped and for a breath of a moment, I questioned my sanity. The light from the fire cast an eerie glow on her face, twisting it into a distorted expression. Her stare, a suddenly vivid, living thing, seem to beckon to me. Above the crackling fire and the sounds of the storm outside, I thought I heard her desperate whispers. "Beware, Britanny... beware..."

I closed my eyes tightly and shuddered. I was sorely tempted to run from the house, not giving a second thought to why I had come in the first place. But I didn't run. I remained steadfast, knowing in my heart that I was needed here. When I opened my eyes, Sorcha's face had returned to the sweet, innocent look I had first seen.

Stop it, Britanny, I scolded myself. *Your imagination is playing tricks on you.*

But it wasn't my imagination that caused the doors of the parlor to burst open with a resounding crash. I whirled around, my heart leaping to my throat.

Another streak of lightning lit up the room and outlined a dark, hulking figure filling the doorway. His face was shadowed, vaguely sinister. I drew a breath. He lumbered into the room, and the floor shook with his heavy steps. I smelled the dampness that enveloped him, saw the droplets of rain glistening on his black cape.

"Who are you?" he bellowed, moving closer to me.

My cheeks began to burn beneath his bold stare. His eyes, black and as cold as marble, surveyed me and proceeded to travel slowly from my tangled mass of hair down to my clothes which clung damply to my body and back up again to my face. A chill ran up my spine. His hair, dark, wet, and unruly, spilled over his forehead. He pushed it back impatiently. His chiseled features were sharpened more so in the glow of the fire, and the power in his expression nearly left me breathless.

"Who are you?" he asked again brusquely.

"I could ask you the same question, sir," I said with a rush of bravado that surprised me. "I am a friend of the Blackwells."

His eyes widened and his features twisted into a maddening leer. Still, he did not move away from me, and I began to shake. No one had ever looked at me quite like this.

"Well, if you're a guest of the Blackwells, then you're a guest of mine as well, I'm afraid." His tone was insolent and the edges of his mouth curved in a crooked sneer.

I wasn't sure how to react to his presumptuous words. Who was he? His hard, unyielding face now evoked my curiosity rather than any uneasiness. Who was this stranger in Sorcha's home?

For a brief instant my glance diverted to the portrait as if to seek an answer to my gnawing question. When I looked back at him, his eyes were shining, hardened with anxiety. The moment's pause seemed like a lifetime.

"You have an interest in that picture, I see," he said, lifting his hand to rake through his thick hair.

"She's very beautiful," I answered. My mouth became dry, my tongue thick.

Finally, his eyes moved from me and he looked up at the painting. "Yes. Sorcha was very beautiful."

My heart jumped. He knew her name!

A sadness pervaded the room. His sadness. Our sadness, I concluded. It was a strange feeling, almost ethereal, as if we were connected in some way.

But when he faced me again, his eyes were defiant. "My name is Colin Rutledge," he said, glaring down at me. "Sorcha was my wife."

Chapter Two

There was a chill in the air but it was not the cause of my shivering.

"Your wife?" I burst out, then lowered my gaze so as not to give away my astonishment.

The room seemed to quiver with his deep sigh. "Yes. My wife," he reaffirmed almost with too strong a conviction. "She died a month ago."

Sorcha married? My mind reeled with the staggering news. I was grateful for the shadows in the room and that his attention was still drawn to the portrait. I was sure that my expression more than revealed my feelings.

"I must tell you, Mr. Rutledge, that Sorcha was my friend. My very dearest friend. My name is Britanny St. James." When I finally looked up, his dark eyes held mine fast, and I was startled by their intensity.

"Britanny St. James." My name flowed with the richness of his voice. He looked thoughtful, almost beguiling. "Yes. Sorcha spoke of you often."

In that moment, not longer than a breath, I saw such agony in his bold face that my heart ached. This man, this stranger, touched me deeply. His expression also took me on a journey into my own past.

On my eighteenth birthday I had waved my last good-bye to Sorcha from the front doorway of my Aunt Elizabeth's house. That day I couldn't stop the huge tears that assaulted my cheeks, yet at the same time I was terribly angry with her.

For, as free-spirited and rebellious as she was, she became strangely submissive when her parents had announced their plans to send her to a finishing school in Switzerland.

"They want the best for me, Britanny," she had said quietly when she saw my expression of disbelief. "They love me."

"But I love you, too, Sorcha!" I cried, my tears staining the white tulle of my party dress. "I'll miss you terribly!"

"It will be all right. You'll see. In a few years I'll be back here with you."

"A few years!" I sobbed. "Oh, Sorcha! It isn't fair. It isn't right that they're taking you away from me!"

She had tried to comfort me with an embrace, and I had held her close, afraid to let go. Afraid that if I did, I would die.

That day, two years ago, was the last time I saw her.

We wrote to each other often. Though her letters never seemed to satisfy the emptiness in my heart, it was a comfort, nevertheless, to have a part of her with me. The letters were always filled with humorous tales about Madame Dupree's School for Young Women and wonderful, mysterious stories depicting her travels through Europe and the Orient. Still, there was a sense of despondency clouding her letters. A melancholia that covered her true feelings.

I could not deny how quickly the year had passed. Though I was involved with my own education back in the city, we still found the time to communicate. Soon, to my joy, her letters were being sent from Raven Manor. Sorcha had come home! And though I wrote to her many times during the next year, telling her I needed to see her, she never responded to my request.

Then a strange thing had happened. Sorcha stopped writing, and any letters that I had sent to her came back unopened. The day before I had received the news of her death was the day I had planned to make an unannounced visit at Raven Manor. I was more than just curious as to what was going on with her. I was deeply worried.

But Margaret's letter came the next afternoon with the unbelievable news that Sorcha had died by hurling herself from the great cliffs that towered over the Saint Lawrence River.

I shivered now, not from fear but from despair. Margaret's heartsick words burned in my memory. Even now, I felt crushed and broken as if mourning my own death, for, indeed, the day that Sorcha died, so did I.

I had sensed that something was wrong, yet never could I have imagined something so tragic. No. More than just tragic. Much more. For I still believed that Sorcha could not have taken her own life. This was a heinous crime, one of diabolical evil. This was murder.

"May I ask, Miss St. James, your reasons for coming to Raven Manor?" Colin Rutledge's gruff, impatient tone shook me out of my painful insights. The coldness in his eyes had melted slightly as they reflected the flames of the fire.

"I have come to pay my condolences, Mr. Rutledge. As I said, Sorcha and I were very close. I was always treated like a daughter by the Blackwells."

A look of contempt suddenly spread across his face like a menacing shadow. It made me wonder. Had he not been treated as a son?

I lowered my gaze. "My only regret is that I did not come sooner." The words lodged in my throat, suffocating me. *If only I had come sooner. If only...*

"If only you had," he said, repeating my thoughts. But the words were not filled with regret. These were taunting, insulting words, ones that made me glare back at him. The room had suddenly turned cold. What was he implying? Hadn't I suffered enough at the loss of my dearest friend? Was he in a cavalier way blaming me for Sorcha's death?

"Mr. Rutledge, your insinuations are most insulting. I'll not stand here and be treated in this manner." My independent nature was getting the better of me. Still, I could not help myself.

The fire spat. Logs slipped in the grate as they burned through. I watched with trepidation as he removed his cape with an exaggerated sweep of his strong-looking hands and tossed it carelessly on the tufted velvet sofa. He drew his lips into a tight, mocking smile. His eyes became a brilliant black. "Oh, but you will stand there, won't you? And you'll stay for as long as it takes to mourn and grieve for your poor dear Sorcha. And you'll cry real tears and say sweet things about her."

My anger was aroused. How horrid of him to assume anything about my feelings. What kind of person was he? How could kind, gentle Sorcha have been attracted to such an insolent man?

He moved toward me now, towering over me

like some predatory creature, poised to pounce and kill. I remained steadfast, my heart pounding in my chest, my breath coming in short spurts.

"And once your conscience is satisfied and your guilt has vanished, perhaps then you'll be on your way. Am I not correct, Miss St. James?"

Impulsively, I raised my hand, eager to slap the impertinent grin from his face. His reaction was swifter, though, as he grabbed my arm and held it tightly. He pulled me toward him, so close that I could feel the heat from his body. An amber light radiated from the dark depths of his eyes. I shuddered as my knees weakened with an unexpected tremor.

"How dare you speak to me like this!" I said, furious because he had forced me to behave in such an uncivil fashion.

A crooked, almost evil smile crossed his lips. He was goading me, delighting in my unladylike behavior. I freed myself from his grasp. My wrist throbbed, yet I did not wince or cry out. I would not give him the satisfaction.

A sudden movement by the doorway drew my attention away from this obdurate man. It was Margaret. Though she was shrouded in the shadows of the room, I could see that her face was twisted in surprise. Her wide eyes reflected fear.

"Mr. Rutledge." She curtsied and the tea cups on the tray she carried clinked. "You're home, sir. You were not expected until tomorrow."

He turned his body ever so slightly,, but his powerful gaze on me did not falter. "I finished my business early, Margaret. I'm sorry if I caused you any trouble."

"No. No trouble, sir." Her sturdy face brightened with a red glow of embarrassment as she set the silver tray down on a table by the hearth. She came behind me, pressing her hand lightly against my back. I had an odd feeling I was being used as some sort of shield. "Mr. Rutledge, may I present Miss St.—"

"I've already had the pleasure," he said, his lips curled with a cruel confidence. "I would prefer, though, that next time we're about to have company that I be warned."

"Margaret should not be blamed, Mr. Rutledge," I said, my voice brimming with disdain at his accusation. "My visit was quite unexpected." I stared at him with deadly concentration. "And if I am not welcome here, I will certainly leave come morning."

In the firelight I thought I saw his face fall in disappointment. He turned away, then, as if to hide his expression from me. He reached for the brass poker that leaned against the hearth and began to stoke the fire. "Miss St. James is welcomed to stay at Raven Manor for as long as she wishes, Margaret. See to it that a room is prepared and that she gets a suitable meal tonight. She is my guest and she will be treated as such."

His sudden change of personality bewildered me—harsh and unsparing one moment, the next obliging and generous. He was truly an enigma, a man filled with dark secrets. Troubled in a way that Sorcha would have found vulnerable, not unlike a stray kitten or homeless waif. But I found the puzzling Mr. Rutledge to be a dangerous man, cunning and cautious. My instincts could have been misleading, though. Perhaps he was only being overprotective where his wife was concerned. For Sorcha's sake I wished it to be so. But a nagging feeling gnawed at me as I watched him warm himself by the fire. He was hunched over, his arms extended, his hands curved, catching the heat of the flames. My eyes were drawn to those large hands, ones that might not give a second thought to snapping a delicate white neck. Fingers powerful enough to squeeze the breath from a trusting young woman.

Waves of renewed fear rippled through me, and I swallowed nervously. They warned me, begged me to leave Raven Manor, but I chose to ignore their portentous advice. My burning interest in Sorcha's death was slowly becoming an obsession. Determined now, I would not rest until I discovered the truth.

"I've already prepared a light repast for Miss St. James before she retires," Margaret said.

"Perhaps you'd like to join her, sir. You must be hungry after your journey, too."

He raised a hand in mild protest. "No, Margaret. I would prefer to be left alone for the rest of the evening."

"There are tea and biscuits, sir, should you be wanting them," she said, referring to the refreshments that she had originally prepared for us.

"Thank you, Margaret." His brooding gaze fell on me. "That will be all."

She curtsied again, nudged me from the room, and closed the doors. Admonition echoed through the foyer as I followed Margaret into the shadows.

The glow from a dozen or so carefully placed candles brought a friendly warmth to the dining room, so unlike the room where I had just been. I breathed in their scent—jasmine—and commented on their loveliness.

"There's a little shop in town that makes them," Margaret said. "I'll take you there." She pointed to the high-backed chair at the head of the mahogany table that filled the center of the room. The massive crystal chandelier above also burned brightly with the same sweet-smelling candles. My skirt swished as I passed the matching sideboard that stood regally against the pretty flower-papered wall and took my seat.

The table was already set with fine china

that was patterned with small honeysuckle buds. Silver utensils rested beside the plate. A crystal goblet held cold, fresh water. Suddenly realizing how thirsty I was, I reached for the delicate stem of the glass. The water soothed my dry lips and parched throat. It was so delicious that I found it difficult not to gulp it down eagerly.

Margaret excused herself, leaving me alone with memories that closed around me and filled me with a longing for bygone days. Thoughtfully, I glided my hand over the shiny surface of the table and smiled, realizing that Margaret had directed me to the same seat that I had always occupied when I dined with the Blackwells. Margaret's sumptuous meals were one of the highlights of the evening, but what I remembered most was the laughter around the table. Sorcha's father had kept us entertained by telling us silly riddles and making funny faces that would tickle our fancies for hours. Even now, I could envision Sorcha sitting across from me, her silver-blue eyes moist with tears of laughter. Dierdre Blackwell would often pretend to scold her husband for his relentless whimsy and Sorcha, the tears spilling onto her porcelain cheeks, would plead for him to continue.

I sighed feebly, my heart sinking into the dark pit of my stomach. What had happened to make everything change so quickly? Why did I now feel so threatened by the strangeness that surrounded me?

"Soup, miss?"

The voice, not louder than a whisper, startled me. I turned my head aware now of a wisp of a girl, no older than my twenty years, standing beside me. She was new to Raven Manor. I had never seen her before. Not a beauty, in my opinion, but exotic-looking with bronze skin that gleamed golden in the candlelight. Her hair, a rich sable, was gathered loosely at her nape. The thick, unruly tresses barely brushed her slender waist. But it was her eyes, as blue and clear as a June sky, that mesmerized me. I was aware, also, of how unusual they were on one whose skin was the color of warm honey.

Gingerly, she struggled with a soup tureen that was almost as big as she was.

"Here," I began, and reached for the large crock. "Let me help you."

She said nothing, yet it was clear by her anxious face that I had treaded where I didn't belong by offering my assistance. I had hoped to assure her with my own amiable expression, but she drew back from me, mutely insistent on placing the vessel on the table herself. As if compelled by a nervous habit, she stroked her hands on the bleached muslin apron that covered the plain brown shift she wore.

"Evangeline! For goodness sake's, child. Haven't you served Miss St. James yet?" Margaret had bolted through the door leading from the kitchen in her usual commanding fashion.

"No, ma'am. I was just about to." Evangeline's voice wavered and her hand shook as she lifted the lid from the tureen.

The hearty aroma of beef broth charged the room.

"Mmmm. It smells delicious," I said. I had not eaten since that morning, and I realized I was ravenous.

My soup dish in her hand, Evangeline carefully filled the bowl with the broth. She set it in front of me and then disappeared into the kitchen.

Margaret shook her head disapprovingly. One of her gray curls had loosened from her upsweep and dangled tiredly over her forehead. She brushed it back impatiently. "You'll have to forgive the girl, Britanny. Evangeline has only been here a few months and has so much to learn about being a competent domestic." She placed a small wicker serving basket to my left and peeled back the four corners of the deep pink linen napkin that lined it. The glorious smell of freshly baked bread made me sigh with a sense longing.

"I'm sure the poor girl is just a bit nervous at my presence here." Eagerly, I reached for a generous portion of the bread. It was still warm. "Margaret, please join me," I said, not wanting her to leave. "We have so much to talk about."

I did not have to implore her a second time. Willingly, she sat to my left.

"So many things have changed," I said, my voice lowered with regret.

Margaret's eyebrows raised. "You mean Mr. Rutledge, don't you?" She whispered his name as if it was something reverent—or evil? I couldn't tell which.

"Were Sorcha and he really husband and wife?"

She nodded solemnly and leaned in closer. "Yes, Britanny, as shocking as it must have seemed to you, Sorcha and Mr. Rutledge were very much married."

"Why didn't you tell me?"

"It was not my place to do so," she answered quietly.

I had the uneasy feeling there was something more she wanted to say, but the words never came. Instead, Margaret talked generally about her beloved Sorcha. While she reminisced, I was aware of the great suffering she had endured these past few weeks.

As I sipped at my broth, leaving the tender beef and thickly cut vegetables until last, I also took particular notice of the lilting way she spoke about Colin Rutledge.

Frustration seized me. I needed to know more about this marriage so that I could understand what was going on at Raven Manor.

For whatever the reason, I somehow knew that it was connected to Sorcha's death.

"How long were they married, Margaret?" I asked.

A blank expression clouded her eyes. "I'm not sure, Britanny. Sorcha was very close-mouthed about that."

"But who is he? Where did he come from?" I envisioned his dark eyes bearing down at me, cutting through my soul. I shivered.

"I don't know. I only know that Colin Rutledge made my Sorcha very happy." She looked away from me. "That's all I cared about."

"But, Margaret—" I began.

She put a plump finger against her lips. I fell silent and then she spoke.

"When the Blackwells, God rest their souls, died in that carriage accident last April, Sorcha was devastated. It was Colin who stayed by her and helped her through that awful tragedy."

A knot tightened inside my stomach. "That's all well and good, and I'm glad she had someone, but why didn't she turn to me, too? I would have been there for her." Remorse ebbed and flowed within me. "Why didn't she write me of her parents' death? Her marriage? Every letter I wrote to her came back unopened." Tears welled up in my eyes and I blinked them back furiously.

Margaret leaned back against the chair. Her

shoulders drooped, her eyes became empty. "There were too many other circumstances, Britanny. Sorcha did not feel comfortable contacting you."

My heart dropped like a stone. "How can that be? We were friends."

She patted my hand apologetically. "I know, dear, but sometimes life forces us to act in certain ways that are so unlike us."

Her words puzzled me. "Are you talking about Sorcha's death?" I felt the anger rising in my throat.

She bowed her head as if in prayer. "Maybe I am."

The disconcerting pause between us was broken when tenacity gripped me and I asked an even more disconcerting question.

"Margaret, do you really believe that Sorcha took her own life?"

She lifted her face veiled in confusion. "The coroner confirmed that, Britanny. What else am I to believe?" Her eyes began to dim with a faraway look. "And there was no one more ravaged with grief than Mr. Rutledge. Poor dear. He's at such loose ends with himself. It's what makes him act so erratic now and again."

I wanted to grab Margaret by the shoulders and shake her. It was clear to me that I was getting nowhere with her. All she had proved to be was Colin Rutledge's staunchest supporter.

Certainly not without qualms did I pose my next question.

"Was Colin Rutledge aware that Sorcha was a very wealthy young woman?" My eyes narrowed. "Indeed, he surely inherited all that belonged to her."

Her face came to life then. Her forehead furrowed, and the corners of her mouth were rigid. "What are you implying, Britanny?"

I drew back from her stony expression. "Nothing. I meant nothing by it. I was just thinking out loud."

My feeble excuse seemed to satisfy her, but what surprised me was the look of doubt glazing her eyes. I had planted a seed. I had yet to find out, though, if her look was because of Colin Rutledge or me.

I would have to wait. Our conversation was finished for now. Margaret called for Evangeline. The young girl hurried into the dining room, gathered my empty bowl and silverware, and returned to the kitchen.

"Come, child. I'll take you to your room so you can get a good night's rest." Margaret stood and gently urged me up. Taking one of the candelabras from the sideboard, she led the way into the foyer and to the stairs.

My eyes shot a restless glance at the parlor's double doors. I couldn't help myself. They were still closed, still portentous-looking. Why was I so curious as to whether Colin Rutledge was in that room?

With Margaret a few paces in front of me, I ascended the stairs. The walnut banister was smooth beneath my hand. Happily and somewhat guiltily, I recalled the times Sorcha and I slid down the beautifully carved railing on our backsides. Of course, the childish fun was done in secret, and it was certainly a miracle that we were never hurt. Ah, youth! How impetuous. How quickly it slips away.

The steps creaked with our footfalls. At the curve of the stairway was a large window. Its colored glass was set with lead in an intricate pattern and framed in thick oak. When the sun shone through, the design had reminded me of a kaleidoscope, sparkling and exciting to look at. Now, in the bleakness of the dimly lit stairwell, the window was almost a frightening thing. I hurried past as it scowled dangerously at me.

We moved down the wide, carpeted hallway and stopped in front of an oaken door with shiny brass fixtures. My heart leaped in my chest.

"This is my room," I whispered, and glanced over at a smiling Margaret.

She nodded, slowly opened the door, then stepped aside so that I could enter first. After a few moments she swept by me and lit the lamp on the dresser. The golden glow made the room come alive with memories.

"Oh, Margaret, it's truly wonderful to be back." Remorse seized me. "It just pains me so that Sorcha is gone."

She grabbed my hand and squeezed it gently. "I know how you feel."

The double bed made of woven burnished wicker still dominated the room. Its plump pillows and quilts invited sleep. An immense armoire stood against the far wall, and a vanity and dresser drawers were opposite it.

Margaret hurried passed me to another door and gave it a slight push. As I watched her, I recalled how each of the bedrooms at Raven Manor had its own bath. A luxury, yes, but also a convenience, especially when I was used to sharing one with five other girls at the Academy or with three families in the flat where I had lived with my parents. And at Aunt Elizabeth's ... Well, I could never get used to taking care of private matters in a such a public place as the outdoors.

Margaret came to me and hugged me close to her. "I'm so glad you're here, Britanny," she whispered in my ear. Her voice shook with happiness. "Get some sleep, now. We'll talk in the morning." She turned away and I thought I saw her wipe something from her eye.

"Good night, Margaret," I said, and watched as she closed the door behind her. The latch clicked. I was alone.

In the lamplight I saw my trunk by the door. Draped over it were my cloak, purse, and gloves. Naturally, I was curious as to how they had arrived in my room. I searched through my memory. Winfield ... yes, Roger Winfield, the Blackwells' caretaker. Vaguely, I remembered him puttering about the grounds during my summers here. Could it be that he, too, still worked at Raven Manor? I would ask Margaret in the morning.

Another thought jarred my memory and my frustrated sigh filled the room. With all the surprises at Raven Manor, I had forgotten to ask Margaret about the letter. I went for my purse and took out the folded piece of paper. With a mixture of habit and burning interest, I opened the note once again. The scribbling, hurried and desperate, was almost illegible, but I ascribed that to the dim light and my weary vision. The message was still the same, though. Now, more than ever, I needed to find the true meaning behind those words. I placed the letter back in my purse for safekeeping.

A wave of exhaustion came over me as I removed my dress and undergarments. I slipped my nightgown over my head. The soft cotton material felt like silk against my skin. It was my favorite, a pale coral color that complimented my red-gold hair. The nightgown was from Aunt Elizabeth, one of many presents she had given to me before I had left for the Academy.

"A pretty girl deserves pretty things," she had said.

I smiled and hugged the cloth closer to my body.

41

The lacy ruffles of the vanity skirt tickled my knees as I sat down on the white velvet-tufted chair. I was not surprised to see a pale, tired-looking face staring back at me from the mirror. Even my green eyes had lost some of their sparkle. It had been a long, exhausting journey, though I knew that the trip had little to do with the way I felt.

Unpinning my hair, I let the tresses fall to my shoulders in a cascade of curls. Some of the strands were still damp from the rain. Slowly, I guided the silver hairbrush through my thick hair, enjoying the luxurious feeling.

A knock on the door caused me to jump. I swiveled in the chair. "Come in."

The door cracked open and Evangeline slipped through the thin space. "Mrs. Tuttle sent me to turn down your bed, miss. Make sure you had everything you need."

"That wasn't necessary," I said, smiling.

Without any concern for my mild protest, she proceeded to the bed, drew down the quilts, and fussed with the pillows. "I do what I'm told, miss."

Finished with the bed, she scurried into the bathroom. Though I couldn't see what she was doing, I could hear the clinking of bottles and tins. Most likely she was checking the sundries, making sure that all was in order for the morning.

"Can I do anything else for you, miss?" she asked, standing behind me now, twisting her

fingers nervously. I could hear the sharp cracking of her knuckles. The noise made me wince.

I did not face her but her reflection in the
mirror, instead. "Yes, Evangeline. There is
something you can do for me. You can call me
Britanny." I wanted to put her at ease, but my
suggestion only served to fluster her more.

"Oh, no, miss. Mrs. Tuttle, she wouldn't like
for me to do such a bold thing as to call you
by your first name." Her speech was like tiny
firecrackers exploding one after the other.
"Good night, miss." It was clear by her rest-
lessness that she wanted to leave my room
quickly.

"Good night, Evangeline." I barely got the
words out and she was gone.

Staring into the mirror, I frowned. She was
a strange girl. I placed the brush back on the
vanity amid vials of perfume and flasks of powder, and sighed. I was not going to bother myself with Evangeline's odd behavior.

As I extinguished the lamp, a blanket of
darkness shrouded the room. Gingerly, I
moved to the window and pulled back the lace
drapes. The fury of the storm had ceased. All
that was left of it was the light tapping of raindrops against the glass.

I slipped my body between the chilled white
sheets. The mattress, though unyielding, was
comfortable and the fluffy down quilts formed
a kind of cocoon. I was suddenly looking forward to a restful night's sleep.

But sleep wouldn't come. I tossed fitfully under the covers, my mind a jumble of thoughts about Sorcha. There were too many pieces that just didn't fit the puzzle of her death—or her life.

"Colin Rutledge."

The name slipped out as a whisper. Again I envisioned the bitterness and hatred that were in his glance when we first met. Even now, it sent a spasm of fear shooting through me. He was so mysterious, so menacing. And yet, Sorcha loved him. Maybe there was more to the man than I could discern.

My mind began to slow now as I felt an urgency to end this day. But something stopped my eyes from closing. A melody, soft and lilting, reached my ears. It sounded so far away yet so clear in tone and timbre. At first I thought I was dreaming the sweet music. I opened my mind drawing in the strains of the tune. Strangely enough, I even felt compelled to hum the melody. After a few moments, I stopped. I remained quiet, letting the music fill me, dance through me, until I realized its familiarity. It was Sorcha's favorite song!

Hastily, I threw back the covers and swung my legs over the side of the bed. My body fought the rush of cold air as I listened to the melody with a knowing ear. Yes, it was the overture from "Romeo and Juliet" by Tchaikovsky. During those long-ago summers, I had often heard Sorcha humming it when we'd

pick flowers or when we'd go for walks. Sometimes it would burst forth from her like flowers
in the spring when the two of us were just
sitting quietly.

My heart skipped a beat. I had to know
where the music was coming from. More important, from whom.

Determination propelling me forward, I
threw on my robe and crossed the floor, finding
the door easily. The cold of the wood numbed
my bare feet. Several wall sconces were lit
along the hallway and, except for the music,
the rest of the house was deathly still.

My feet barely touched the carpeted steps.
My night clothes billowed out behind me as if
trying to pull me back up the stairs. As I neared
the bottom, the music became louder and with
it the beating of my heart.

I began to cross the foyer but the loud clang
from the grandfather clock made me stop
abruptly. Barely breathing, I stood as still as
a marble statue and silently counted the
chimes. Midnight.

It was then my gaze fell upon the doors of
the parlor. The music, still vibrant, was coming from inside. I pushed the door open a crack
and peeked in. The wood squeaked but the melody disguised the noise.

The fire was still blazing, causing shadows
to plunge along the walls. The furnishings
seemed to take on a monstrous look and their

silhouettes wavered in ominous discordance with the music.

I steadied myself, the surreal apparitions making me dizzy. It was then I spied him. Colin Rutledge was at the piano, his dexterous fingers handling the keys with an obstinacy that could be considered utterly mad. Only a small portion of his face was obstructed by the darkness. His mouth and chin were firmly set. I pulled back afraid at first that he might notice me. But on second glance I saw that his eyes were closed.

As he played the haunting melody, his body swayed as if in a self-induced trance. Yet, as erratic as his behavior was, his expression drew me to him. A tender, loving look diminished the hard edge to his appearance.

My heart felt heavy and I wiped a single tear from my eye. What was it about Colin Rutledge that touched me so? Had I been wrong about him? Was it the way he played the love song that was slowly changing my mind about this brutish, somewhat selfish man? I couldn't be sure. In my own mind, though, I had come to a reluctant understanding. Colin Rutledge and I did have something in common. Both of us were thinking about Sorcha.

I closed the door. The strains of the music were lightly muffled now. A slow, rising heat seared my neck and cheeks. I was suddenly embarrassed, feeling as though I had barged in on a very private moment. I stared at the door, the vision of Colin burned in my memory.

Certain that sleep would help me see things differently in the morning, I started for my room. But as I turned, I sensed something. It was soft, shallow breathing, other than my own. Fear clutched at my heart. Someone was here with me.

"Margaret?" My voice trembled and I swallowed nervously. There was no answer. I walked slowly toward the stairs, collecting what was left of my bravery. "Evangeline? Is that you?" Still no answer.

I was beginning to doubt my own sanity when a sudden movement caught my eye. I looked up, squinting to see. There, at the top of the stairs, a figure came into view. In the thick shadows, I could not make out the features. Long, dark hair hid the rest of the shape.

I froze in shock, struck dumb from what I thought was impossible. My throat closed over the name that tumbled from my mind to my dry lips. My hand shot out before me, reaching toward the figure. Finally, I cried out, "Sorcha! My God! Sorcha! Is it really you?" My eyes blurred and my throat tightened. I felt as if I was going to suffocate.

I stumbled backward across the foyer until I ran into something hard and unyielding. I spun around wildly. Strong hands seized my arms and held them fast. I had no other choice but to look up into the angry, black eyes of Colin Rutledge.

Chapter Three

"What is the meaning of this?" Colin's voice boomed like the thunder of the earlier storm. His eyes were bolts of lightning. "Why are you sneaking around down here?"

"I was not sneaking around!" I said, struggling against his hold. He let go, glowering more fiercely than ever. Free now, I dashed across the foyer, climbed several of the steps, and then stopped. The murky shadows glared down at me from the top of the stairs. I searched for an answer. Nothing. No one was there. The figure had disappeared. Had I dreamed the whole thing? Was it a combination of my obsessiveness, the music, and coming back to Raven Manor, that had suddenly conjured up Sorcha's ghost?

Or—I held my breath—was the specter real?

"What is wrong with you, Miss St. James? Have you suddenly gone mad?"

I turned back to him and answered quite honestly, "I'm not sure."

His dark brows curved furrowing his face in a perplexed frown. The realization of what I had said and his expression made me shake with a nervous twitter.

He cleared his throat. "Well, mad or not, you haven't answered my question. What are you doing down here?"

I had quickly decided that I would not breathe one word about what I had seen—or thought I had seen—lest he really believe me insane. But there were other reasons why I chose to remain quiet about the incident. Until I was certain that all of this had to do with my overactive imagination, I would trust no one.

My mind clicked. "Please forgive my curiosity but the music woke me. I only wanted to find its source." It wasn't a lie, just half the truth. "Tchaikovsky is one of my favorite composers, Mr. Rutledge, and may I say that you do play beautifully."

He looked amazed. "Thank you." His words seemed to falter. "From one so young that is praise indeed."

It was my turn to be surprised. "Did you think I would not appreciate the finer things for one 'as young as I,' as you have said? Or was it my compliment that startled you?"

He was silent, but his impenetrable stare suddenly made me conscious of the fact that all that covered me was a flimsy dressing gown. I pulled the robe around me to cover my half-nakedness. My gaze dropped to the floor, yet I was aware of the scorching intensity of his interest. A shiver slithered up my spine like a snake. Did he know he was the cause of my trembling uneasiness? Did he derive pleasure in making others—me—feel intimidated?

I looked fully into his eyes. Something new appeared in them, something deeply serious.

"Would you like to hear more?" A thin smile cracked his lips.

The invitation stunned me, even more so his momentary change of mood. All too soon, though, the brightness in his face was gone. "Come," he ordered, not waiting for my answer, yet somehow knowing what it was. He stretched out his arm indicating that I enter the parlor first.

The room was warm and considerably more friendly than it had been when I first peeked around the door.

"Please, sit down, Miss St. James," he offered, and nodded to a soft leather armchair near the piano.

He took his place behind the keyboard, while his eyes focused on me.

"Do you play?"

I blinked. "Pardon me?"

He laughed a little at my accusing stare.

"The piano, Miss St. James. Do you play the piano?"

"Oh," I answered, my cheeks growing as hot as the fire. "Not as well as you, I'm afraid. My Aunt Elizabeth, whom I lived with for a while, had attempted to teach me, but I never had the patience to sit and play those tiresome scales."

A flicker of a smile that was so unlike him crinkled the corners of his mouth and I thought I heard the low sound of laughter. "I see." He seemed amused.

The amber glow from the fire streaked across his face in a frenzied dance, sharpening his already-striking features. Darkness encompassed the rest of him like a black sheath. Only silky white fragments of his shirt shimmered through the shadows. Though quiet and still, he had full command of his surroundings, and for the first time I found him disturbingly attractive.

"If I know anything about the piano, it's because I learned from—" I caught my breath so quickly that I was sure he noticed.

"From Sorcha?" he finished, looking troubled.

I cleared my throat and forced myself to go on. "Yes. She and I would sit at this very piano, sometimes for hours. She loved to play, to be a part of the music." My glance darted spontaneously to the portrait above the mantel. Sorcha's silver-blue eyes gleamed with a liveliness that jolted me. "Beware, Britanny ... beware..." I stiffened as once again the disquieting sound of her voice pounded in my brain. Though I knew it was only my imagination, I couldn't help feeling I was being warned. But why? And about whom? With the unsettling thought fixed in my mind, I turned back to Colin Rutledge.

"The selection you were playing, the Fantasy Overture from *Romeo and Juliet*? It was Sorcha's favorite."

He nodded slowly, his dark eyes mirrored by memories. "Yes. I know."

The despondency in his voice saddened me, but it was the compassion in his expression that wrenched my heart. I pressed my lips together in exasperation. Colin Rutledge was indeed a difficult man to understand. In the short time I had been here, he had shown so many sides of himself, so many moods. I was more than aware of the conflict that raged within him, yet I found myself silently doing battle with Margaret's explanation. Had he been so in love with Sorcha that in losing her, he had lost some of his sanity? Was it Colin Rutledge whom I had to fear?

"And what is your favorite piece? A concerto by Bach? Haydn, perhaps?" His fingers moved swiftly across the keyboard, the music sounding and resounding its magic.

The vibrant tone trailed off in an echo. A strange sensation played havoc with my senses. Was it the heady scent of the fire that made me feel dizzy, or was it his penetrating gaze that bothered me so?

"Play for me. Play me the music that you and Sorcha enjoyed." He beckoned me with the faint beginnings of a smile.

I wanted to resist his invitation. Though it seemed innocent enough, I knew that I should not yield to someone whom I considered suspect. But I was caught in some sort of spell. A spell woven with the treacherous threads of temptation. It summoned me forward, slowly but very willingly.

My nightgown swished softly as I sat next to him on the polished bench. My body rigid, I was conscious only of his nearness. His arm brushed up against mine and I pulled away, flustered by the brief contact.

"Is something wrong, Miss St. James?" he asked.

I swallowed the lump in my throat. The sweetness of port wine was on his breath, but the reckless scent of him alone was just as intoxicating. I appeared to concentrate on the keyboard, keeping my eyes down for fear my expression would reveal my uneasiness.

"I haven't played in quite a long time," I said, glancing quickly at him. With a quivering hand, I brushed some stray tendrils of hair away from my face. The gleaming ivory keys stared at me tauntingly. I took a breath to sustain what courage I had left, curled my fingers, and poised them above the keyboard.

The soft, beautiful strains of Beethoven's *Pastoral* filled the room. I played it just the way Sorcha had taught me, surprising myself that I had committed such a difficult piece of music to memory. I watched in awe as my fingers danced across the keys with complacent alacrity. The Muses were smiling down on me, and I thought if Sorcha could only hear the wonderful sounds, she, too, would be pleased.

Then it was over. The music stopped as I lifted my hands from the keys suddenly. For a moment the music seemed to go on, then drifted away to a deafening silence. My hands felt like lead. My fingers, hovering above the keys, were paralyzed, useless.

"Do go on, Miss St. James." Colin Rutledge raised a dark brow. "Please."

Clenching my fists, I lifted my chin and looked at him. "I . . . I can't. I'm sorry," I said, composing myself long enough to say the words. The keyboard seemed to turn to liquid before my eyes. My throat was on fire. My head pounded furiously.

"You're thinking about Sorcha, aren't you?" His question required no confirmation. He had read my mind, my heart.

For a brief moment, I had felt her next to me. Like many times before, she was showing me each note, patiently explaining my mistakes, lavishing praise when I had succeeded. Only now it was my overwrought imagination that had felt her presence. I shuddered as the memories closed around me, filling me with an aching that had embedded itself in my soul.

"Perhaps I can help." Colin Rutledge's deep, rich voice stirred my painful reminiscing.

Before I had the chance to react, the resonance of the piano charged my senses. The melody, unfamiliar this time, was slow-paced and I found myself relaxing to the soft strains. I watched, mesmerized, as his hands lorded over the keys, each tone clear and definite.

My heart fluttered, and my lips were half-parted in an attempt to smile. He was pleased with my delight and his expression revealed an air of conquest.

His eyes, like live coals, began to glow with a hungry look as the intensity of the music rose in a tremulous vibrato. The power behind it frightened me. He frightened me. I felt a tingling at the base of my spine. It was almost as if he was playing me—every chord, every note. He was in control.

With wide-eyed trepidation, I gasped as he tossed his head back wildly in the throes of pain and pleasure. So fierce was his action that I could not bridle my excitement. What was happening to me? Hours ago I had wanted to slap him for saying such cruel things to me. Now, I wanted to caress his face, hold him close to me. I had never encountered anything so shameless before.

He moved against me now, fanning the sparks of my arousal into a leaping flame. Again and again his rock-hard body pressed into mine, then retreated. His hands wildly caressed the keys in a demanding display of domination.

Strong and vivid desires coursed through me, and a gentle moan of passion escaped my lips. Mortified at my scandalous response, I looked away from him and tried to resist the frenzied melody. But in the dark recesses of my mind it spread like a flash fire throughout my body. A primitive instinct enveloped me, unleashing my senses with sweet abandon. I felt my willpower slipping away, as unsuspecting tremors pulsated through me in an untamed dance of desire. My eyes swept back to him. A cruel smile of confidence illuminated his face. Somehow he knew I was at his mercy.

And then, the last strains of the music ended with brutish finality. My breath was ragged and my cheeks flushed hotly with the aftermath of an explosion that was causing my body to shake uncontrollably. There was no explanation, no logical reason for the way I had carried on. Silently, I counted to ten as my pulse started to return to normal. The spell was broken.

"Is something wrong, Miss St. James?" He spoke low, close to my ear, and it made my heart jump. "Didn't you enjoy it?"

I pulled away from him as my body rippled with tension. "No ... I mean, yes, I did enjoy your playing," I said, gulping in the acrid air. "It was quite ... exhilarating."

He nodded, clenching his jaw in a deliberate expression of self-assurance. I could tell he had expected me to say something like that. Bold, black, defiant eyes pinned me with a long, silent scrutiny. I blushed. Was he aware of the feelings he had so brutally released in me? Could he know? Unabashed thoughts and images swam in my mind, but I chased them away. I was not about to allow these ridiculous urges to obscure the reason I had come to Raven Manor.

I rose from the bench and moved around the bend of the piano. I stood facing the hearth and watched the flames grow weak and helpless. A chill came over me. Once again my gaze rested on Sorcha's portrait.

"I miss her," I said, the words tumbling from my lips.

"So do I." Colin Rutledge's deep, unruffled voice answered with the same sincerity. He had followed me and now stood close behind me, so close I could feel the flaring warmth of his nearness.

I was hesitant to turn around. The sinking feeling in my stomach only fortified my decision to end this conversation. I was afraid I might say something that could give away my true feelings about her death.

"She was too young to die. Too young and too beautiful." His words were sudden and direct and very angry.

My mind snapped. Was he, too, holding something back?

"It's late. Perhaps you should get some sleep." The nebulous mood of the room had changed. Slowly, I turned around. Colin Rutledge seemed lost in his own thoughts, staring into space.

"Yes," I agreed, wondering if he had even heard me. "I shall see you in the morning then."

"I'm afraid I leave rather early. Business, you know."

"Oh, I see." Had I sounded too disappointed?

He pushed his bottom lip forward in thought. "Perhaps dinner? If you are still here."

His probe into my visit did not fluster me. "I will be here this evening. If I remember correctly, it was you who invited me to stay as long as I liked."

He gave a short laugh touched with embarrassment. "So I did, Miss St. James. So I did."

"Good night, Mr. Rutledge." I nodded politely, turned, then started to leave. I beamed with a secretive smile of triumph.

"Good night, Miss St. James," he called after me.

I did not look at him again, though I wanted to. I was only too aware of his piercing gaze. It followed me, and it was only when I began to climb the stairs that I finally felt alone.

Most of the candles in the sconces had burned down to nubs, leaving the hallway sparse with light. Gingerly, I made my way to my room. I knew I wouldn't sleep. There was too much to think about, too many plans to go over in my head. Tomorrow I would ask Margaret about the letter, and have her show me the place where Sorcha died, where she supposedly had taken her own life. I wasn't sure what I would find or how I would react. I only knew I had to go there and see for myself. I needed to know if my instincts about her death were correct. Only then would I be able to put all of this behind me.

The whimpering was almost inaudible. I first I thought I was hearing things. After all, with the "vision" I thought I saw, my imagination seemed to be working overtime since I had arrived. I stood very still and listened. The faint sounds were not in my mind; in fact, they were growing louder.

Nervous flutterings erupted in my chest as I cautiously made my way down the hall. The whimpering had turned to sobbing now, very mournful, and the sound wrenched my heart. I followed the sound to the end of the hallway. It was coming from Sorcha's bedroom! I pressed my ear against the door. My whole body tightened, and I took a breath. Pictures floated in my mind. Maybe it was Margaret crying over the loss of Sorcha. Or Evangeline, for whatever reason. It did sound more like a young person's wailing.

Should I interfere? I wondered. Feelings and

common sense warred with each other now. The sobs sounded so helpless, so out of control. Suppose someone was in trouble?

The latch opened easily. I peered around the corner of the door.

"It's Britanny," I whispered into the darkness. "Does someone need help?"

I waited for a moment, but the only answer was more tearful sobbing. One thing I had noticed, though. Muffled by the closed door, the crying had sounded distant, remote. Now clearer, it was very different. Nervously I walked into the room. When my eyes adjusted to the darkness, I spied the outline of a shadow at the opposite end of the room. A harsh odor, acrid and sharp, assaulted my nose.

I stopped, my heart pounding furiously in my chest. The crying had quieted a bit, and I felt my presence had something to do with it. My gaze caught and I held the silhouette. I closed my eyes and shook myself, thinking I was seeing things. I wasn't. The outline was still there when my eyes opened.

It was a cradle. A rather large, beautifully carved one. Through the undraped window, I saw the clouds part, exposing a half-moon. Its dim, white light pierced the rain-streaked glass and cast a surrealistic glow over the cradle.

The whimpering had turned into curious gurgling. I peered down and caught my breath. Numb astonishment filled my whole being as the small, sweet face of a baby stared up at me.

Chapter Four

Regaining my composure, I pushed away my feelings of astonishment and thought only of the baby. The whimpering had begun again. I reached into the cradle, carefully lifted the helpless creature, and hugged it to my breast. Its bottom was damp. The poor little thing needed changing.

"There, there, sweet baby," I cooed gently, patting its back. "Everything is going to be fine. I'm here now." The soft bundle nuzzled against me. I could feel the warm moistness of its tears through my nightgown. "Who do you belong to?" I whispered in its tiny ear.

As if to answer me, the baby pulled its head off my chest and stared into my eyes. The small, round face was a picture of content-

Suzanne Hoos

ment. It was then I knew whose precious baby this was.

Instinctively, I hastened about the room, searching for a change of clothing for the baby, but the light that trickled in from the hallway was too dim to help me find anything.

I had to get Margaret. She would know what to do.

The baby wriggled against me and I thought it best to return it to the cradle. "I'll be right back," I said, smoothing its dark wisps of downy hair from its damp brow.

A golden light made the shadows of the room jump. "You have no right to be in this room, Miss St. James. Now leave the baby alone."

My head snapped around at the sound of the menacing voice. Colin Rutledge filled the doorway. The eerie glow of the candelabra he held distorted his hulking shape, making him appear even more ominous.

Ignoring his stern expression, I swallowed and found my voice. "This child needs attending to, Mr. Rutledge."

"Margaret will see to that," he answered petulantly.

"Then, please get her. I'll stay with the baby."

He drew back, his eyes questioning. My firm directive had surprised him. Restless sniffles were once again drifting from inside the cradle.

"Hurry," I hissed, and turned my attention

62

to the baby. From the corner of my eye, I was aware that the candlelight had quickly disappeared from the room. Gently rubbing the baby's belly, I smiled, indulging in my small triumph.

I wasn't sure why but I stepped back into the shadows when I heard Margaret come into the room. Colin was behind her but did not follow her to the cradle.

"Hush, Melinda. Don't cry, sweetheart," Margaret said, now holding the baby close to her.

"Melinda." The name played over and over in my head like a lovely melody. I smiled.

Unaware that I was in the room, Margaret walked directly toward me. We were almost face to face when she realized I was there. Then her eyes widened and she embraced the baby protectively.

"Britanny." She choked on my name. "What . . . what are you doing here?"

"Miss St. James heard the baby crying," Colin answered before I had the chance to.

She said nothing, only nodded, but the corner of her mouth twitched slightly.

"We must talk, Margaret," I said in a low voice.

She hurried past me and I wasn't sure if she heard me. She placed the baby gently on the bed that was in the room, and which I recognized as Sorcha's.

Offering my help, I was promptly pointed in

the direction of a dresser. In the drawers, I found baby clothes and clean linens for the cradle.

Though Colin was silent, his eyes regarded me with an intense, watchful stare. I stiffened, not knowing whether to be uneasy or angry.

As Margaret attented to Melinda, I changed the soiled sheets and blanket in the cradle with fresh ones. The baby's gurgling made me laugh quietly. She sounded happy and content.

"Will she be all right, now, Margaret?" The accusation in his voice irked me. If anyone was at fault, it was he. Did he not think I would have found out about Melinda? Was he going to keep her a secret from me? Even more curiously, why would he want to?

Frowning, I glanced at him and wondered what sort of thoughts were running through his obviously troubled mind. If he saw me studying him, he didn't respond.

"Yes, Mr. Rutledge. Melinda will be just fine now," Margaret said as she adjusted the tiny nightgown on the baby's rather sedate form. Melinda's eyes were closing. Her little mouth puckered in a pink rosette.

"Then I'll leave you to the rest of your tasks." About to go, he turned and looked straight at me. "Are you coming, Miss St. James?"

"I wish to speak with Margaret before I retire," I answered, then added, "if that meets with your approval."

He seemed amused. "As you wish." He nodded curtly, left behind the candelabra, departed from the room, and closed the door.

Margaret had already placed Melinda in the cradle. I went to her and smiled down at the baby. Her eyes were closed, her breathing steady and peaceful.

"She's asleep," Margaret whispered as she gently rocked the crib.

"She's beautiful," I said dreamily. "How old is she?"

"Nearly a full year," Margaret answered.

I reached down and tenderly stroked her tiny hand. The skin felt like silk and I marveled silently at the perfectly shaped fingers. "She's Sorcha's baby, isn't she, Margaret?"

If my question surprised her, Margaret didn't show it. "Yes," she confirmed. "Melinda is all I have left of Sorcha." The sadness in her voice nearly broke my heart.

"Why were you keeping something so important from me?" I had expected her to be either defensive or embarrassed, but all I received was a shrug.

"I wanted to tell you about Melinda." There was a slump to her shoulders and a darkening under her pale blue eyes that spoke of fatigue. "I . . . I just didn't know how."

"Or you were told not to," I said, anger seeping through my words.

Her arm slipped around my waist and she guided me away from the cradle and toward the bed where we both sat down. She held my hands and rubbed the tops with her thumbs in a soothing gesture.

"Don't blame Mr. Rutledge. He's a very private person. Even more so since Sorcha's death." Her expression pleaded for me to understand. I did not know what to make of this whole situation, but I knew it would be useless to argue with her.

A sudden feeling of need mixed with grief overcame me. My anxious heart started to beat with a quickened pace. "Margaret, I want you take me to the place where Sorcha died."

Letting go of my hands, she frowned as if to scold me, but her eyes were wide with fright. She drew a careful breath. "I don't think that's a good idea, Britanny—"

"Please, Margaret. I have to go there. I have to see." The sense of urgency was growing stronger and a tremor passed through me.

Her face was grim. "It's impossible. I have to care for Melinda."

"Surely Evangeline can care for the baby for one day."

Margaret scoffed. "Evangeline? She's too young, too inexperienced."

"Then we'll bring Melinda with us," I announced.

"Mr. Rutledge would not approve of such a thing."

"Mr. Rutledge doesn't have to know."

She looked horrified.

"Margaret, please," I said, determined to

convince her. "Will you take me?" I held her hands in mine.

Her eyes darted quickly to the closed door and then she leaned closer to me. "Do you still believe that Sorcha was murdered?" she asked, her voice low, her hands shaking.

"Yes, Margaret," I answered without hesitation, knowing now that I had been right about having planted doubt in Margaret's mind during our earlier conversation.

She shook her head but it was more in exasperation than disbelief. It made me question her true speculation.

"Tell me about the day Sorcha died," I said, hoping she was willing to talk. "What did she do? How did she act?"

Margaret thought for a long time, or maybe it seemed so to me because of my eagerness to learn everything I could about Sorcha's death.

"Sorcha awakened early that day. She was already in the nursery with Melinda by the time I arrived."

"The nursery?"

"The room next to yours. Since Sorcha died, Mr. Rutledge prefers that the baby sleep here in Sorcha's room."

"Why?" I asked, frowning.

She shrugged. "I suppose it's because he's right across the hall."

An odd feeling crept into my bones. Separate bedrooms? Of course, I wasn't an expert in marital bliss, but I did know that husbands and wives usually slept together. I did not pursue the issue further for fear Margaret would put an end to our conversation. Still, the thought puzzled me.

"Did she act strangely?" I asked. "Did she see anyone that day?"

Margaret looked down at our intertwined hands and shook her head. "I don't know, Britanny. All I remember was that she asked if I would look after Melinda for a while. She said she had an errand to attend to. It was raining heavily that afternoon and I told her not to go, but she said that it was too important." Margaret's eyes, shining with tears, met mine. "If only she had listened to me, Britanny. If only I had seen the signs. She had been depressed for so long after her parents' accident. I had no idea she would take her own life."

Sorrow tightened around my heart. I reached up and stroked Margaret's cheek. "Don't blame yourself. You know how determined Sorcha was about anything she set her mind to."

She nodded, agreeing with me, yet my words did not erase the hurt from her tired face. She wanted to turn away but I would not allow her to hide her eyes from me.

"Where was Mr. Rutledge that day?" I finally asked.

She pulled away from me suddenly, stood up, and frowned in irritation at my question.

"He was at his place of business. That's all I know."

"Are you certain?"

Her features tightened. "Britanny, if you intend to pursue your ridiculous theory about Mr. Rutledge having something to do with Sorcha's death, then our conversation is finished as of now."

She had no right to be upset with me. "I'm only trying to put the pieces of this puzzle together, Margaret."

"Not if you continue to suspect Mr. Rutledge. He loved Sorcha. He would never have harmed her." She went to the cradle to check on Melinda, but I had the feeling that she wanted to get away from me.

I would not have it. I followed her, grabbed her arm, and made her face me. "I don't understand you, Margaret. I should think you would want to learn the truth. After all, it was you who pleaded with me to come to Raven Manor. It was you who needed my help."

She blinked and confusion clouded her eyes. She had no idea what I meant.

"The letter, Margaret," I said perhaps a little louder than I should have. Melinda stirred. I lowered my voice. "I received it a few days ago. That's why I'm here. You begged me to come."

Margaret touched the baby's brow, stroking it until she quieted. Then she turned to me. "The only letter I wrote was to tell you of Sorcha's death. Your visit came as a complete surprise."

It was my turn to be confused. "If not you, then who sent me the letter asking me to return?"

The room was shrouded in an eerie silence. We looked at one another for a long time, each of us trying to come up with a viable answer. There was none to be found—at least for now.

We both gazed down then upon the sweet, innocent baby's face. "I still have to learn the truth about Sorcha's death, Margaret," I said quietly. "Melinda will grow up without knowing a mother's love. Doesn't she have the right to know someday what really happened?"

There was a long, tense silence. Then Margaret raised her eyes to mine. "I'll take you there tomorrow. I'll take you to the place where Sorcha died."

My heart leaped and I hugged her tightly. "Thank you," I whispered in her ear.

Gently, she pushed me away. "Mr. Rutledge will have my job if he finds out." She pursed her lips and for a moment I thought she would waggle her finger at me, too.

"He won't, Margaret. I promise."

Briefly, something passed through the both of us. A feeling that somehow gave us hope. We smiled and embraced each other again.

"Come now. Off to bed." Margaret turned me around and we headed for the door. "We'll talk more in the morning."

Holding the candelabra, she walked me to my room, said good night, and proceeded down the stairs to her own quarters.

Alone, I mulled over all that had happened in the past few hours. Sorcha. Melinda. The writer of the mysterious letter. Even the "ghost" I had seen, or more likely, thought I had seen at the top of the stairs. Believing now that the figure was only a product of my imagination, I was glad I did not mention it to Margaret. It would have only served to upset her further.

I stared out the window and watched the dark flurry of dark clouds eclipse the moon. A thought from the deep recesses of my mind pushed its way forward. Colin Rutledge. Somehow, I could not conceive the idea of Colin as the fatherly type. He was so cold, so distant. A child needed tender care. Love. Something I was certain he was unable to give to anyone.

But as his face vanished slowly from my mind, it suddenly occurred to me that I was only assuming the baby's parentage.

I scoffed now, thinking the question ridiculous. Of course Colin Rutledge was Melinda's father. Who else could it be?

Chapter Five

I was awakened the next morning by the startling squawks of geese. As my eyes adjusted slowly to the sunlight tumbling into the room, I noticed that the window was slightly ajar, and a warm breeze was fluttering the lace curtains.

I frowned. I was certain I hadn't left the window opened last night. I rose from the bed, wondering if someone had been in my room while I was asleep. I scanned the surroundings, making a mental image of what I could remember from last night. Everything seemed to be in its place.

Puzzled, I ambled into the bath. To my surprise, the claw-foot tub was filled with water and sweet-smelling oils. I dipped my hand into the water. It was hot. I grinned knowingly. The window, the bath—all of it Margaret's doing. I should have been used to it by now. The many times I had stayed with the Blackwells, she had always "spoiled" me in this manner. Secretly, I had loved it.

I heard the squeak of the door, and I hurried from the bath.

"Margaret?" I called out.

But it wasn't Margaret. It was Evangeline who stood there, with fluffy white toweling cloths in her arms. On top was a pretty silver box, round in shape, with a small crystal knob on the lid. She was dressed in the same shapeless brown frock she had worn yesterday, but her hair was pulled back and braided. She stared at me blankly through those arresting blue eyes.

"Excuse me, miss. I brought you drying cloths and some of this dusting powder. You might be a-wanting it after your bath."

I frowned, bothered somewhat by her intrusion. "Are you responsible for opening my window? For drawing my bath?"

Her lower lip began to tremble. "Mrs. Tuttle told me to."

"Didn't Mrs. Tuttle also tell you to knock first?" I did not want to be mean but I did not appreciate a stranger in my room while I slept, either.

"I did knock, but you were still sleeping, miss." She lowered her eyes and peered at me

73

through thick lashes. "Have I done something wrong?"

I was about to explain my feelings when she cut me off with a quivering sigh.

"If I have done wrong, I'm sorry. Just please don't tell Mrs. Tuttle. Please."

Concerned at her outburst, I went to her and touched her shoulder gently. "It's all right, Evangeline. I won't tell Mrs. Tuttle. I promise."

She looked up at me and a glimmer of a smile reached her lips and then disappeared. Without another word, she left the towels on the bed, placed the dusting powder on top of the dresser, and vanished from the room.

I shook my head. Odd girl. Simpleminded. I wondered if she truly realized her mistake, or was she more frightened that Margaret might learn of it?

But Evangeline's shortcomings were not my main concern. Today the terrible truth might rear its brutal head. I wasn't sure how or when, but somehow just being at the place where Sorcha had died, I felt confident that I would know. The thought also scared me.

Though the water felt wonderful, I hurried with my bath. The perfumed oils clung to my skin as I dried the droplets of water. The dusting powder was scented with roses; its diaphanous layering on my skin made me feel as though I was wrapped in the finest satin.

Anxiously, I fumbled with my peacock-blue

skirt and white blouse with a silk embroidered collar. Sitting before the mirror, I brushed my hair, then pinned it in neat coils on top of my head. I pinched my cheeks and bit down on my lips to enhance the glow of the bath that was like a warm breath still lingering on my skin.

The day would not be an easy one. Being there, seeing the place where Sorcha had died was going to be difficult. Already the feeling of remorse weighed heavily upon me. I blinked back tears that threatened to spill onto my cheeks.

Stop it, Britanny, I told myself, *You must uncover the truth. You must avenge Sorcha's death.* With the strength of those words echoing in my mind, I grabbed my jacket and left the room.

The clock in the foyer announced my arrival with seven melodious chimes. Bacon and freshly brewed coffee awakened my appetite. I followed the glorious aromas into the dining room, only to stop before entering.

There, sitting at the head of the table, was Colin Rutledge. He was engrossed in reading a newspaper, or so I thought. My pulse began to quicken and I stepped back from the doorway.

"Good morning, Miss St. James," he said, slowly raising his dark eyes. He pulled me into his gaze.

Unconsciously, I smoothed my hair and

straightened my clothing, though neither needed arranging. "Good morning," I answered, catching my breath.

He folded the newspaper, set it down on the edge of the table, and motioned to the chair on his right. "Please, sit down. Breakfast is just being served."

I swallowed and crossed to the table. My heart skipped a beat when he stood suddenly and pulled out the chair for me. I was flustered, surprised at his display of chivalry.

"Thank you," I said, easing myself into the seat.

He did not return to his own chair, but leaned into me, his warm breath fluttering against my ear. "I trust you finally managed to get some sleep."

I had barely answered with a civil response when I found him back in his chair at the head of the table. He unfurled the white linen napkin and draped it over his knee.

Slowly becoming acclimated to his striking presence, I felt myself relaxing considerably. Though our initial meeting was anything but cordial, Colin Rutledge looked very different to me in the light of day. Unreserved. More approachable.

"You said last night that you probably wouldn't be here for breakfast. Did something change your mind?" My voice was so low when I spoke that I was surprised he heard me.

He tilted his head and looked directly at me.

The light in the room reflected in his eyes and caused a glow that seemed to come from behind the pupils.

"Rutledge and Blackwell Shipping Company can manage without me," he said.

Panicking, all I could think about were my plans with Margaret. Would his being at the house disrupt them?

"At least for an hour," he added with a half-smile.

His announcement calmed me considerably. Much to my surprise, I found myself smiling, too. Was I just being polite? Or did I feel an attraction to this man? I shook myself, trying to push the absurd thought aside.

"Are you all right, Miss St. James?" The curiosity in his expression made me suddenly self-conscious. I was certain he was reading my thoughts.

I nodded to his question. We talked briefly about his shipping business. His explanation of the ships and imports of fine fabrics, teas, and spices from the Far East sounded almost romantic, and though I tried to fight it, I was enthralled by his every word.

"You must come down to the docks with me one day. I would be happy to show you around." But in the next breath he added, "Of course, you're probably familiar with the place."

I looked at him questioningly.

"The company belonged to Kingsley Blackwell. Sorcha inherited it when he died."

"And now it belongs to you," I said without hesitation.

He rose from his chair once again, his eyes shaded. "Yes. It belongs to me."

A chill crawled up my spine at the cold, prideful arrogance of his words.

"May I get you some coffee, Miss St. James?" He walked to the sideboard and helped himself to some from a silver carafe.

"Yes. Thank you," I said as politely as I could manage. He placed the filled cup in front of me then sat back down. I did not look at him, I could not, but stared instead into the steaming, aromatic liquid.

"And what are your plans for today?"

He asked so matter-of-factly that I opened my mouth to answer him with the truth, then caught myself in time.

"I'm really not certain," I lied. I could feel my cheeks growing hotter with each word. Then an idea came to mind. "I thought I'd spend some time with Melinda. It looks like such a beautiful day that a stroll around the grounds might do both of us some good." I looked up. He was watching me carefully, but I smiled. "Of course, if it's all right with you."

He seemed thoughtful for a moment, then his face brightened. "I would like that very much." His eyes suddenly took on a faraway gaze. "I believe Sorcha would have wanted you to be with Melinda, too." He suddenly leaned over and placed his hand on my arm. "And I do apologize for last night, Miss St. James. If I frightened you in any way, I am sorry."

His touch shot through me like a flame, yet I could not pull away. If the truth be known, I did not want to.

"Good morning, Britanny." Margaret's lilting voice wafted through the room.

Colin withdrew his hand but his gaze still lingered. I blushed again.

"Good morning, Margaret," I greeted, hoping she could not tell how flustered and confused I felt.

Margaret carefully set down before us a tray brimming with breakfast treats of sausage, bacon, eggs, cinnamon rolls, and honey. The aromas alone were a delight.

After Margaret departed, smatterings of polite conversation seemed to ease the tension between Colin and me. He was still a mystery. So changeable. So elusive. There was so much yet to learn about him, especially how he fit into Sorcha's death. I knew I had the initiative. I wondered if I also had the courage.

Colin brushed the napkin against his lips and set it down next to his plate. He pushed himself away from the table, stood, and straightened his dark gray morning coat.

"Well, Miss St. James, do have a good day. Kiss Melinda for me."

Margaret re-entered just as he started to leave the room.

"I'll be home early this evening, Margaret. Make something special for dinner tonight." His eyes lit up with pleasure. "Perhaps Miss St. James would consider spending some time with me this evening."

A tremor passed through me and I was at a loss for words. It was just as well, for when I turned to answer, Colin was gone.

"I just don't understand your Mr. Rutledge," I said as Margaret began to clear away the breakfast dishes.

She sighed. "He does take some getting used to." In the same breath, she added, "But he's a good man, Britanny. I don't know him that well, but I can feel it"—her hand covered her heart—"in here."

For some reason, I wanted to believe her. But even though I trusted Margaret, it was difficult for me to be convinced of Colin Rutledge's honor. There was something amiss. Something terribly wrong that was gnawing at my common sense, and whether he was involved in Sorcha's death or not, I would not rest until I found out what it was.

The air was refreshing after the night's rain, crisp and savory. The sun was still warm even at summer's end and burned brightly in a deep blue sky. Some of the trees were already changing their colors from dying greens to dazzling oranges, yellows, and reds.

Margaret held Melinda tenderly against her

bosom as we made our way to the stables. She wore a pretty pink frock and was bundled loosely in a tartan blanket. In the light of day, I could see that her eyes were blue with a hint of silver just like Sorcha's. They were wide with wonder, darting about like two bouncing balls.

The ground was muddy and I wished I had worn my walking boots instead of my dress shoes. The walk was long but pleasurable and it gave Margaret and me an opportunity to talk.

"Does Roger Winfield still work at Raven Manor?" I asked, remembering that he was the one who took care of the stables for the Blackwells.

Margaret fussed with the blanket so that a portion was covering Melinda's head from the sun. "Goodness, no. Mr. Blackwell, rest his soul, had him fired."

I frowned. "He seemed a nice enough man."

"Roger Winfield liked his whiskey a little too much," she snorted. "He was drunk the night the stable caught fire and Mr. Blackwell blamed him."

"Was he responsible?"

She shrugged. "I'm not sure, but Mr. Blackwell was furious. The fire killed some of his prize stallions."

I pressed my lips together thoughtfully. Margaret, however, was compelled to continue.

"A few days later the Blackwells were killed."

"Killed?" The word writhed in my stomach. "You said it was an accident."

"It was," she answered quickly. Distracted for a moment, she then turned to look at me. "They were on their way to town when the back wheels broke loose. Both of them were thrown from the carriage." There was a tinge of sadness in her eyes. "They were killed instantly."

Spontaneously, my arm wrapped around her shoulders. "I'm so sorry, Margaret. I know how much you cared about them." Deep inside, I was fighting my own morose feelings. How awful for Margaret to lose her entire family, for that's what they were to her.

The stable was as I remembered it, simply styled with dark red clapboard. Part of it, though, was charred and damaged from the fire Margaret had spoken of.

"Mr. Rutledge intended to have the stable fixed," she said as a matter of information. "But since Sorcha ... well, he hasn't been able to concentrate on anything but her."

Her words brought a twinge to the depths of my soul. The sensation troubled me. Was it jealousy? Was I actually jealous of what Sorcha had had with him? Ridiculous notion. I could never have feelings for such an enigmatic man as Colin Rutledge seemed to be. I shook my head, ridding myself of the absurd idea, and welcomed back my sensibility.

"And of course there's this precious thing," I said, and peered under the blanket. Melinda's eyes caught mine and I could almost swear that there was a hint of a smile on her tiny face. "I'm sure Mr. Rutledge spends most of his time with Melinda."

"Oh, yes." Margaret said it quickly, too quickly, as if she too had to convince herself.

Two fine copper-colored horses were hitched to a handsome sturdy wagon that was waiting for us at the entrance of the stable.

"Mornin', ladies. Fine day for a ride if I do say so." An older gentleman with gray hair and spectacles greeted us. He tipped his green woolen cap and then placed it back on his head.

"Good morning, Thomas. It is a beautiful day, isn't it?" Margaret said, agreeing. I smiled and nodded. "Thomas, this is Miss St. James, a friend of the family. She'll be staying with us for a while."

He strode toward me on long, thin legs. Only friendliness resided in his smile. I offered my hand. He took it in his own large, calloused one and, to my surprise, kissed it sweetly.

"Thomas Reilly," he said with a certain flair to his voice. "Pleased to meet you." Humor glinted in his gray-green eyes.

"Thomas is our new stable hand," Margaret said.

I noticed that something passed between

them. A smile. A nod. Whatever it was, I had the distinct impression that Thomas Reilly was flirting and Margaret was reciprocating. My curiosity was aroused along with a happy feeling in my heart.

"I see you've also brought the wee one," Thomas said, motioning toward Melinda. The baby stirred in Margaret's arms.

"Is everything ready for us?" Margaret asked, heading toward the wagon.

"Yes, ma'am. Are you sure you don't want me to drive you into town? It would be my pleasure."

Margaret declined and I could see disappointment in Thomas's eyes.

I climbed in first, then held the baby while Margaret, helped by Thomas, got into the wagon seat. She grabbed the reins and with a wave to Thomas, commanded the horses to be on their way.

"Thomas won't tell Mr. Rutledge, will he?" I yelled over the noise of the moving wagon.

"Thomas thinks we're going into town, but, no, he won't tell."

I hugged Melinda to me. Soon Thomas, the stable, and Raven Manor were just specks behind us.

For a solid half-hour the wagon bumped along the open trail, jolting me. Melinda seemed to enjoy the uneven movement and giggled and cooed with every buffet. I laughed with her.

There was a change in the wind. It was cooler, feistier, and I wondered if we were nearing the bluff. Margaret was strangely quiet during the ride, and I knew it was because of our destination. Silently, I chastised myself. How thoughtless of me to ask her to do this, to relive this tragedy. I should have come here alone.

The sun's warmth had disappeared. I looked up to see that the sky was a mass of dusty clouds. I covered Melinda with more of the blanket and wished now that I had brought my own cloak.

With a firm tug on the reins, Margaret brought the wagon to a halt. She didn't need to say anything. I read the sorrow in her face. This was the place where Sorcha's body was found.

Chapter Six

Knowing that Margaret wouldn't follow me, I gently placed Melinda in her arms, climbed out of the wagon, and headed for the promontory a few yards ahead of where we had stopped.

I stood there, trembling. Why had I insisted on coming? I wanted to flee this place. Nothing made sense. Nothing.

But my instincts were stronger than my fear. Something or someone had caused Sorcha to come here. Something or someone had ended her life. For my sake, for the sake of that sweet child, I could not risk turning back.

Already anger was replacing my fear. Anger at whoever or whatever had cast its shadow over Raven Manor, over Sorcha. I walked to the edge of the cliff, not a helpless victim, but ready to confront the evil that lurked there.

The snarl of the raging St. Lawrence River pounded in my ears as I drew closer. Massive black rocks roared up from the water's edge. The place was shrouded in a pallid mist, and I felt the dampness seeping through my clothes and skin.

I peered over the periphery and into the gray-green gloom of the river. The restless water collided with towering rocks and the rough winds swept over me like lost souls. A narrow ledge of jutting stones surrounded the bottom of the bluff just above the river. Starting to shake, I looked away quickly. Was it there they found Sorcha? Was it there that her body lay broken and bruised, her life ebbing away? A life that she herself decided was worthless? Or was her death worthwhile to someone else?

I gulped the chilled air and tried to slow down my pulse. I had seen enough, felt enough. My head held high, I returned to the wagon.

I looked up at Margaret. Her lower lip trembled and there were tears in her eyes.

"Someone murdered Sorcha. She did not take her own life." I said it with such conviction that I noticed she hugged Melinda tightly for fear the baby might hear the awful truth.

She shook her head. "That cannot be, Britanny."

But I saw something come into her misty

87

eyes. She believed me. What was more important, she now believed what her own heart had been telling her all this time. Somehow she had always known that Sorcha had been murdered.

Melinda's brief wail distracted us.

"We had better be heading back, Britanny," Margaret said, gazing up at the sky. "It looks like rain."

I agreed with her, and though I found it hard to leave this place, I knew in my heart that I would be back.

It did not rain as we headed back to Raven Manor. The clouds parted and the sun shone on us as if happy that we were gone from that evil place. Margaret steered the horses toward the stable. Thomas was there to greet us, said he hoped we had enjoyed our outing, and then untethered the horses while we walked back to the house.

I was exhausted, not from the trip but from the unleashing of too many of my emotions. I needed to relax and think about other things if only for a little while.

As Margaret fed and cleaned Melinda, I too freshened up. Then Margaret and I had a light repast of fruit, cheese, and bread. When finished, I talked her into letting me take the baby for a walk around the grounds. After all, I had told Colin that that was what I had intended to do today.

I placed the baby in her honey-colored wicker pram once her eyes began to close as I covered her with a blanket and wheeled her outside.

The sun was high in the sky as I ambled through the gardens in the back of the manor, gently rocking the baby buggy. Geraniums and other hardier summer flowers were still alive with color. Welcoming the autumn were asters and zinnias just beginning to bloom from their green casings. Rose bushes lined a pebbly pathway, and their velvet petals blushed with a sweet perfume. The rather grand gazebo, I recalled, stood amid the tranquil beauty and it was there that I sat to rest.

So many pictures went through my mind at the same time, as my eyes took in the scenery around me. So many memories of Sorcha and me running through these gardens, playing tag or hide and seek, or tumbling down the grassy knoll just beyond the footpath.

"Oh, Sorcha," I whispered into the warm breeze. I thought of her portrait over the mantel, the way I imagined it had cried out to me. "I want to help you but where do I begin? What do I do? *Help me*."

My gaze fell upon the buggy and sweet child inside. Asleep, Melinda looked so peaceful, so free from the burdens of the world, especially those that plagued Raven Manor. But in a few years, she too would have questions about Sorcha. Why wasn't her mother here to read or sing to her, to hug her and laugh with her? Why had she left her all alone? What would Margaret and Colin tell her? What could I tell her?

Sleep the sleep of the Innocents, my love, I wished for her in my thoughts. *I'll always be here for you.*

My silent promise encouraged more contemplating. It was the strange message that tormented me now. Margaret had denied sending it. Who else knew that I would come here to seek the truth about Sorcha's death? Surprisingly, in that quiet moment of thought the answer came to me. Why hadn't I realized it before? Colin Rutledge. He knew. He knew I was Sorcha's best friend. "Sorcha spoke of you often." His words echoed in my brain. Had he sent the letter? Did I dare ask him?

The tramping of hooves and the rumble of a carriage disturbed my enlightening, if not intriguing, thoughts. Could it be Colin? My eagerness got me to my feet. Steering the buggy, I hurried to the front of the house.

I squinted and shielded my eyes against the sun. A handsome black coach was traveling up the path toward Raven Manor. The driver pulled back on the reins and brought the carriage to a stop right in front of me. Hastening from his seat, the gaunt figure opened the door and assisted a woman from the carriage. Behind her, a younger man followed promptly. Disappointment clouded my anticipation. I was so hoping that Colin had come home early.

The woman wore a pearl-gray traveling suit that looked quite expensive. The skirt and jacket were bordered by a black velvet ribbon. I watched as she fussed over her clothing and tucked strands of her light brown hair beneath the brim of a matching hat. She said something to her companion and the two turned and headed straight for me.

It was the man who reached me first, his curious expression now giving way to a pleasant smile. His eyes were blue, his chin angular, and his blond hair had a natural wave that reminded me of a Greek hero. He was handsomely attired in a tweed Chesterfield coat. I smiled back at him. He responded to my gesture with a bow.

"Douglas Garwood," he said by way of introduction. He turned halfway toward the woman. "My mother, Eleanor Garwood."

I nodded politely and she did the same. For a moment I found myself staring at this rather attractive woman. I realized I was being unmannerly yet I couldn't help myself. I was certain that I knew Eleanor Garwood. I just couldn't remember where we had met.

Her gloved hand reached up and touched the lovely black onyx brooch pinned to the middle of her high-necked blouse. "We're here to see Mr. Rutledge," she stammered, her dark eyes narrowing. I couldn't blame the way she was acting. My gawking was most likely making her nervous.

"I'm sorry, but Mr. Rutledge is not at home."

"Then may I ask to whom we have the pleasure of addressing?" Douglas Garwood asked. His eyes reflected the brightness of the sun and I noticed how good-looking he was when he smiled.

"Britanny St. James," I said without hesitation.

"A very pretty name, but then someone as beautiful as you deserves nothing less."

I could feel my cheeks growing warm at his blatantly flirtatious ways. Or was it the presence of his mother that was causing me embarrassment? I lowered my gaze, avoiding both their stares.

"Are you new to Raven Manor?"

"Pardon?"

"Do you work here?" He glanced down at the baby buggy. "The new nanny, perhaps?"

I couldn't contain my amusement. "Goodness, no. I'm a friend of the family." On a more serious note, I continued, "I'm ... that is, I was Sorcha Blackwell's friend." The past tense of the words nearly choked me. At the mention of Sorcha's name, a morose air blanketed the three of us. It was obvious that they had known her, too.

Eleanor Garwood shook her head. "That poor dear girl," she said, and sighed deeply. "My son and I are also friends of the family.

Her death was such a tragedy. You must be beside yourself." She started to reach for my hand, then seemed to think her gesture brash and drew away. Her expression was filled with compassion, though, and I found myself agreeing easily with the sturdy, yet sleek woman.

But it was Douglas Garwood who captured my attention. He looked older suddenly, his face worn with a grief he could not express. Once again, his gaze fell on Melinda. I thought it strange that he seemed so lost and at the same time his look was a veritable vessel of affection.

"Can we find Mr. Rutledge at his place of business then?" Eleanor asked, her quiet question easing her son from his trance.

"Yes," I said. "He left early this morning."

"Thank you, my dear," she said abruptly, giving me the impression that she was in a hurry. "Come, Douglas." She turned and made her way back to the carriage.

But Douglas lingered. "You mentioned that you and Sorcha were friends. How long did you know her?"

"Nearly ten years."

"That is a long time." He looked thoughtful. "You must miss her very much."

My expression must have given my feelings away for in the next moment he was apologizing. "Please, forgive me if I've upset you. Sorcha and I . . . well, I know how you feel."

His comment seemed odd to me, confusing.

For that brief instant, he acted as if he had known Sorcha as long as I had. In all the years we had been friends, she had never once mentioned a Douglas Garwood. Were the Garwoods friends of the Blackwell family as Eleanor had said? Not likely. At least I didn't recall them to be.

"That's quite all right, Mr. Garwood. You didn't upset me," I said.

He winced and his lips drooped at the corners, making him seem rather appealing. "Would you please call me Douglas? 'Mr. Garwood' was my father."

My uninhibited laughter transformed his face into pure sunlight. "Then you must call me Britanny."

He agreed and I was quick to realize that the informality between us did not lessen my uneasiness.

"May I be so bold as to ask how long you intend on staying at Raven Manor?"

"I'm not certain, though Mr. Rutledge has invited me to stay as long as I like." There was a sudden darkness behind Douglas's clear, blue eyes at the mention of Colin's name. It disappeared, quickly replaced by a flicker of interest.

"I don't mind telling you, Britanny, that you are a very lovely young woman. It may be the wrong time to say this, and I hope you will not find it inappropriate if I tell you that I would like to get to know you better."

His remark startled me and, at first, I did not know how to respond. But his hopeful expression seemed to make my reply easier. "If you wish," I said.

A dazzling smile once again broke out across his face.

"Douglas, we should be going," Eleanor Garwood called from the carriage, waving her hand impatiently at her son. "You know that it is important that we see Mr. Rutledge today."

He turned to me and shrugged, looking a trifle forlorn. "Mother. Always thinking about business. Never considering the important things in life." He took my hand, raised it to his lips, and gently kissed it. His stare made me blush. "I will see you again, Britanny."

"I'll look forward to it," I answered.

He did a strange thing then. At least I thought it strange. He touched the hood of the baby buggy. No, not a mere touch, but a caress. A careful, almost negligible caress. He said nothing but merely smiled, and then went to the waiting carriage.

The driver slapped the horses' reins and I watched as the coach headed back down the path away from Raven Manor.

I sighed deeply. My instincts burned with curiosity and the uncomfortable feeling disturbed me. Why, in such a few short moments, did the Garwoods' presence nourish such a suspicion in me? Images swam in my mind. Visions I could see clearly but not explain, even if I had been forced to do so. We were all connected somehow—Sorcha, me, Colin—and oddly enough the Garwoods, too.

Though I had not bargained for all these disquieting thoughts, nevertheless I knew with a certainty that I belonged here. Finding the truth about Sorcha's death was more than my responsibility. It was my destiny.

Melinda's faint stirrings made me aware that she would awaken soon. I reached down and lifted her out of the buggy. She wiggled a bit, then settled herself against me, content and undisturbed.

I was about to climb the stairs to the porch but stopped when I felt a chill. Something, a premonition, made my eyes fly to an upstairs window. Someone was watching me.

Sorcha. The thought flashed across my mind like a bolt of lightning. Was it happening again? Hadn't I imagined my dear friend standing at the top of the stairs only last night? I was frozen to the spot. My heart pounded like a drum. I held Melinda tightly, wanting to protect her. But from whom? Sorcha?

My panic lasted only an instant. When I looked, really looked this time, I saw that the person in the window was not Sorcha but Evangeline—and she was not staring at me. Her intense gaze was following the Garwood carriage as it disappeared around a bend of stately oaks.

Chapter Seven

"Eleanor Garwood?" Margaret's voice was as sharp as the knife she was brandishing. She brought the blade down, slicing through the leaves of a large head of cabbage. I jumped at the resounding thwack it made against the maple cutting table.

Hastily, I stuffed a small morsel of one of Margaret's feather-like biscuits into my mouth. Seeing her in this agitated state unnerved me and the sweet-tasting bread seemed to soothe my anxiety.

"What did she want?" Margaret snapped.

"She wanted to see Mr. Rutledge."

"Indeed she did."

The comment was a strange one, yet I ignored it. "Who is Eleanor Garwood?" I asked quite innocently.

Margaret gave the cabbage another whack, sending some of the pieces tumbling to the blue-and-white tiled kitchen floor. I gulped and reached across the table for the jar of strawberry preserves.

"Don't you remember her, Britanny? She used to work at Raven Manor." She pursed her lips and emitted a disgruntled sound. "She was one of the upstairs maids."

"Ellie?" I almost shouted, now realizing where I had seen the woman before. "Ellie McDonald?"

"The very same."

Sorcha and I were already fast friends when Ellie McDonald came to work for the Blackwells. Looking back now, I did recall that she had barely been in the family's employ when she just picked up and left. The reason for her hasty departure was unknown to me. But what did come to mind was Sorcha. Even though we were both scarcely twelve years old, I was aware of Sorcha's behavior whenever Ellie was present. She acted anxious around the woman, uncomfortable. She would sometimes intimate her uncomfortable feelings to me, too, by sporting a worried frown or dragging me from whatever room Ellie happened to be puttering in. It was an unusual way for Sorcha to behave. In the years that I had known her. Sorcha had never shown dislike toward anyone, never with an unkind word or even a nasty thought. Yet she was different with Ellie McDonald, and now, with these thoughts swimming through my mind, I couldn't help but wonder why.

"How did she come by the name of Eleanor Garwood?" I asked, my curiosity now surfacing. I took a quick sip of the strong tea that Margaret had prepared for me.

Using her apron like a basket, she gathered the wedges of cabbage in it, walked to the sink, and unloaded them into the basin. "Tricked Lance Garwood into marryin' her. Poor man. Had no idea what he was getting into." She turned on the spigot and a rush of water sputtered from its spout.

I leaned against the high-backed chair, my mouth opened in surprise. "Lance Garwood? The wealthy Pennsylvania coal baron?"

She glanced over her shoulder at me. Displeasure was etched in the lines around her eyes and mouth. "Britanny, could you fetch the carrots for me?"

After collecting the cluster of orange-gold vegetables from the spacious work table in front of the large window, I joined Margaret at the sink. She was vigorously scrubbing the leaves with a small brush, clearing venting her anger on the poor, innocent cabbage.

"Ellie went to work for Mr. Garwood soon after she left Raven Manor. Oh, she was a sly one. Always was. Always looking for an opportunity and sparing no one who got in her way."

I saw Margaret's brow furrow deeper with each accusation. Her attitude surprised me. I had no idea of her animosity toward Ellie.

"Mrs. Garwood wasn't dead six months before that—that trollop ingratiated herself into the bereaved widower's life." Margaret made an irate clicking noise with her tongue. "Shameful. Utterly shameful." She closed the spigot with a forceful turn, then dried her hands vigorously on her apron.

Frowning, I reached into the sink for a piece of a cabbage leaf. "How do you know all of this?"

She shot me a stinging glance. "I'm not a snoop," she said defensively.

"I'm not implying that you are, Margaret. I only wondered—"

She touched my arm. "I'm sorry, child. It's just that talking about Ellie McDonald sets my blood to boilin'." She marched over to the ponderous wood-burning stove and carefully lifted the lid from an iron pot. Seeing that the water inside was not yet simmering, she replaced the cover and went back to the sink to tend to the carrots. "Mr. Garwood was often a dinner guest at Raven Manor. All during the meal all he could talk about was his 'wonderful Ellie.' Made my stomach turn, it did."

I nibbled thoughtfully on the sweet cabbage

leaf. "Maybe she was just being kind to a sad, old man."

"Kind? My Uncle Pat's posies."

Margaret's familiar expression caught me off guard. I bit down on my tongue to stop myself from laughing out loud.

"Took advantage of the man, she did. Made herself indispensable to him. Made him fall in love with her."

My eyebrows raised with interest. "Then what happened?"

"She convinced him to marry her, that's what happened," she said as she yanked the thick green fronds from the carrot tops. "A year later he was gone, leaving everything to her and Douglas."

"Her son?" I asked. A picture of Douglas Garwood's blue eyes and angular face crossed my mind.

"Stepson," she corrected. She stopped attacking the carrots and stared, "I often wondered if she did the poor man in for his money."

I gasped at her accusation. "Margaret, that's an awful thing to say!" I thought about Colin then, and my own allegations about him. I suddenly felt uncomfortable.

She snapped out of her macabre daydreaming. "I suppose," she said, sounding undecided.

"Did Sorcha know Douglas?" I couldn't stop the words from tumbling out of my mouth.

"He called on her a few times. Mr. Blackwell

always welcomed him but Mrs. Blackwell . . . That was a different story. She didn't trust him. Said he was too good-looking, too charming. 'Charm the honey from the bees,' she would say." Margaret's eyes locked with mine. "It wasn't a compliment, believe me."

I frowned and shook my head. "I don't remember any of this, Margaret. Sorcha never told me about Douglas's intentions toward her."

Something about my words bothered her. Her mouth drooped at the corners, collapsing the rest of her features in a troubled expression. "I suppose it wasn't all that important to Sorcha." She looked away from me quickly, yet I could see that her face carried a startling wealth of information. Or was it secrets?

I leaned against the sink, as my mind raced. "Margaret, I've been thinking about that letter."

"The one asking you to come to Raven Manor? The one you thought I'd written?"

I nodded. "Do you suppose it was Mr. Rutledge who sent me that message? After all, he did tell me that Sorcha often spoke of me. Is it he who wants me here?"

"Whatever for?"

I shrugged. "It was just a thought. But someone sent me that letter and I intend to find out who."

I wanted to further this particular conversation, but Margaret had other plans.

"You said Ellie was here to see Mr. Rutledge?" she asked. She went back to the stove to check on the water once again. This time it was bubbling to the top of the pot.

"She said it was business."

"Hmmph. That's what she always says." Sweeping up the wedges of cabbage from the sink, she placed them in the boiling water. With a wooden spoon, she stirred them gently until they sank into the pot. "If you ask me, she has her sights set on Mr. Rutledge for her next victim."

"Margaret!" I couldn't contain my shock. "She's attractive, yes, but she must be at least ten years older than he is."

She turned to me and placed her forefinger under my chin. "My sweet innocent thing. Don't tell me you know nothing of feminine wiles? There are ways Miss Ellie can get what she wants. Mr. Rutledge is very vulnerable right now, and as you said she is an attractive woman."

I felt my cheeks grow hot, not from embarrassment, surprisingly, but from annoyance. I was not totally innocent where men and women were concerned. I knew about the flirting and the ruses that the "weaker sex" used to get their way. I, myself, had even acted coquettish with a few gentlemen callers.

But Margaret wasn't alluding to harmless dallying. It was lovemaking between man and woman in the passionate throes of their own desires. Colin and Ellie? I shifted uneasily, assaulted by a terrible sense of humiliation. Not for myself, but for Sorcha.

I watched Margaret add the thick slices of carrots to the already limp cabbage. She seasoned it lightly with rosemary and tarragon. Next, she bent over and pulled down the heavy iron door of the stove. With a large ladle, she basted the roast that she was also preparing. The aromas were delightful but they did not sway my mind from the subject being discussed.

"You don't think Mr. Rutledge and Ellie—"

"Oh, my stars, no," Margaret cut in with a twitter in her voice. "Mr. Rutledge is not too fond of Mrs. Eleanor Garwood. Besides, he has too much respect for Sorcha to get involved with a woman like her."

I sighed. But why, I wondered, did it seem to be a sigh of relief?

"Mr. Rutledge and who?"

The voice made Margaret and me jump. We both turned to see Colin leaning against the kitchen doorway, his arms folded, his eyebrows raised, with a smile that heightened his curious look.

"Mr. Rutledge," Margaret said, choking on his name.

I caught my breath, swallowed, and took in his full length.

He strode to the stove and gulped the air greedily. "Something smells delicious, Margaret. I hope you have enough for two more."

"Sir?"

"I've invited some guests for dinner."

Something pricked at the back of my neck. It was a stab of an unsettling thought.

"Mrs. Garwood and her son will be joining us this evening."

I fought with myself not to look at Margaret and I knew she was doing the same.

"Very good, sir," she said.

He consulted his gold pocket watch. "It's four o'clock now. They will be here in about two hours. Will that pose a problem?" The lid of the timepiece snapped shut.

"No, Mr. Rutledge. Of course not."

He nodded, his eyes sparkling with a dark determination. I could see in his expression that the Garwoods' company was very much desired. Or was it Eleanor he longed to see?

He turned toward me then, and with heavy-lidded eyes and a slight lopsided smile, he acknowledged my presence. "And how was your day, Miss St. James? I trust you weren't too bored."

I discreetly distanced myself from him. I was not about to let him even suspect that I had gone to the place where Sorcha's body had been discovered. "I am never bored, Mr. Rutledge. I don't allow myself to be."

His brow rose in surprise.

"Margaret and I talked the entire day away. We had a lot of catching up to do." I saw Margaret flinch at my obvious stretching of the truth. "And, of course, being with Melinda kept me busy, too."

At the mention of the baby's name, I noticed his cavalier expression soften. "I'm glad you spent some time with her. I would like her to get to know her mother's best friend." He sounded sincere and his smile reached clear to my heart.

I smiled back, and for what seemed to be too short a time, we stood there staring into each other's eyes.

Colin was first to break the connection. "Well, our guests will be arriving soon. I'll be in my study, Margaret. Let me know the moment Eleanor arrives." His gaze swept back to me. "I don't wish to keep someone like her waiting too long."

The sincerity was gone, and his tone set my teeth on edge. So satisfied with himself, so arrogant. Maybe Margaret was wrong. Maybe Colin Rutledge and Eleanor Garwood were attracted to one another. Or had their relationship gone even further? I blushed at the thought. But a faint feeling of anger began to work its way through my embarrassment. I didn't look at him. I couldn't.

"Margaret, I'll set the table in the dining room," I offered. Without waiting for her reply. I lifted my skirt and hastily brushed past Colin in a huff.

It was my loyalty to Sorcha that made me

uneasy. She had been dead a little over a month. How could Colin Rutledge be so heartless? Margaret was mistaken, I convinced myself. He had no respect for Sorcha's memory.

The dishes clattered in my hands as I carried them from the sideboard to the table. The light from the late-afternoon sun shimmered lazily through the window. A warm breeze fluttered the curtains, bringing with it the sweet perfume of the roses in the garden.

I tried not to dwell on Colin Rutledge and his condescending ways. I was never going to understand the man and I would not waste my energy trying. I had more important matters on my mind.

Across the room I felt the surging power of his sudden presence. I looked up and felt a sudden flutter in my chest.

"Have I upset you, Miss St. James?" Colin asked pensively. He walked into the dining room, stopping at the head of the table. He clutched the top spindle of the chair and studied me with a probing gaze.

I chose to ignore him and went about the business of gathering the silverware from the center drawer of the sideboard. I placed the knives, forks, and spoons on top of a neatly folded pile of napkins and brought it all to the table.

"You're angry with me, aren't you?" he asked again, trying to bait my emotions.

I looked into his dark eyes. "And what if I am?"

"May I know the reason why?"

"I thought you didn't—" I stopped myself, wary of my intrusion. It was his life, after all.

"Didn't like the Garwoods? Is that what you were going to say?"

I pursed my lips, irked that he had read my thoughts.

"You've been talking to Margaret." He grinned, amused at my annoyance. His bright look of success made me even angrier. "She's right. I'm not particularly fond of those two, but Eleanor Garwood has something I want. Something very important."

I frowned. Did this "something" have to do with the shipping company? I wondered.

"Sometimes one must make allowances to get what one wants, Miss St. James."

"Is that how you do business, Mr. Rutledge? By wooing prospective clients?"

He gave me a strange look yet continued to play along. "Perhaps. Of course, the prospective client must be a woman. All a man needs to do is say the right words and they respond."

I wanted to scream. I had a vision of grabbing one of the knives, hurling it through the air straight into his cold, dark heart. Instead, I snatched a few of the napkins, snapped them opened, and began to refold them into tight triangles.

"Not every woman succumbs to male charm

and prowess," I said defensively.

The unfaltering sound of his footsteps warned me he was nearing me. He touched my arm, easily turning me toward him. Slowly, he pulled the napkin from my shaking fingers and tossed it with the others. With a curled forefinger, he lifted my chin so that our eyes met. His were smoldering, their heat burning away my anger.

"Does that include you, Miss St. James?"

Something passed between us. His expression relaxed and his eyes, which searched my face, lingered on my mouth. He reached up and touched my cheek, and I felt as if a coil wound up inside me unsprang. We looked into each other's eyes and a tiny thrill raced through me, but my heart was pounding so hard, I couldn't move. The light and shade in the room played on his face. His eyes were like clear black glass, raking me with a fiercely possessive look.

I felt that same sense of yearning that had tormented me last night as Colin had played the fiery sonata. I could not understand what was happening to me, and for some strange reason, I didn't want to.

"You didn't answer me, Britanny." He said my name softly, as if praying. "Could you surrender to a charming, attractive man?"

A wave of heat shot through me and tremors of excitement caught in my throat. I pulled away from him, as my heart quivered. "Excuse me, Mr. Rutledge. I must dress for dinner."

Without a second thought, I hurried past him and out of the room. I ran like a mad-woman through the foyer and up the stairs, not stopping until I reached the door to my room. I grabbed onto the latch tightly and tried to compose myself. I did not move until my breathing had returned to normal.

"Yes, Colin," I whispered, suddenly frightened of my own feelings. "I could surrender to a charming, attractive man—if that man was you."

Chapter Eight

The cold water I had splashed on my face had not washed the confusion away. My perplexed expression was still there, staring back at me from the mirror. Unpinning my hair, I let the curls fall to my shoulders. I brushed it slowly, hoping the gentle motion would relax me. But I felt drained, exhausted, and at the same time elated. I shivered suddenly, knowing it was Colin Rutledge who had prompted such a state.

What was he after? Why all the fuss about Eleanor Garwood? Was he teasing me? Trying to make me jealous? *Ridiculous, Britanny*, I chided myself. We hardly knew each other. Besides, it was too soon after Sorcha's death to invite such flirting. I was now certain that there was much more to his inviting the Garwoods than to spark my envious nature.

Discarding my skirt and blouse, I pampered myself with some of the sweet-smelling powder that Evangeline had brought to my room yesterday. It felt like silk against my skin, and though I tried to lose myself in its luxury, I couldn't help but think about the young servant girl. I could still see her staring out the upstairs window after the Garwoods' carriage. She had looked so forlorn, so lost in her thoughts. I did not know what to make of her.

Finished with my primping, I chose my cream-colored faille dress trimmed in green velvet bows. The puffy sleeves swept below my shoulders, revealing maybe more neckline and collarbone than I had anticipated. Nevertheless, the dress made me feel pretty, and that was exactly how I wanted to feel this evening.

Instead of fashioning my hair on top of my head, I decided to let remain as it was, long and free. I did, however, pull back the sides, fastening them with my favorite mother-of-pearl combs. A few tendrils framed my face.

A light tap came at the door. I opened it to Evangeline. Her quick glance took in every detail of my appearance. Something flickered in her clear, blue eyes, but her only comment was, "Mr. Rutledge sent me to fetch you, miss. The Garwoods are here."

Together we descended the steps, Evangeline leading the way. She too looked especially pretty, but she left my room so hurriedly that I did not have the time to compliment her.

In the foyer, she pointed toward the opened doors of the parlor. "In there," she said, then turned and hurried off in the opposite direction.

The candlelight from the chandelier above made the foyer invitingly bright, and the atmosphere put me in a much better mood. I had almost forgotten about Colin and his fatuous responses earlier. What I couldn't erase from my mind was the mesmeric way he had looked at me, his touch that had made me tremble. Even now, as I readied myself to meet the Garwoods—this time on a more formal note—my senses began to flutter at the thought of Colin Rutledge.

Smoothing my skirt and flouncing my hair off my shoulders, I took a deep breath and stopped in the doorway of the parlor. Save for the crackling fire, I heard no voices coming from inside the room. The eerie silence puzzled me. Was I late? Had the three already started dinner without me?

Miffed at the thought, unfounded as it was, I walked into the room. My eyes were drawn to the shadowy figure by the fireplace. It was Douglas Garwood. His back was toward me, yet I could see a glass in his hand. He had positioned in such a way that it seemed as though he was offering it to Sorcha's portrait as some sort of tribute to her memory.

Though I found his behavior strange, I reminded myself that he had alluded to knowing Sorcha, mysterious as that implication had been.

"Douglas?" I called softly, not wanting to startle him. He did not turn around and I wondered if I should disturb him at all. Just as I was about to leave the room, I heard him call to me.

"Britanny. How wonderful to see you again." He walked toward me, looking more dashing than he had when we had met this afternoon. He studied me with a practiced eye. Though I was flattered by the attention, it nevertheless made me feel slightly uneasy.

"May I get you something to drink? Perhaps some sherry?"

I declined his offer, but noted his familiarity with Raven Manor. He seemed very much at home, and it surprised me.

"Are you alone, Douglas?" I asked, unwilling to look at him yet finding I couldn't help myself. "I thought you and your mother would be joining us this evening."

He laughed wickedly. "Mother and your Mr. Rutledge are in his study. They wanted to be alone." His eyes sparkled with mischief.

"He is not my Mr. Rutledge," I said, sweeping past him and his insinuations.

"Well, whoever he belongs to, I'm very glad that he left us alone for a while." Douglas followed me to the hearth. He took my hand in his, brought it to his lips, and kissed it. "May I say that you look exceptionally beautiful tonight, Britanny."

As I looked into his cool, liquid blue stare, a trembling thrill raced through me. Douglas Garwood was indeed exquisite. There was no other word for him.

He smiled and his smile warmed me, making me suddenly realize how guarded my feelings had been since my return to Raven Manor. Yet I also knew it was neither the place nor the tragic circumstances. It was Colin Rutledge who had forced me to become wary. True, I found him exciting but in a dark, sinister way, and I was not about to abandon my suspicions that he was involved in Sorcha's death.

Douglas was so different. A rascal, yes, but not a brooding, enigmatic sort. He was straightforward and friendly and all I had to guard myself against was his boyish charm.

I retrieved my hand from his hold and though difficult, I managed to pry my eyes from his handsome face as well. I turned back to the fireplace. The logs burned cheerfully in the grate, and a blush of pleasure as warm as the fire rose in my cheeks.

"How long have you known the Blackwell family?" I asked.

He was standing next to me now, and I stole a sideways glance at him. His brow was furrowed and he looked as though he was deep in concentration.

"My father was acquainted with Kingsley Blackwell through business." He snorted giving the impression he was not too fond of the alliance. "They had so much in common. They both loved to make money." His words were filled with contempt, harsh and unrelenting.

I was hesitant at first, not wishing to upset him with further questioning, but my curiosity overshadowed my reluctance. "Is that how you came to know Sorcha?"

He took a half step forward and raised his eyes to the portrait. A smile, sweet and genuine, graced his countenance. "I knew Sorcha long before I had even laid eyes on her lovely face."

I frowned, puzzled at his odd statement. He turned toward me and tilted his head, amused at my bewilderment.

"Sounds strange, doesn't it? But when I was younger, a mere child, I often had these dreams of a beautiful girl with long black hair and haunting eyes. She never spoke to me in those dreams. She would just appear and seeing her loving, gentle expression made me realize that someday I would find this beautiful creature and we would be together forever."

Douglas had me clinging to his every word. I was assailed by his uneasiness, felt his apprehension.

"I never told that to anyone before, Britanny. I hope I haven't upset you."

I had an incredible urge to run my hand

gently across his cheek, to do anything to ease the pain from his expression. "No," I said. "You haven't upset me. Please tell me more."

He nodded, obliging me. We sat opposite one another. He looked somewhat relaxed in the leather chair by the fire. As for me, I was poised on the edge of the other chair's cushion.

"One day, when I was older, my father had a meeting with Kingsley Blackwell, and so, he took me along. I imagined he was anxious for me to follow in his footsteps. But I was bored by their business talk. I sneaked away to the gardens. Anything was better than listening to two stodgy men discussing how they were going to make a fortune."

I watched his eyes suddenly reflect sparks of joy that could only have come from deep inside him.

"And then, I saw her. She was sitting in the gazebo, watching the sunset. I had no idea who she was. I only knew I had to speak with her. So, I summoned all my courage and introduced myself. My mind reeled when I saw her lovely face and smile. I knew it was she—the girl in my dreams!" He took a deep breath and his gaze settled on Sorcha's portrait.

"It's a wonderful story, Douglas," I said.

"It's the truth." His eyes flashed back to me. "I suppose you think that it's just some romantic fantasy, or the ravings of a madman, but I swear to you, Britanny, it is the truth. I did dream of Sorcha before we even met."

"I do believe you," I assured him. "Please go on."

"There's nothing more to tell other than we became good friends..." He paused, then whispered, "Very good friends. You see, I loved Sorcha."

"Everyone whoever met Sorcha loved her."

"No, Britanny. I was really in love with her and she really loved me. That's why I couldn't understand..." His voice trailed off into the darkness when the lilting sound of laughter wafted into the room.

I turned, annoyed at the interruption. But my irritability was slight compared to the anger I began to feel when I saw Eleanor Garwood on Colin's arm. They sauntered into the parlor, totally oblivious to Douglas and me.

"Oh, Colin, dear," Eleanor twittered. "You are quite the cad!"

I watched him throw his head back in a wicked laugh. It turned my stomach. He was flirting shamelessly with the poor, unsuspecting woman. Whatever Colin wanted from her, I was sure that he would have no trouble obtaining it.

"Good evening," I said, interrupting their frivolity.

Colin's dark eyes cut into me like a blade. A cruel smile twisted his mouth. "Good evening, Miss St. James," he answered in a low growl.

Eleanor nodded to me. "We meet again, Britanny."

"Again?" Colin looked surprised.

"Mrs. Garwood and Douglas came to the house to see you today," I said.

"And she was kind enough to let us know that you were at your place of business." Eleanor smiled warmly and for the first time I could see the Ellie McDonald I used to know in her youthful face. She was attired in a gown made of strawberry satin enhanced with creamy silk embroidery. The style accentuated her firm figure. A lovely pearl choker graced her neck and matching earrings glistened in the glow of the fire.

Douglas stood, his body tall and rigid. Though he remained silent, I was aware of the animosity between the two men. It made me uncomfortable.

"Finished with your business talk, Mother?" he asked, then drained the last of his drink with an impassioned gusto.

Eleanor laughed and looked at me. "Douglas never had a head for business. Just an eye for the ladies." She turned toward her son. "Isn't that right, dear?"

"Whatever you say, Mother." His face had changed to stone.

My gaze drifted to Colin. He seemed to be enjoying this mother-son tiff. I found his hard, cruel smile abominable.

"Excuse me, Mr. Rutledge."

We all turned to see Evangeline in the doorway. She wore a black muslin uniform and a neat white apron.

"Yes?" Colin asked.

"Dinner is served, sir."

"Shall we?" Douglas said, offering me his arm.

I accepted it willingly. He led the way with an unyielding ardor as if trying to prove something to the smug, self-righteous Colin Rutledge.

Though annoyed with the game these two seemed to be playing, I was more perturbed with Evangeline. As Douglas and I slipped past her, I saw the hate in her eyes, the twisted features of her expression. My pulse began to quicken, frightfully aware now that her maddening look was directed at me.

Everything about the dining room overflowed with elegance. The scent from the jasmine candles filled the air. The table sparkled with crystal and silver. I assumed that Margaret had finished what I had started before being interrupted by Colin's sharp tongue.

It was a rather bold move, but I chose the seat at the opposite end of the table, directly across from Colin. The place was traditionally reserved for the mistress of Raven Manor. Mrs. Blackwell had always sat here. More recently and likely Sorcha had also.

I raised my eyes over the lovely flower arrangement that adorned the middle of the table. Colin's own dark eyes reflected the candlelight and a curious gleam.

He uncovered the steaming dishes that Margaret had prepared. A fine-looking roast, a cabbage-and-carrot medley, and crisp potatoes were the main fare.

I was less than aware of the delicious aromas that came from the wholesome food, however. I was puzzled. I imagined Colin would be angry with my choice, but his face harbored a pleasant look, as if he expected me to sit opposite him.

The dinner conversation, though forced at times, remained light, and to my disappointment, unrevealing. I heard Sorcha's name mentioned once or twice, but by neither of the two men. It was Eleanor who again lamented my friend's tragic demise.

Douglas, who sat to my right, paid particular attention to me. His jokes made me laugh and his compliments made me blush. They also disturbed Colin. The strange part was that I couldn't distinguish between enjoying his jealousy and being troubled by it.

Douglas pushed his empty plate aside. "Tell me about yourself, Brittany," he said, his face showing his interest in me.

At first, I refused politely, knowing my life was not all that interesting. But when I looked at Colin, his eyes shone with a subtle eagerness that compelled me to change my mind.

I spoke briefly about my parents and my upbringing with Aunt Elizabeth. I found tales of my friendship with Sorcha took up most of my conversation.

Colin watched me the entire time. His handsome face lit up brightly when I mentioned the wonderful times I had had with Sorcha. It was almost as if he was reliving some part of his own past. The bond that I had felt between us seemed to grow stronger, impervious to any outside force, and I secretly wished that we were alone.

Realizing that this notion was a foolish one, I wanted to erase it from my mind. But not completely. Some part of me, perhaps my romantic side, wished the fleeting whim to linger just awhile longer.

Soon, I forced myself back to the situation at hand. At once I noticed that Eleanor, too, was quite interested in all I had to say about Sorcha. If she recognized who I was, she made no move to announce it publicly. After my talk with Margaret earlier, I wondered if Eleanor had chosen to block completely her servant days from her mind. She was a wealthy woman now, even if Margaret viewed her means of obtaining that fortune as questionable.

The dishes were soon cleared away by Margaret and Evangeline. Compliments on the dinner were heartily echoed by the four of us. Dressed in the same type of black uniform as Evangeline, Margaret looked even more severe when she gathered the plates from Eleanor's place. I could only imagine what was going through my dear friend's mind as she kowtowed before one of her kind.

Douglas continued to pose questions to me and for a while it seemed as if we were the only ones in the room. Margaret soon appeared with a silver carafe of coffee. Evangeline trailed behind, balancing a tray that was larger than herself.

Seeing the young servant girl made me think back to only a little while ago when I had passed her to enter the dining room. Her vicious expression had shaken me a bit. Though I had not a clue as to why I deserved such a look, I nevertheless took it very much to heart.

"Dessert, sir?" she barely whispered to Colin.

"And what flavorsome confectionery has Margaret prepared for tonight?" he asked.

I saw a secret smile on Margaret's lips as she poured the steaming coffee in my cup.

"Apple cobbler with cream, sir. She said it was your favorite," Evangeline answered.

"And she's right." His smile surpassed the dazzling candlelight.

Not surprisingly, I felt myself smiling, too. Margaret's warm apple cobbler with fresh cream was one of my favorites, also. I would have liked to think she had prepared it just for me, but knowing it was Colin's choice somehow made it seem even more special.

Deep in my thoughts, I didn't see Douglas

lean forward and reach across the table until his hand covered mine. My heart jumped.

"Britanny, Mother is giving a small informal party in two weeks for one of the more prominent businessmen in town." Though slight, the statement was a direct stab at Colin's business status. But he didn't seem ruffled at the inference; in fact, he looked more amused than annoyed.

Douglas continued, "I'd like you to be my guest."

To say the least, I was caught off guard by his invitation. "I'm not sure if I'll be here, Douglas," I said, uncertain of my plans. My gaze found Colin's eyes again.

"Miss St. James and I have an agreement, Douglas. She is more than welcome to stay at Raven Manor for as long as she wishes." He leaned back in his chair, his hulking form commanding the room.

Douglas's eyes sparkled with a longing that began to melt my heart. "Please make me a happy man, Brittany. Say yes."

"Yes Britanny, please accept," Eleanor said all atwitter. "Then this handsome gentleman can be my escort." She flashed a girlish grin at Colin. He smiled back at her, a wicked, playful smile, and I cringed.

I turned back to Douglas, hoping he couldn't detect my discontent. "Of course, Douglas, I would be pleased to be your guest."

It all happened so fast that I hardly had time

to react. Evangeline was offering me dessert one moment and the next, the warm apple cobbler had spilled from the dish and onto my lap.

I pushed the chair back and stood up. With one quick movement, I flung the cobbler off my skirt and feverishly brushed away the residue with my napkin.

"Evangeline! Look what you've done!" An angry Margaret upbraided the young girl for her clumsiness.

I looked up to see Eleanor, her expression aghast, and Douglas's sporadic movements depicted his uncertainty of how to react. Only Colin remained calm. He sped down to where I was, took the napkin from my shaky grasp, and soaked it in my water goblet. His hand reached between my skirt and petticoat and with firm but gentle strokes, he persisted at the stain until it was gone.

He glanced up at me eager for my approval. I smiled, reacting with more gratefulness than embarrassment.

"I think this beautiful dress is saved, Margaret," he said, cutting off the housekeeper's ranting.

I glanced over at Evangeline, who was still standing behind me. Though accidents happened, I had expected some sort of apology to which I would have probably forgiven her without so much as a blink of an eye. But she said nothing. Instead, there was darkness in her eyes and I felt numb. A self-satisfying smug expression twisted her features into a maddening leer, and nervous flutterings began in my stomach. This was no accident. She had planned to embarrass me.

"Excuse me," I said, nearly choking on the words. I did not give an explanation for my hasty departure. I just needed to be alone. I hurried from the room, leaving, I was certain, a bewildered Colin and guests behind.

Holding the dress in my hands, I studied the stain by the light of the lamp in my room. It was gone. All that was left was a damp spot where Colin had so doggedly cleaned the affects away.

I shivered as I placed the dress on the bed. Covered only by my robe, I could have assumed it was my lack of clothing that caused me to feel the cold, but I knew better. In my mind, I could still see the cruel expression on Evangeline's face. The entire incident puzzled me. I had been friendly to the girl since I had arrived. What would make her do such a thing?

I pondered the question for what seemed a long time, but there was no answer to be found, at least not for now.

The knock at the door interrupted my thoughts.

"Miss St. James?" Colin's muffled voice filtered into the room.

Though a surge of expectation coursed through my veins, I took a deep breath and paced myself, not wanting to seem anxious. I opened the door.

We stood there, staring at each other, perplexed in a way. Then the corners of his mouth lifted slightly. His look was clear and direct.

"Are you all right?" he asked, studying me up and down. For some reason, his probing glance did not make me self-conscious; in fact, it relaxed me.

"Yes," I answered, not wanting him to worry.

"May I come in?"

I stepped aside readily and closed the door behind him. "I apologize for leaving you and your guests so abruptly."

"No apology necessary. I understand."

"Yes, but do Douglas and Eleanor?"

He smirked. "To hell with them."

I felt my cheeks grow warm. "I'll get dressed and come downstairs as quickly as—"

"No need to, Miss St. James. The Garwoods have left." He almost looked relieved.

"Was it because of me? I'm sorry."

"You did me a favor. Their presence was beginning to bore me."

I found the statement curious. For one so persistent in wooing Mrs. Garwood, Colin was certainly revealing another side of himself.

"I do wish to speak to you about the Garwoods, though," he said.

"Of course," I agreed, not knowing what I could possibly offer him as information.

A dour, dark look enveloped his face. "Why didn't you tell me you had met Douglas and Eleanor prior to this evening?"

It was a strange question, but one that I answered. "I didn't know it was so important to you. We only spoke briefly. I was outside in the garden with Melinda—"

His body went rigid. "Melinda?"

"Yes." A wave of apprehension rushed over me. "I told you I'd spent the day with her." I paused, dizzy from trying to keep pace with his moods. "Have I done something wrong, Mr. Rutledge?"

He studied me with a clear expression of hatred, and it sent a spasm of fear shooting through me. "I never want Douglas Garwood to come near that child. Ever. Do you understand?" His words were enough to stun me, but it was the horrific look in his eyes that rendered me speechless.

He grabbed me by the shoulders, his grip tight and unyielding. Roughly, he pulled me closer to him. The front of my robe parted suddenly revealing my underclothing. But my near nakedness meant nothing to him. His fingers only dug deeper into my flesh until I thought I would cry out for mercy.

"Do you understand?" he shouted.

Tears sprang to my eyes as I fought my way out of his powerful hold. In haste, I wrapped the ends of my robe tightly around me. "Why?" I stammered, trying not to show him how frightened I really was. "Why are you saying this?"

His dark eyes shone now with a keen awareness that he had terrified me with his outburst. "It's none of your concern, Miss St. James. Only know that I am right in what I say. Douglas Garwood is *never* to go anywhere near the baby."

Amid Colin's ravings, a sudden flash of memory came thundering back to me. I envisioned Douglas as he was this afternoon, his hand stroking the hood of Melinda's buggy in a loving or, I now wondered—a possessive way?

I frowned, banishing the latter thought from my mind. "You act as though he would hurt the baby. Are you afraid he might do such a dreadful thing?"

He wanted to turn away from me at that moment, but I would not let him. My hand grasped his arm and I forced him to face me. The haunted look in his eyes was his answer.

"You are afraid, aren't you, Colin?" I whispered. "You're afraid Douglas might harm Melinda. But why? How can you even think such a thing?" My heart was pounding against my ribs. Blood roared in my ears.

Tenderly, he covered my hand with his and a new sensation filled my being, its tingling effects spreading through me like wildfire. He searched my face as if to find the answer that would end his torment.

"Britanny." It was the second time he had

129

called me by my given name. It sounded as beautiful as the first time, and I smiled. "I know I said you can stay at Raven Manor, and God knows I want you to, but it is too dangerous here. For your own safety, I want you to leave."

"No, Colin. I can't. I can't leave. Not now."

He started to protest, and once again my decision to stay remained steadfast. Only now, something else was troubling me. Would I be staying to carry out my original plan? Was it finding the truth about Sorcha's death that would keep me here? Or was Colin now the reason I wanted to remain?

"Britanny . . ." he began, looking away from me.

I raised my hand to his cheek and turned his face back to me. "Let me help you, Colin. We can fight whatever it is that's causing you so much pain. We can fight it together."

He smiled then, a sweet, singular smile and for one brief moment, all the agony on his face vanished. "Sorcha was right. You are a good friend."

For a moment his stare held me fast. His lips parted as though he were going to say something, but then he hesitated. Instead, he looked down into my face, paralyzing me. In his dark eyes, I could see my reflection. He brushed my cheek with his hand. The softness of his touch sent a shiver throughout my body.

"Colin," I whispered, not knowing why I

spoke his name. The blood pounded in my ears as I felt his fingers weave their way through my hair.

His lips moved closer and my senses throbbed with the scent of him. My heart skipped again and again. His hand swept to the back of my neck and he drew me into him. He kissed me then, his mouth warm and demanding upon mine. The sweetness of his lips made me move even closer until I was aware of his entire rigid length.

"Britanny," he murmured against my mouth.

A small sound of wonder rippled from my throat as he slowly pulled away. Our gazes locked and we both breathed heavily. But when I opened my lips to speak, he placed a finger on them.

"No. Do not say anything." He backed away from me, his dark eyes shimmering sadly. "I'm sorry, Britanny."

Before I could stop him, he turned and fled the room.

The night stretched out before me like a dark endless tunnel. Lying in bed, my body felt like a limp rag. My eyes were heavy and smarting. I tossed and turned and tried to talk myself into some semblance of sleep, but it was to no avail. I would not get any rest tonight.

I touched my fingers to my lips which still tingled from Colin's kiss. My head sank deeper into the softness of the pillow. It caressed me, reminding me of Colin's touch. His powerful masculine scent lingered in the darkness of the room, and I could hear his deep voice urgently whispering my name.

It had all happened so quickly. His touch. The kiss. The rush of heat that surged through my body. Inexperienced in sensual matters, I had only my feelings to guide me. But I was not totally ignorant. If we had allowed our desire to control our emotions, we very well could have done something we might have regretted.

I sighed suddenly but not happily. Though difficult for me to admit, I was grateful that Colin had left when he did. In a flash, I succumbed to an overwhelming sense of guilt. I now knew the reason for his hasty departure. It was because of Sorcha. Yes, she was gone but not forgotten. Not by me and certainly not by her husband. She had been dead only a little more than a month and was still Colin's wife, even if only in memory. With a heavy heart and a tear stinging my cheek, I vowed silently never to let this happen again.

I closed my eyes tightly, hoping to shut out the frantic demons that tormented me. I needed to rest, to become one with the night. I needed to pray that things would seem different in the morning. Better.

A sound hurled me back from the edges of sleep. It was slight but audible, and when I opened my eyes and turned my head, I noticed the light that was trickling in from the partially opened door.

I raised myself up on my elbows. My whole body tensed. "Is someone there?" I whispered hoarsely.

There was no answer, yet I was sure that someone was in the room, lurking in the shadows . . . watching me. My heart thumped wildly in my chest.

"Show yourself or I'll scream!" I said, hoping to scare the intruder.

It was then the figure rushed out from the darkness, hurling itself toward me before I had the chance to cry out. Something soft—a pillow was brutally crushed against my face, pushing me back down on the bed. I wanted to gasp from the suddenness of the fiendish act, but when I tried to breathe, I couldn't. Someone was trying to smother me!

Like a snarling beast, I fought, kicking and scratching, trying to pry the pillow from my face. But my attacker was strong and the pillow was pushed against my nose and mouth fully. My lungs burned as I tried to gulp in air that wasn't there.

My arms and legs weakened, my body was becoming limp and useless. A dark dizziness engulfed me and I felt myself slowly plummeting into death's abyss. But I was still alert to the horror and my will to live was undaunted. *No!* my mind screamed. *I will not be the willing victim of some crazed murderer! I will not die!*

Amassing my spirit, I felt my strength growing. At the same time I was aware of my assailant's somewhat relaxed hold on me. Perhaps not thrashing about for a brief moment had given the impression that I was dead or at least nearly so. If that was true, I had to act quickly.

Stealthily moving my hands, I managed to get them next to my face and under the pillow. With a power propelled only by raw courage, I pushed the pillow away, catching my would-be killer off guard.

Air rushed into my lungs at full force as I wheezed and choked on my first breath. I wiped the wetness from my eyes and searched the room. It was empty. Obviously, I had stunned my attacker only momentarily.

I leaped out of the bed. The quilts tangled around my legs, detaining me for a few frustrating seconds. Anger quickly replacing my fear, I kicked my way out of the bonds, dashed through the opened door and into the hall.

Running steps echoed from the foyer. Whoever had brutalized me was getting away! Throwing caution aside, I bounded down the stairs after my attacker. I heard the front door open, its mournful squeal signaling the intruder's escape.

"Stop!" I shouted. The words burned my throat. My cry startled the assailant and I saw the figure jump and the head snapped around and looked at me. I wanted to scream but no sound came from me. I clasped my hands over my mouth as the horrible feeling of suffocation returned. In that brief moment, my hammering heart seemed to stop beating and my gaze froze on the figure that clutched the opened door.

It was Sorcha!

Chapter Nine

"No! No! No!" The terrifying sound of my torment reverberated unmercilessly. Through a blur of tears, I watched, helpless, as the figure, its long, dark hair billowing behind, turned and scurried out into the night.

My mind reeled with horror. Was I truly going insane or was Sorcha, my dearest friend, really trying to kill me? But Sorcha was dead, I reminded myself as I shook from head to toe. She was dead.

"My stars! What is going on here? Who left this door open?" Margaret's shouting echoed off the walls of the foyer and found their way to me. I watched her hurry to the door. The single candle she held lit her way. Her dressing gown and night cap looked ghostly in the pale moonlight that was seeping into the spacious entrance way. Struggling a bit, she closed the door cutting off the night air and doing away with my only link to the awful incident.

I sat down upon the step, wrapped my arms around myself, and huddled against the unknown. I started to cry then, from fear, confusion, or maybe sheer happiness that I was alive. I wasn't sure. My mournful sobs stabbed the darkness engulfing me.

I was aware of Margaret's voice now, vague and perplexed, calling up to me from the bottom of the stairs. I was conscious of her confused questioning, her motherly concern, but the words didn't register in my brain. I was too overwrought to make sense of anything.

Then I heard my name. Before I turned around, I knew Colin was there. I could feel his hand gently grasping my shoulder. I gulped and my sobs began to ease at his touch.

"Britanny," he whispered again, his voice wary.

Before I could speak, he tenderly pulled me up into his arms. I leaned into his strapping length for support as ragged whimpers of sheer need escaped my lips. He responded by holding me closer to him and running his fingers through my hair. I shuddered expectantly.

"Go back to bed, Margaret," I heard Colin order gently. "I'll see to it that Miss St. James is taken care of."

"But, sir ..." Margaret protested mildly.

"Everything will be all right. I promise. Now go."

"Yes, Mr. Rutledge," she answered obediently yet reluctantly.

His arm still embracing my waist, he helped me turn around on the narrow steps. A feeling of dizziness rushed over me and I stumbled as if drunk. With a swift and decided movement, he whisked me up into his strong arms. I gasped slightly, then surrendered, wrapping my own arms around his neck and laying my cheek against his lightly stubbled face.

I was soon back in my bedroom, and Colin eased me onto the rumpled quilts.

"I seem to be nothing but trouble for you," I said, hesitating before relinquishing my hold on him. He enjoyed the fact that I had paused and showed his reaction with a brief, but warm, smile.

"You're talking nonsense," he said, placing a finger against my lips. He left my side for a moment to light the lamp that was on the dresser. His shadow loomed on the wall behind him, but I felt the dark presence comforting, protective.

"What is this doing here?"

The surprise in his voice caught my attention. I followed him with an intense gaze and watched as he bent down to retrieve something from the floor. He turned to me, holding something in his hand.

I blinked, adjusting my eyes to the dim light.

He took a few steps closer to me and I froze. The pillow. He had the pillow that had been so brutally pushed into my face. My attacker must have dropped it before fleeing from the room.

I was reluctant to look at it. My throat became tight and dry. The air around me was thin and scant. It felt as though I was being suffocated all over again.

I had to stop this. If I didn't, Colin would certainly realize that something was dreadfully wrong.

He questioned the appearance of the pillow again, but I didn't answer. I couldn't. My self-induced muteness did not seem to make him suspicious, though, and I was grateful.

Shrugging his shoulders, he tossed the pillow onto the overstuffed chair in the corner. He came back to the bed, sat on the edge close to me, and reached for my hand. "Now, tell me what happened."

I touched the sleeve of the royal blue silk robe he wore and shuddered. My insides began to churn with dread. My thoughts were a jumble of confusion. There were so many things to reveal—my reason for returning to Raven Manor foremost. Now this attempt on my life had pushed all that aside. Should I tell him of my horrible ordeal? Of the specter that I believed to be Sorcha? My mind snapped. Indeed, it was no "ghost" that I had seen. Whoever this intruder was had tried to kill me.

But would I be wise to reveal such a thing? Could he protect me? Would he want to? Would I only be plunging deeper into danger? True, my feelings for Colin were changing, but could my trust in him be turned around as well?

He was staring at me, his dark eyes shimmering with concern. I searched his face for something, anything that would set my mind at ease. My gaze focused briefly on his lips and I thought of our kiss. My heart fluttered reliving the taste of passion we had shared. Was he thinking about our kiss, too? Was he bothered by it? I suddenly felt vulnerable. Naked. Exposed. Still, defenseless as I was, I could not bring myself to tell him what had happened.

"I feel foolish," I said, trying to manage a smile, but my mouth would not cooperate. The best I could hope for was a pained grin. I shifted on top of the quilts. "I—I had a nightmare."

Colin pursed his lips warily. "A nightmare? Britanny, you were trembling like a captured bird when I found you." He took hold of my other hand. "Why, you're still shaking. Are you sure it was just a bad dream that put you in this state?" He was staring at me, his dark eyes shimmering with concern. Gazing closely now, I also saw wisps of suspicion flickering in them.

Did he believe me? I held my breath. Reluctant to look at him, my glance moved to the floor. But he lifted my chin and forced me to meet his gaze.

"Are you feeling better now?" he asked.

I nodded as my heart quieted. I had convinced him, at least for now.

"Will you be all right? No more bad dreams?" His smile warmed me.

"No more bad dreams. I promise." I smiled back at him.

His hand slowly drifted away from my face. The urge within me to keep his touch next to my cheek was overwhelming. I thought about how near death had been, how close I had come to never seeing Colin again. I shuddered openly.

"I'll let you sleep now." He rose from the bed, his gaze still fixed on me. He turned to go, then faced me again with a look that made my breath leave my body. "Britanny, I—"

"I want to stay with you tonight. I want us to become lovers." Were those the words he was about to speak? My mind nearly exploded with anticipation.

"Good night, Britanny," he said finally.

My heart sank and sadly, I watched him go. The room was so dark and empty without him. Or was it I who felt so lost and empty? I got up from the bed, went to the door, and peered into the hall. Colin was already gone from my sight.

Disheartened, I was about to close the door when I noticed the pillow again, its shapeless form taunting me. I should have been terrified, but a stronger feeling took over. This time a quiet fury began to build inside me. I grabbed the pillow, flung opened the armoire's doors, and threw the hideous thing into the darkness of the uppermost shelf. My throat began to constrict again as flashes of my brush with death violated my thoughts. Angrily, I pushed them from my mind, closed the doors tightly, and breathed a heavy sigh.

Stopping by the window, I watched the moon drift lazily along a black velvet sky. Its pale light washed over me, causing me to shiver. As my eyes grew heavy with sleep, a different thought crossed my weary mind. Was there truly someone who did not want me here? And in what other ways would that being make it known that I was not welcome?

I slept poorly and rose as the light was just barely visible through the window. Though awake, I stayed in bed, pulling the quilt up under my chin.

Real nightmares had invaded my sleep, but now with the morning, my fears of last night had subsided. Understandably, I still felt violated, and I knew without question I would have to be vigilant of everyone and everything around me. I was certain that whoever wanted me to leave Raven Manor would stop at nothing to see that the deed was done.

I took time to wash and pamper myself for

the day ahead, hoping my indulgence would make me feel better. Surprisingly, it did. From my wardrobe, I chose a simple plum-colored skirt and ecru blouse to wear. I pinned up my hair, pinched my cheeks to bring out my natural color, and blotted some face powder to hide the dark circles under my tired eyes.

It was early, too early for anyone but Margaret to be awake. Quietly, I stole down the stairs and headed to the kitchen where I knew I would find her.

"Good morning, Margaret," I whispered so as not to startle her.

She was bent over the sink, diligently chopping a huge block of ice. She turned at the sound of my greeting. "Land sake's, child. What are you doing up at the crack of dawn?"

I went to her and kissed her cheek. "I couldn't sleep," I said, shrugging my shoulders.

Tenderly, she stroked my cheek. Her hand was cold and I shivered from her touch. "What happened to you last night, Britanny? Your cries gave me quite a scare. Even Mr. Rutledge looked a mite piqued with your behavior."

A wave of fear fluttered through me as I reluctantly recalled my brush with death. "It was only a nightmare, Margaret. People do have those occasionally."

Her face puckered in a doubtful look, but then it quickly disappeared.

I hated lying to Margaret, but I felt I had not

choice. She would only worry more if I told
her the truth. For the sake of my safety, she
might feel compelled to tell Colin. No, I
thought firmly. Until I could unravel the mystery that surrounded Sorcha's death, I had to
keep certain things to myself.

Eager to change the subject of our conversation, I nodded toward the cake of ice. "May
I help you with that?"

She glanced back to the sink. "Blasted ice-
man! I'm always telling him to bring two
smaller cakes, but he ignores me. Less work
for him and more money, too." With chisel and
mallet in hand, she continued her tedious
chore, murmuring some unsavory exclama-
tions that surprised even me.

"Poor Margaret," I teased. "Here, let me do
it." I gently steered her out of the way, took
the tools from her grasp, and proceeded to take
up where she had left off.

She dried her rosy, but chafed, hands on her
apron. Bringing them up to her mouth, she
tried to warm them with her breath.

"Mr. Rutledge usually does that for me," she
said as a matter of information. My mind became immediately alert at the mention of Colin's name. "But he left the house so early this
morning."

Disappointment clouded my thoughts. "He's
not here?"

She shook her head. "It was I who was awakened by his leaving. He must be attending to

something important at the shipping company."

She offered me nothing more about Colin, and though I wanted to, I did not pursue the issue. I had furrowed only halfway through the block of ice when I felt my fingers become numb from the pressure and cold.

Margaret noticed me struggling, too. "Leave it be for a while, Britanny. Come and talk to me."

I was glad to be rid of the job if only temporarily. With one hand, Margaret busily stirred a pot of oatmeal on the stove and tended a pan of frying sausages with the other. The sweet and pungent aromas blended together in one delicious scent, but did nothing to whet my tastebuds.

"I hope you're not cooking just for me, Margaret. I'm really not very hungry."

She frowned. "Since when did you ever refuse breakfast? Why, I remember times when you and Sorcha were underfoot in this kitchen, sneaking sausages and bacon, stealing the oranges before I could squeeze them into juice for the family." She paused for a moment and seemed to drift off.

I smiled to myself. I too recalled those happier days. Breakfast, like all the meals in the Blackwell home, was a time for togetherness and gaiety. Sometimes during the very hot weather, Margaret would serve the food on the front porch. Other times, we would all grab our plates and follow Sorcha's father out to the gazebo. I particularly enjoyed those days. the air was so cool and fresh, the food delicious, and the company delightful. It was a wonderful way to begin the day.

Margaret tilted her head and studied my face. "Are you feeling well, child? You look a wee tired."

"I am," I said, agreeing with her keen observation. "I guess I'm not used to dinner parties."

She answered me with an inaudible sound. "Dinner parties," she scoffed. "Indeed."

I braced myself for a barrage of insipid comments about Eleanor Garwood, but all Margaret seemed interested in was the state of my dress and Evangeline's clumsiness.

I assured her that all was well thanks to Colin's quick thinking. The thought of him warmed me. How I wished he was here now.

"Britanny, are sure that everything is all right? You seem distracted."

I glanced at her, touched her arm, and smiled. "Yes, Margaret. Everything is quite all right." Her concern made me sad. How I longed to confide in her about my feelings for Colin. Would she be happy for me? Or would she scold me for those feelings, saying I had no right to them? No right at all.

A rhythmic rapping banished my troubled thoughts at least for now. Margaret patted my hand; then giving me a look that told me to stay where I was, she hurried to the kitchen door.

It was Thomas who had come calling. A morning mist outlined his sturdy figure, its pallid dankness accentuating even more the smile that illuminated his ruddy face.

"Good mornin', dear lady." His greeting was buoyant, as he tipped his hat politely. "You might be a-thinkin' that I've come for me breakfast."

"If not that, then what?" Margaret said, teasing him with a scampish suspicion.

"Well, to see you, of course. It'll be a guaranteed good day when I first lay me eyes on you."

I watched as Margaret tapped him playfully on the shoulder. "You rascal!" She laughed.

Though her back was toward me, I was sure she was blushing. She stepped aside and Thomas strode into the kitchen, cap in hand.

"Well, fancy seeing you, miss," he said, his surprised gaze falling on me.

I nodded. "Good morning, Thomas. Now I see why Margaret was preparing such a feast. Alas, 'twas not for me." I tried my best to imitate Thomas's Irish brogue, not to abase him, but to make him laugh. And laugh he did.

"Hush, child," Margaret said, her face piqued at my playfulness. The rosy color in her cheeks glowed darkly. Trying her best to look annoyed, she waggled a finger at me as a mother would at her belligerent child.

147

I smirked, not the least bit embarrassed. Thomas winked at me, enjoying my teasing.

"Sit down, Thomas. I'll fetch you a bowl of oatmeal." Like a butterfly, Margaret fluttered to the stove and with a large wooden spoon filled a bowl to its brim with the pasty cereal.

Thomas, his gray-green eyes shining with mirth, took his place at the table in the chair that Margaret had previously occupied. I smiled back at him and reading his thoughts, I rose from my own seat.

"Just where do you think you're going, young lady?" Margaret imposed disapprovingly.

I sashayed to the large window alongside the door. "Is it not a marvelous morning, Thomas?" I asked, ignoring Margaret's insistent stare.

"There's a bit of a low fog upon the ground," he said, winking. "But I'm sure it will disappear once it beholds your lovely face."

Now I blushed at Thomas's flirting. "Then I shall go for a walk," I announced, my hand poised over the latch of the door.

"Not until you've had something to eat," Margaret said as she started to fill a bowl for me.

My gaze fell upon a wooden dish on a small table just within my reach, brimming with oranges. Quickly, I snatched one of the red-golden beauties and bounced it in the palm of my hand like a ball.

"This will do nicely," I said. "Now, don't give another thought to me, you two. I'll be back later." I turned to go.

"Britanny." Margaret's voice was stern.

I looked over my shoulder, wincing. Expecting another reprimand, I watched as Margaret's face lit up at the prospect of being alone with Thomas. "Don't forget your cloak," she said. "Autumn mornings are a mite chilly here."

The three of us burst into laughter. Holding my orange close to me like a coveted prize, I whisked past them and out of the kitchen. After retrieving my green woolen cape from the armoire in my room, I decided to exit by the front door instead. I could still hear their merriment echoing through the foyer.

Margaret had been right. The morning air carried a chill that buried itself deep within me. White, ghostly mists floated aimlessly about the grounds. My intended stroll became more of a frenzied march as I made my way toward the garden. But I fought the coldness by conjuring up warm thoughts of Margaret and Thomas together.

The ground was unyielding as I tramped across it, hard and dusty. The heels of my shoes kicked up tiny pebbles behind me. I breathed deeply, then exhaled. I shuddered, reached for my hood, and pulled it over my hair.

I pressed the nubby skin of the orange against my nose and smelled its sweetness. It reminded me of summers long gone, warm, lazy days spent with Sorcha. My mind was a prism of beautiful colors, a spectrum of dreams and happier times. But through all the brilliance, one thought dominated the rest, that of Colin Rutledge.

Truly, I had missed not seeing him this morning. I carried a dull ache within my heart and the memory of his kiss burned through me like wildfire. How I longed to have him by my side.

Was I being foolish? Were my romantic notions and girlish whims overriding my sensibilities? There was still the matter of Sorcha. In my eyes—in my heart—he was very much married to her. There was so much heartache for the man to overcome. And then, there was the question of truth. Was the sadness real or was Colin Rutledge hiding some dark secret that linked him to the death of his young wife?

My concentration was so intense that I did not notice how far I had walked. I had passed the rose garden, the gazebo, and a trio of wrought iron benches scattered along the gravelly path.

Coming to an abrupt and disoriented stop, I realized that I was standing on top of a grassy knoll looking down into a glen. The fog was thicker here, making me feel ill at ease. But dense as it was, it did not obscure my vision. A shuddering sorrow seized my heart as my gaze was drawn beyond the chapel to the headstones and the gray granite of the Blackwell family vault.

Slowly, as I made my way down the small hill, a curious atmosphere settled around me. I heard none of the usual morning bird cries, or the sound of the breeze rustling through the trees as before. Everything was strangely still.

I pushed open the gate to the little cemetery and kept a respectable distance until I no longer felt like an intruder. I had seen this place many times, but had had no desire to explore such morbid surroundings. Now, I walked softly between the graves, hardly noticing the worn, and to me, insignificant inscriptions upon the stones. Lost in my own thoughts, I paused before taking another step toward the vault. I knew what would be waiting there.

The vault was a plain structure save for a simple sculpture of a wreath above the iron door. The name "BLACKWELL" was carved into its center.

I felt the beginnings of a quiver as I perused each inscription that surrounded the door. Kingsley Blackwell, 1833–1874; Deidre Blackwell, 1834–1874; Olivia Blackwell, their first daughter born dead at birth, 1854.

I wanted to avoid the last name that was carved apart from the rest. My nerves began to tingle and I flinched. I was scared. But somehow my feelings didn't matter. My eyes were drawn to her name as if it was the only source of my life. Sorcha Blackwell, 1855–1875.

It seemed to jump out at me from the mist, beckoning me the same way her portrait had done. Though I did not believe in ghosts as a rule, I nevertheless wondered if spirits remained around their graves to haunt intruders—or to play cruel and violent tricks on their friends, I thought bitterly. Tears welled in my eyes. I stared at Sorcha's name again, and the deeply etched letters wavered. *No!* my mind screamed. Sorcha was dead, and whoever was impersonating her was doing his or her deadly best to rid Raven Manor of my presence. But why? What was I not supposed to discover? Who had lured me to this place? Who had killed Sorcha? Who tried to murder me? The questions seemed endless. The answers impossible.

Shaking the eerie thoughts from my mind, I concentrated on the granite tomb looming before me. It was now I noticed the meticulous touches that had been overseen with such painstaking care. I reached out and drew my fingers down the cold stone, stopping just above Sorcha's name. While the opposite side of the vault was darkened by weathering and bore traces of a greenish stain, this part was bleached to its original, if not better, condition.

Below, upon the still supple grass, was a small bouquet of white roses tied together with a white satin ribbon. A knot tightened in the pit of my stomach. Roses. Sorcha's favorite. I caught my breath sharply. Roses—the flower of a passionate love.

I crouched down and touched the petals. They were soft, pliant, and felt like velvet against my fingertips. Someone had recently placed them here. My heart wrenched with sorrow as I made the quiet discovery in a matter of moments. Colin. Colin had brought these flowers to Sorcha's grave.

Though wishing to remain at the gravesite, I could not. My heart was too heavy with sadness. But were my distressed quiverings for Sorcha or because of Colin's obsession with her even in death?

A few yards away was the chapel. As I headed toward it, I hoped to find a quietness to calm the turmoil within me if only for a little while.

But the chapel was cold, bone-numbing cold, and its sullen darkness only served as a catalyst for my jumbled and disconnected thoughts. Everything about the sanctuary— the finely carved altar, the stained glass windows—whispered of hopelessness.

I wanted to leave this place and return to the house but my own guilt and sorrow held me fast a few moments longer. In my mind's eye, I saw Sorcha's name carved for all eternity on the lifeless granite that marked her final resting place. A chill of reality crawled up my spine. But as the vision slowly blended with my other bleak thoughts, my concern shifted to the living. It was Colin and my feelings for him that were causing me so much confusion.

How could I have allowed myself to be attracted to a man who was still so in love with his dead wife?

My head bowed against the cold, bleak air, I left the chapel. My shoulders drooped, my gait was slow and unsteady. I felt as though I was drowning in a whirlpool of emptiness.

Despite Thomas's assurance, the fog remained, hanging close to the ground.

"Britanny. Britanny."

The sound of the flat, inflectionless whisper brought me to a halt. I looked around, my gaze straining through the thick mist. I saw no one.

I shrugged, believing my imagination was playing tricks on me, and I quickened my pace.

"Britanny. I'm here. I'm waiting for you to come and play with me."

My head shot up. "Who's there?" I said, a shaft of fear crawling up my throat.

"Britanny. It's me. I'm frightened. It's so dark here. So dark and cold. Please come and get me." The voice had become louder, more desperate, and it chilled me to the marrow.

"Who are you? What do you want from me?" My body rigid, I spun around quickly, for the echo of the voice sounded as though it was pressing down on me from all sides now.

My pounding heart seemed to stop beating and my gaze froze on a shadow that had appeared from the mist. I could not see its face, yet I could tell the figure was a woman. Hair, black as a raven's wings, clung to the slight form like a cloak.

I clamped my hands over my mouth to stifle a scream. It was the ghost I had seen at the top of the stairs. The same ghost who had tried to kill me!

"Brit—an—neey!" The wailing voice turned my blood to ice. Arms reached out toward me and I recoiled in horror.

"Who are you?" I screamed through gritted teeth.

There was no answer.

"Sorcha?" The name tumbled from my mind and onto my lips.

The figure turned suddenly and ran, disappearing into the thick fog.

"Wait!" I cried. "Come back!"

Hesitating no longer, I picked up my skirts and took off after the figure. This time I would not let this menace get away.

My eyes burned from the stinging mist, my nostrils flared with determination. I could hear the plodding of hurried, frightened footsteps. They seemed to be louder now. Was I getting closer? Would I finally discover my enemy?

Something loomed in the near distance. I blinked. It was the carriage house. I saw the figure clearly then run toward the structure and vanish around the back.

But as I rounded the corner of the carriage house, a scream lodged in my throat. The bloodless face of an old man had jutted out from the fog.

"Beware, my pretty thing," he snarled at me, his features twisted in a maddening leer. Jagged teeth filled his mouth and the stench of alcohol was so strong that I almost choked. "Leave this place. Leave this place while you're still alive!"

A numbed terror froze me to the spot. I tried to catch my breath, to scream, anything to take me away from this frightening world.

I closed my eyes tightly for only a second, and when I opened them, the face had been stolen away by the fog.

Chapter Ten

As I hurried toward the house, a prayer of deliverance on my lips, the only sound I heard was the thundering of my heart against my chest. The horrid face of the old man plagued my thoughts. Now, there was someone new to this scenario. Someone else who wanted me to leave Raven Manor.

At that moment the sun broke through, dissipating the swirling mists. Suddenly, the colors and sounds of autumn were all around me. But inside, I shook, feeling as though the dead of winter covered me.

As if I had willed her presence, Margaret opened the front door as soon as I stepped onto the porch.

"Where have you been, child?" she asked,

looking down at me. She seemed more worried than annoyed. "Do you realize it's almost noon?"

Even though overcome by my terror, her words surprised me. I had no idea I had been gone so long.

"I'm sorry, Margaret," I managed to utter. "I went to the cemetery."

She frowned, studying me. "What's wrong, Britanny? You look as though you've seen a ghost."

I wanted to laugh out loud at her choice of words, but my fear would not allow it. Finally, I caught my breath and felt my pulse slowing. "Margaret, does Thomas have an assistant? Someone who works with him at the stables?"

"Why, no, Britanny. Why do you ask?"

I swallowed, then shrugged. "It's nothing. I just wondered."

My question did not make her curious. She was more anxious about her own news.

"You have a guest, Britanny," she said.

Tilting my head, I frowned. "A guest?"

"Douglas Garwood." She seemed just as surprised as I was.

"What does he want?"

She shrugged, not hiding the fact she was annoyed at his unannounced visit. "I'm not sure."

Margaret opened the door wider and I stepped inside. She nodded toward the parlor, then hurried across the foyer, and disappeared into the kitchen.

I removed my cloak and draped it across my arm. I fussed with my hair and hoped that the color had returned to my cheeks. Taking a deep breath, I stood in the doorway of the parlor.

The last time I had seen Douglas he was drinking a toast to Sorcha's portrait. Now, his hands behind his back, he was staring into the dark hollow of the fireplace.

"Douglas?" I said, still wary of his presence.

He turned at the sound of my voice and a smile lit up his face like the sunniest of days. "Britanny. It's so good to see you."

The greeting amused me. His tone carried a strange inflection as though we were good friends who had been apart for many months.

"Did you forget that you and your mother were guests for dinner last night? Have you missed my company that much?" I was teasing him, but apparently by the expression on his handsome face, he didn't see it that way.

He walked to me, reached for my hand, brought it to his lips, and kissed it gently. His sky-blue eyes locked with mine. "Yes, I have missed you. That is why I am here. Yesterday, when we first met, you mentioned it would be quite to your liking if we could get to know each other better."

I nodded, though not remembering the exuberance he seemed to believe I showed when he had posed that question. I did recall that I

Suzanne Hoos

had been a bit surprised at his proposal.

He gave my hand a tender squeeze. "Well, I've come calling. I pray it's not an inconvenience."

Douglas Garwood was charming all right. The mischievous twinkle in his eyes, the impish smile, everything about him was utterly attractive. A thought flashed across my mind. What would Colin think if he knew that Douglas was here?

Colin's reaction had been so strong when he had learned that Douglas's previous visit had included seeing Melinda. That mystery aside, what would he say about this delightful man's intentions where I was concerned?

"I find no inconvenience in your visit, Douglas," I said, smiling. "In fact, I'm glad you're here."

He had not released my hand so I steered him in the direction of the burnished leather chair. His brow rose in surprise at my assertiveness. but a look of pleasure quickly replaced it. I felt the eyes of Sorcha's portrait following us as we crossed the room. I wondered if she would approve of my behavior.

I practically sat him down in the chair. "Would you like to stay for luncheon? I'm sure Margaret can fix us something." Before he had the chance to answer, I was off in the direction of the kitchen. "I'll only be a moment," I promised.

Away from Douglas now, I came to an abrupt

halt in the foyer. What was I doing? And why was I doing it in such a bold fashion? Was my invitation to Douglas actually a way of making Colin jealous? Could I be so petty? No. At least I hoped not.

I thought for a while and then realized that I did have a more sensible motive for wanting Douglas to stay. I wanted to know more about his and Sorcha's relationship. My heart ached with the pain of betrayal. Why hadn't she trusted me enough to confide in me about Douglas Garwood? What had she been hiding? I was her friend, her best friend. At least I believed that to be so. Now, all I could do was wonder if we ever had a kinship at all.

"Britanny, what is he doing here?" Margaret's question attacked me the moment I appeared in the kitchen.

"He's here for a visit. To see me, I might add."

"Oh, is he now?" She wagged her chubby finger close to my nose. "If Mr. Rutledge finds out about this—"

"Let him. After all, he invited me to stay. I suppose it would be all right to have some of my friends here as well."

Her eyes widened like saucers. "Friends? Douglas Garwood is no friend. Especially to Mr. Rutledge."

A happy, cooing sound caught my attention. There, by the window, was Melinda. Squirming around in a tall wooden chair, she banged her tiny hands on the matching tray that enclosed her in the seat. I couldn't be sure but I thought I saw her smile as though she recognized me. I threw her a kiss and she giggled.

"Be that as it may, Margaret. I've invited Douglas to luncheon." The voice was not mine. It was too firm, too opinionated, and without the slightest hint of apology.

Margaret clicked her tongue against her teeth disapprovingly. "Brittany—"

"Please, Margaret," I said, my childlike demeanor apparent now. "Could you make something special for us?" I looked at her from under my eyelashes. "Could you do it for me?"

A smirk twisted her mouth. "I suppose," she said, relenting.

I pecked her cheek with a quick kiss. "Thank you, Margaret. I can always count on you."

Before I could hurry from the kitchen. she grabbed onto my arm, pulling me back to her. "Why is Douglas Garwood suddenly so important to you? You just met the man."

"I know. And I can't tell you why. You'll just have to trust me."

Her look was skeptical. "Watch yourself, Brittany. Don't be taken in."

It was my turn to wonder. "What do you mean, Margaret?"

"Never mind. Just heed my warning." She released my arm. "Go on. I'll call you when the meal is ready."

With Margaret's strange words pounding in

my ears, I thanked her again and hurried back to the parlor ready to make the most of Douglas's impromptu visit.

Cold chunks of chicken and cubed ham mixed in a light, creamy dressing were the main fare. A hot vegetable salad and freshly baked bread completed the meal.

We ate in the dining room, enjoying not only the tasty food that Margaret had magically prepared but also each other's company. Aware of his charms and good looks, I was nevertheless attracted to him as one would be to a good friend.

Talking with him proved frustrating, though. Yesterday, he had been so eager to share his stories about Sorcha with me. Now, when I mentioned her name. he carefully avoided speaking of her. Instead, he directed the conversation around to me and about trivial matters in the form of his mother's party. In passing, he did ask about Melinda and though Colin's threats rang loudly in my ears, I saw no harm in telling him that the baby was just fine.

"Luncheon was delicious," Douglas said to Margaret when she came into the dining room to see if we were finished.

She nodded, averting her eyes from him. "Thank you, Mr. Garwood," she said politely yet curtly. Like a whirlwind, she went about the task of clearing away the dishes. Her conduct did nothing to hide the fact that she wanted Douglas out of the house. Though I understood her actions, I nevertheless was annoyed at her. I was sure that Douglas was aware of Margaret's disapproving attitude but being a gentleman, he kindly overlooked it.

"Margaret, why are you rushing so?" I asked, feeling as though I should apologize for her blatantly rude behavior. Her head snapped around and her eyes pinned me with a hard look. I shifted uneasily in my chair.

"Perhaps Margaret has better things to do with her time than cater to us," Douglas said, giving me a wink. He dabbed at his mouth with the linen napkin. "Might it be the thought of a gentleman friend that has you in such a dither?"

Margaret came to a dead stop. Boldly, she stared down at Douglas, her eyes flaring. "Pardon me, sir, but my private life is none of your concern."

I rolled my eyes in exasperation, but Douglas seemed to take her rudeness in stride.

"Then there is someone else. Oh, Margaret, you have broken my heart." He clutched his chest and leaned back in the chair. "I thought you would always wait for me."

His teasing was flagrant, and I cringed, knowing Margaret was in no mood for such playfulness, especially with Douglas Garwood.

I reached out and placed my hand on his arm, hoping he would stop. "Douglas . . ." I began. The corner of my right eye started to twitch.

"Oh, Britanny, do you know what this means?" he asked, his expression forlorn.

"I can only guess," I said, wincing. I glanced at Margaret, certain that there would be nettling sparks in her pale blue eyes. But, to my surprise, she looked almost interested in what Douglas was going to say.

"It means my rival will be getting all of Margaret's famous sugar cookies. There will ne'er be one left for me."

He voiced his predicament with such conviction that I actually felt sorry for him. But I held my breath and braced myself for Margaret's angry words. Imagine my amazement when the faint beginnings of a giggle tumbled into hearty laughter.

"Oh, Mr. Garwood. There'll always be plenty of my sugar cookies for you. I'll see to that!" Margaret's eyes were bright with pride. "In fact, I baked a batch just this morning. I'll fix you some tea and you can have all the cookies you want."

My jaw dropped as I watched Margaret flit off to the kitchen, her laughter trailing behind her in a merry tune. I turned to Douglas, who wore a very satisfying grin.

"How did you do that?" I asked, totally in awe of him.

His smile widened. "Do what?"

"Get Margaret to warm up to you so quickly."

"It's one of the things I do best," he said.

"Then you're a dangerous man, Douglas Garwood." I looked at him through narrowed eyes.

He gave a short laugh. "Admittedly so, my dear Britanny." His handsome face was brimming with mischief, and I could swear that the devil himself was taunting me.

I could not help myself as laughter occupied all my senses. It was good to be this happy. After my harrowing experience, it was good to be enjoying a lovely day with a new friend. Douglas joined me in my merriment. I felt light-headed and my eyes were wet. We seemed to be in our own little world and I savored the moment.

But something . . . someone had suddenly appeared in the entrance of the dining room, causing my laughter to stop and my heart to race. Colin. Like some ominous premonition, he stood there, his dark, angry gaze causing me to shiver.

Aware of my silence, Douglas too became quiet.

"Britanny?" I heard him say, his curiosity evident. When I did not answer, his look followed mine to the doorway.

"Colin," I said, managing to catch my breath.

Colin's features twisted then. His jaw was as

hard as granite and I could see the pulse in his neck throbbing with fury. "What in bloody hell is the meaning of this?" His angry words were for Douglas but directed at me.

"Colin, I—"

"Answer me, Britanny. Why is that scoundrel here?"

Douglas stood suddenly. The chair toppled over with a resounding crash. "Insult me all you damn well please, Rutledge, but it is not Britanny's doing that I am here, and I will not stand for your speaking to her in that tone."

Although fearful as to what would result from this volatile situation, I had the odd feeling that this type of confrontation had somehow occurred before. Another time, perhaps, in another place. But it had transpired—and it had been just as lethal as it was now.

"If it is not Britanny's doing, then why are you here?" Colin's voice seemed to deepen almost menacingly.

"I came of my own volition," Douglas told him.

Colin lumbered into the room, stopping at the head of the table. "Then may I suggest that you leave of your own volition before I throw you out!"

"Colin, please!" I blurted out. "Douglas is my guest."

His face distorted dangerously, his eyes glowed like smoldering coals as he came toward us—toward Douglas. Quickly, I rose from my seat and hurtled myself in front of Douglas, hoping to thwart Colin's terrifying impulse.

"Britanny! Mr. Rutledge! Come quick! It's Melinda! She's not breathing!"

The moment Margaret's frightened voice reached my ears, everything around me came to an abrupt halt. The three of us stood there, unable to move. An ashen-faced Margaret pleaded with us again. Now, the realization of her words began to take shape in my brain. Horrifying words. With my heart beating furiously in my chest, I ran into the kitchen.

Melinda was slumped in her chair, her tiny head flopped over to the side like a rag doll. She was still, so very still.

Colin rushed past me, nearly knocking me over. Douglas followed, but stood next to me, his face pale.

With a swift agile movement, Colin picked up the baby and hurried over to the table where he lay her down. She looked so helpless that tears sprang to my eyes.

"Margaret, what happened?" I cried, somehow managing to get the question out through my quivering lips.

"I softened one of my sugar cookies in milk and gave it to her," Margaret said, wringing her hands, tears falling freely down her cheeks. "The next thing I knew she was like this. Oh, Britanny. What have I done? She's not breathing!"

From Margaret's fretful explanation, I concluded that a piece of the cookie had somehow lodged itself in Melinda's tiny throat.

"Margaret, tell Thomas to ride into town to get Doctor Barrens," Colin ordered.

"I'm so sorry, Mr. Rutledge. I didn't mean for this to happen," she sobbed.

"I know that, Margaret. Now, please hurry!"

Taking the initiative, I firmly pushed Margaret out the kitchen door, while listening to her pleas for forgiveness.

When she was finally gone, I turned my attention to the serious matter at hand. "No!" I screamed at Colin as he placed his finger down Melinda's throat.

"The baby is choking, Britanny. I have to dislodge—"

Before he could finish, I had already grabbed Melinda from his hold and turned her over my knee. With her head pointing to the floor, I began a series of sharp raps between her shoulder blades with the heel of my palm. I could feel beads of perspiration breaking out on my forehead as the sounds of dull thuds continued. I prayed with all my strength, asking God to have mercy on this little one's life. It was Sorcha who entered my desperate pleas then. Her face was a clear vision in my mind. *Please, Sorcha,* I begged, *please help me. Don't take this beautiful child away from Colin. She's all he has left. Please, help me save her.*

And then, like a miraculous answer to my prayers, I heard a slight sputtering, then coughing. The glorious sound of crying rushed over me like a sweet song. It came from Melinda. Her tiny body shuddered in my grasp.

I turned her over and looked down at her sweet face. The pink color had returned to her cheeks. Her eyes were squeezed shut and she was sobbing and gasping for breath. On the floor was the small piece of sugar cookie surrounded by a puddle of her spittle.

"That's right, my darling. Fill those lungs. Keep crying. Everything is going to be fine." I held her close to me, cradling her protectively.

Colin reached out for her then. I saw his hands shake as I placed her in his arms. I gasped as the realization of what I had just done swirled in my head.

"You saved her life, Britanny," Colin said quietly. "How did you know what to do?"

Feeling faint, I held onto the table. The sensation passed when I looked at Colin's grateful expression. "I ... I was taught things like that ... in my training to be a teacher ... I had to know what to do in case of an emergency ..." My legs felt like jelly. Strong arms steadied me. I glanced over my shoulder. It was Douglas who was easing me over to one of the chairs by the table. I sat down. My entire body was as heavy as an anchor and just as cold.

Melinda wriggled in Colin's arms. She was still crying but softly now. He came to me. His dark eyes, no longer hardened, were like pools of black water. With a free hand, he lightly stroked my warm cheek.

"Thank you."

My body grew warm at his sincerity. How I wanted him to sweep me up into his arms and hold me close to him. Colin, Melinda, and me. The three of us together. Forever.

But even in this tender moment, I could not erase from my memory Colin's violent temper. If Margaret had not interrupted, heaven knows what he would have done to Douglas.

Margaret's sudden reappearance shook the troubled thought from my mind. Seeing that Melinda was all right, she burst into tears of joy. Gently, Colin placed the baby into her waiting arms. Then he too sat down on another chair and placed his head in his hands.

He looked so powerless, so vulnerable that I ached inside. A wave of dizziness rushed over me as I gazed at his distraught figure.

"Britanny saved Melinda's life, Margaret."

I heard Douglas proclaim my heroic effort as his hand gently stroked my hair. His touch was comforting.

Margaret could only smile at me, but that was enough. In my heart, I knew what she was thinking.

The doctor arrived with a frightened Thomas just as Melinda was closing her eyes. Though the baby was asleep, Colin insisted that she be examined, as did Doctor Barrens. A stout and sturdy man, he gently took the baby from Margaret's anxious grasp.

There was nothing more I could do except silently voice a short prayer of gratitude. Drained of energy, I decided to go to my room to rest. There would be much to deal with later and I wanted to be clear in my mind when that came to pass.

The others were gathered around Melinda and the doctor. Quietly, I left the kitchen without anyone noticing—or so I thought.

Douglas stopped me before I ascended the stairs.

"Britanny," he called. There was a slight tremor in his voice.

I turned, a bit bothered by the fact that my departure was thwarted. We stood apart, facing each other. He looked withered, his watery eyes clouded with a hazy sadness. Something took hold of my heart and twisted it, forcing me to share in his sorrow.

He was about to say something but I intervened. "I'm sorry about the way Colin treated you. I know he didn't mean to act that way."

His mouth formed a crooked smile. "You don't know Colin Rutledge as well as I do. He meant every word."

I blinked back the tears that were forming in my eyes.

"But it's all right, Britanny. I'm used to his barbaric manner. I don't expect any apologies, especially from you." He paused for a moment, as his gaze dropped to the floor. Then he looked up into my eyes. "I wanted to thank you. With every fiber in my being, I am grateful to you."

I stared at him, curious as to what he was alluding to. Certainly, it was not because of my hospitality. "I'm not sure I understand, Douglas."

He smiled back at me. It was a sweet smile, one that invited a warm feeling. "Perhaps someday you will understand." He took a deep breath. "Rest now, Britanny. I'll see myself out."

Retrieving his gray overcoat and black felt hat from the settee in the foyer, he turned toward me once again, nodded, and exited the front door.

A chill suddenly shook me. At first, I thought it to be an aftershock of some sort, my body protesting the calm that had seemed to settle around me. But there was more to the way I was feeling. It was Douglas who had placed me in such a state. In my mind's eye, I saw the vision of him stroking Melinda's buggy, his face aglow as he looked at her, and the fright in his eyes when he realized her life was in danger. Everything about him was so intense, so deliberate. And then there were his strange words of gratitude. It was almost as if . . . I stopped. What was I assuming?

With every step up the stairs, the thought became stronger, more alive, until I could no longer consider it just a foolish whimsy. I hurried to my room and closed the door behind me. Alone now, I did not feel at ease.

I settled in the corner chair and huddled against its soft cushions. My arms wrapped tightly around me, I tried to protect myself from the ghosts and demons that were creating havoc with my life.

Was it possible? Could it be that Sorcha and Douglas had been more than just friends? My mind fought against it, and even though I was afraid to face the truth, my heart knew better.

It was Sorcha and Douglas who were Melinda's parents.

Chapter Eleven

Dreams of a faceless entity plagued my restless sleep until I could no longer keep my eyes closed. I had no sense of time, no sense of myself, of who I was, or what had happened. Just a numbness filled me along with a dull ache in my head.

A light rap upon the door gently interrupted my confusion.

"Britanny?"

It was Margaret and hearing her voice brought back the images of Colin and Douglas and, of course, Melinda.

"Come in, Margaret."

She opened the door and peered around it. "Did I wake you?"

I shook my head. "How is Melinda?"

"Doctor Barrens said that she's going to be just fine." She looked as relieved as I felt. She entered the room. "Praise be, Britanny, if it wasn't for you . . . well, I shudder to think what might have become of that darling baby."

I saw tears shining in her tired eyes. "I'm only glad I was here to help. Where is she? I'd like to see for myself that she's all right." I tried to get up from the chair where I had fallen asleep, but my twisted body ached with every move.

A wave of dizziness overpowered me as Margaret helped me to my feet. Seeing my frazzled state, she questioned my own health. I assured her that I was still tired and disoriented from all the excitement. She believed me. Why wouldn't she? It was the truth, after all.

Margaret took me by the hand. "There will be plenty of time to spend with Melinda. Dinner is ready and by the looks of it, you need to build up your strength."

With the mention of food, I heard my stomach growl. I was hungry. In fact, famished would be more to the point.

"May I freshen up a bit?" I asked. "After everything that's happened, I must look a fright."

Tenderly, she stroked my hair away from my face. "You look beautiful," she insisted.

I smiled but gently argued that I would only take a few moments to indulge myself.

With one more question burning on my

tongue, I stopped her before she left the room.

"Colin. Mr. Rutledge. How is he?"

A knowing grin graced her face. "He's downstairs waiting for you. Now, hurry."

Alone now, I wondered what her words really meant. She had said them innocently, yet I couldn't help but imagine Colin Rutledge, poised and ready, waiting to upbraid my choice of companionship in Douglas Garwood.

Colin was waiting for me at the bottom of the stairs. I was surprised to see him there and drew back at first when he offered his hand to me. With my heart pounding in my ears, I took hold of it and he led me down the rest of the steps.

Silently, we walked into the dining room together, my arm entwined with his. The dull aching in my head had vanished. Only a giddy feeling remained.

The delicious aroma of the dinner Margaret had prepared wafted around me, filling my senses to overflowing.

"Would you like some champagne, Britanny?" Colin asked, after seating me in the chair closest to his.

"Champagne?"

"Of course. We're celebrating tonight." His dark eyes reflected the candlelight sparkling them with an excitement he was finding hard to contain.

I looked at him questioningly.

"We're celebrating you, Britanny. Celebrating the fact that you saved Melinda's life."

"Colin—"

"I will never forget what you did." His burning eyes focused on mine. "Never." His intense stare caused a tingling to flow through me.

I did not want praise. I did not feel like celebrating. Knowing that Melinda would be all right was enough.

My protesting was to no avail. He filled two delicate crystal goblets with the sparkling wine and offered me one.

"To you, Britanny." He raised his glass. "I am truly grateful."

I opened my mouth to speak but no words came. Instead, a curtain seemed to unfurl before my eyes, obscuring Colin and replacing him with the vision of Douglas and the night I had seen him lifting his drink to Sorcha's portrait.

"Britanny?"

Colin touched my arm, causing the image to vanish as quickly as it had appeared. I now saw him. Only him.

"Is something wrong? You seem so distracted."

"I'm still tired, I imagine." The explanation sounded credible, though I knew there was more to what I was feeling than mere exhaustion.

Gingerly, I took a sip of champagne. I had never partaken of the fancy wine before. The bubbles tickled my nose and the taste was sharp on my tongue. I made a face and Colin laughed.

"Tonight is just the beginning, Britanny. Tomorrow we will truly celebrate. We will dine at the Chanticleer, the finest restaurant in Hudson—"

"It sounds lovely, Colin," I interrupted. "But I'm afraid I can't accept your generosity."

He tilted his head and frowned.

"What I did, I did out of instinct, that's all."

"You saved Melinda because you love her," he corrected.

"Yes, I do love her. She's Sorcha's daughter, after all." I stopped, afraid to say anything else. Had he noticed my sudden reluctance to continue? What would he say if I told him what I suspected about Melinda's parents? I could not rid myself of the scene of Colin's violent temper toward Douglas. The thought unnerved me. Was this changeable behavior part of his personality? If someone displeased him, would he threaten their life? A stab of a feeling, like a message of danger across the darkness, attacked my senses. I cringed. Had Sorcha been a victim of Colin's rage?

If Colin was suspicious of my abrupt silence, he did not show it. "Come now, let's not argue. Margaret has prepared a fine meal. I think it's time that we do it justice."

The roast beef was succulent, the fresh green beans sweet and tender. The potatoes, crispy on the surface, were fluffy inside and melted easily in my mouth. Colin ate slowly, savoring the delicious food as one would a good book or fine wine. Perhaps, I thought, even a kiss.

I appeared to concentrate on my roast, keeping my eyes downward for fear my expression would give away my thoughts. But after a while, I found it difficult, almost impossible, not to look at Colin's face. Something had changed in him once again. He was refreshingly amiable, determined to please me, and although I was already attracted to him, he seemed even more appealing. A nagging feeling was slowly replacing my admiration and what I had feared was indeed becoming a reality.

Who really was Colin Rutledge? Instinctively, I had been on my guard since my arrival. Why then was I now fighting the impulse to reach out and take hold of his hand? To weave my fingers through his thick hair? The heat from my body came in such a rush that I gasped. My throat became dry.

Was I being careless with my heart? My life? No matter how much he had insisted that I stay, he had wanted me to leave Raven Manor for my own safety, so he said. But was that the truth and would he stop at nothing to make me leave? I thought of the graveyard, the figure that resembled Sorcha, the old man's leering face, and I shuddered. Was Colin responsible? Could it be I was falling in love with a murderer?

Dessert consisted of vanilla custard floating in a generous pool of caramel sauce. It was good but very sweet, and even at the risk of insulting Margaret, I only took one bite.

When Colin noticed that I was finished, he got up and went to the sideboard.

"Brandy?" he asked, a crystal carafe in hand.

Quickly, I declined his offer. Just the small sip of champagne had caused my head to spin. My skirt rustled as I stood and moved back from the table.

"I'm afraid I must put an end to this pleasant evening, Colin." I was sure that the sadness in my tone was detectable. He looked disappointed, but I continued, "I'm very tired and I'd like to check on Melinda before I go to sleep. Please tell Margaret I said good night."

But as I started to leave, Colin took hold of my arm and made me face him. Though his touch was gentle, I felt crushed by his strength. A trembling thrill raced through me. Our gazes locked and I struggled with the temptation of plummeting into the smoldering depths of his eyes.

"Britanny, thank you. I don't know how I can ever repay you." His voice was soft and breathy and brimming with desire.

I looked away as he spoke but he would not allow me to hide my eyes from him. He lifted my chin and forced me once again to meet his gaze. He smiled at me and suddenly all my fears vanished.

He bent toward me and trailed a path along the side of my cheek with his mouth. I tried to still the wild pounding of my heart as his lips wandered down the tingling cord of my neck. The sweet throbbing of his mouth against my skin impelled me to move closer to him, and a small sound of wonder came from my throat.

He took my lips then in a soft, moist kiss. his mouth moving against mine with exquisite tenderness. He wrapped his arms around my waist and, instinctively, I reached to embrace his neck.

Parting my lips, I allowed him to possess my mouth. Languidly, his tongue entwined with mine in a deep, achingly sweet exploration. This was what I wanted. I could not help it if I seemed brazen.

I felt his hand move slowly up my hip and waist and then caress my bosom. A dizzying sensation overcame me once again, but this time it was not the champagne. It was Colin who was intoxicating.

I clung to him in reckless passion. My hands seemed to have a life of their own as they wandered over his rock-hard body.

"Britanny," he whispered hoarsely. "You are so tempting. You do not know where this will lead. I'm not sure I can trust myself with you."

As my heart skipped again and again, I knew

he was right in his warning. My mind tried to caution me that all my foolish justifications would not come to my rescue if I did something I would later regret.

I tried to pry my hands from his body, tried to will my head to turn from his wildly breathless kisses. Feelings and sense warred with each other as I became slowly yet doubtlessly aware of Colin's fingers undoing the buttons of my blouse with deliberate haste. My blood blazed like liquid fire when he pressed his lips against the rise of my bosom. I threw my head back in wild abandonment, wanting to unleash his hunger and satisfy my own.

With his mouth against my ear, he spoke low, slurring his words with an urgent passion. "I want you, Britanny. It is dangerous for me to want you so much, but I must have you."

I broke away from him then, the fervency of his words still echoing in my brain. Panting for breath, I buttoned my blouse and waited for my heartbeat to return to normal. Colin's advances stopped and though I could see the disappointment in his expression, I was aware he too knew our passion should go no further.

At the same time I felt something I had not experienced before with Colin. There was a certain wisdom about him that made me certain that I could trust him. He desired me. That was evident. But he was also concerned with my welfare and that warmed me beyond the thrill of excitement we had just shared. Silently, I thanked him for his look of reassurance.

Colin tucked my arm in his and we made our way into the foyer. He left me at the stairs, kissed my hand, and said a quiet, almost sorrowful good night. Wisely, I fought the urge to throw myself into his arms. With a heavy heart, I watched him walk away, his brooding figure taken away from me in a slash of a shadow.

It was wrong. All of it. Wrong. My feelings for Colin. His feelings for me. All of it terribly wrong. He was Sorcha's husband, after all. She'd been dead a little more than a month. And yet, his bold overtures were certainly not those of a grieving widower. A grayness seemed to press down on me. Suppose Colin's advances toward me had been made because of his loneliness and grief? But his kiss. His touch. The way he held me so close. His passionate whispers. Confusion and guilt racked my thoughts, my soul. Had he really loved Sorcha?

Slowly, I made my way down the hall. The sound of a melody, strained and brooding, reached my ears. It was Colin playing the piano once again. My heart ached remembering the first time I had heard him play. Was he still playing for Sorcha? Or was the music this time for me?

I tiptoed into Melinda's room. It was unbelievable to me that only hours ago there was such turmoil over her precious life. The over-powering fear that she too might have been lost to us forever continued to plague my thoughts even now. Looking down at her in the cradle, I was suddenly envious of the peaceful glow of sleep that enveloped her. I said a silent prayer as I bent over to brush her forehead with a kiss.

Instead of going to my own room, I stayed with her a while, listening to the rhythm of her breathing, catching her little chirps as she dreamed.

The room was plunged in a semi-darkness, making it easy to see my surroundings. Not that they were unfamiliar. This was Sorcha's room, after all. Hers as a child and still hers as a grown woman. Margaret's revelation had truly surprised me. Why had Sorcha slept apart from her husband? Images of Colin wafted through my mind. With a man like Colin Rutledge holding her, kissing her, why would she choose to?

I was painfully aware of how little I really knew about my dear friend. I took a deep breath hoping that some part of Sorcha might come alive in me to disperse this confusion.

Something took hold as a happier memory crossed my mind. As children, we had spent many hours in this room, playing and dream-ing. That was when my gaze rested on the col-orful Oriental rug that cushioned my feet. I

Suzanne Hoos

stepped off it, crouched down, took hold of the fringed edge, and pulled back the corner. My hand wandered gingerly along the cold, wooden planks of the floor until I found what I was searching for. The loose floorboard. It was still there. Our secret hiding place was still there!

Wedging my fingers into the thin space, I yanked back the plank, hoping the scraping noise wouldn't wake Melinda. I waited for a moment and when I heard the sound of her undisturbed breathing, I sighed.

So many memories rushed over me that they all seemed to blur into one. As children we had hid our "treasures" in this dark hollow. Could it be that those once-cherished objects of the past had been left untouched?

Impulsively, my hand dove into the space and immediately collided with something round and hard. A ball. A ball with colorful stripes and designs. The ball Sorcha and I had tossed about in the garden. My heart beating faster, I continued my own treasure hunt, and found a picture card, a very worn rag doll, and a wooden top. The objects, though recognizable, left vague impressions in my mind. I touched each one, hoping to remember a time when Sorcha and I had fussed over such childhood gems. I smiled, feeling warm inside.

Driven by a strange compulsion, I reached into the hollow one more time. My fingers encircled a smooth, flat shape. Pulling it from the

186

darkness, I examined it and excitement mounted within me. It was a book—a journal. Sorcha's journal!

Quickly, I put back the toys, replaced the floorboard, and covered it with the rug. Holding the journal close to my bosom, I glanced one more time at Melinda, then hurried from the room, and went down the hall to my own door.

The flint shook in my hand, yet somehow I managed to light the lamp on the dresser. Bathed in the eerie yellow glow, I ran my fingers across the soft brown leather cover. At the bottom, embossed in gold, was "SORCHA BLACK-WELL."

Remembering the champagne, I felt those same bubbles bursting in my head. The magic was not in finding something that belonged to Sorcha. Everywhere I looked, every corner of Raven Manor held memories of her. No. That in itself had not caused my heart to race, my blood to tingle. Within these pages might be the answer to what I was searching for. Maybe, through her own words, I would finally be able to solve the mystery surrounding her death.

Taking a deep breath, I opened the cover. Something was written there and I brought the book closer to the lamp. The words seemed to jump out at me from the page and I gasped as my eyes paused over each one. "I knew you would come."

There was no mistake about who this message was for. Clearly, it was meant for me.

Chapter Twelve

Was I losing my mind? Was this message truly meant for me? Impossible! Sorcha was dead.

The room began to spin and the journal slipped from my trembling hands. Gripping the edge of the dresser for support, I bowed my head, praying that the dizziness would leave me.

A sharp rap on my door caused my whole body to tighten.

"Yes?" I said weakly.

"Britanny? It's Margaret. Mr. Rutledge said you retired for the evening. Is everything all right?"

Thinking quickly, I nudged the journal underneath the dresser with my foot and blinked away the tears of frustration that were threatening to dissolve what was left of my fortitude.

I opened the door just enough to hear Margaret inquire about my health once again.

"Yes, Margaret, I'm perfectly fine," I assured her. "It's just been a tiring day. Don't worry so."

She pursed her lips, her expression looked doubtful. "At least let me draw you a bath. It will relax you."

Though I smiled at her thoughtfulness, I declined her offer. It was then I saw she was not alone. Behind her, hidden by the shadows, was Evangeline.

"Something is wrong, Britanny," she insisted. "I can tell from the sound of your voice."

I was losing the battle. Rather than risk more of Margaret's relentless questioning. I opened the door wider and invited both her and Evangeline into the room.

Once inside, Margaret took charge in her usual manner. First, she sat me down on the bed and pressed her lips against my brow.

"You don't seem to have a fever," she announced.

I rolled my eyes and looked to Evangeline for a supportive smile. Instead, a tight smirk hardened on her face, making me suddenly uneasy that she was in my bedroom.

"Evangeline, ready a bath for Miss St. James," Margaret ordered.

"Yes'm," the young girl answered, and left

us to do what she was told.

As I opened my mouth to oppose Margaret's fussing, she placed her finger on my lips.

"Hush! A hot bath is exactly what you need. Now, I shall hear no more arguments from you, young lady."

As much as I wanted her and Evangeline to leave, there was nothing for me to do at the moment but accept my temporary situation as decreed by the stubborn housekeeper.

Margaret helped me undress, making me feel like I was a little girl again. The sound of the rushing water from inside the bathroom was already relaxing me. I fought the feeling. The last thing I wanted to do was sleep.

My gaze quickly traveled to where I had hidden Sorcha's journal. So badly did I want to be alone with her written thoughts that my insides ached.

Margaret gathered my clothes in her arms. "I'll have these things washed and pressed for you, Britanny."

I thanked her, my spirits lifting.

"I'll be saying good night, now." She kissed me lightly on the forehead. "Evangeline will stay and see to your needs."

My heart sank and a curious tingle slithered up my spine like a snake. There was nothing I wanted less than to be left alone with Evangeline.

"That's not necessary, Margaret," I said quickly, hoping to hide my uneasiness with a tight grin. "Contrary to what you may think, I am a capable woman. I'm sure Evangeline has more important things to do than to assist me."

Her laughter was brief. A stern expression was fixed on her face, reminding me all too clearly of some of my teachers back at the Brynwood Academy.

"Nonsense," she said, leaning closer to me. "How will she ever learn her trade then? Heavens, child. Good help isn't born, you know." There was a sparkle in her eyes and she winked. "They're trained by the best of us."

As anxious as I felt, I could not contain my smile, and I relented, though reluctantly.

With "pleasant dreams" upon her lips, Margaret left the room.

My better judgment caused me to keep the door ajar, even though I wasn't certain why I should be mistrustful of Evangeline. Perhaps I should ask her to leave. After all, she was a servant, someone who was used to taking orders.

A flutter of movement startled me. I turned. It was Evangeline. How long had she been standing there?

The shadows in the room played upon her face, obscuring her features like a death mask. I shivered at the sight of her. Desperately, I tried to piece together jagged edges that were slashing through my mind. Why suddenly did

Evangeline look so frightening? So...so deadly?

She took a small, insignificant step toward me, yet I immediately drew back.

"Your bath water is ready, miss."

Her sharp tone made my mouth go dry. I wet my lips and nodded. "Thank you, Evangeline. You may leave now." My words sounded conspicuously pressing.

She blinked and stared at me as though I had suggested something bizarre. Her captivating blue eyes turned as cold as granite. I wrapped my robe tighter around my body, trying to ward off the chill that suddenly filled the room.

Ignoring my order, Evangeline turned away from me. Like a sleek jungle cat, she stalked toward the bed, stopping to draw aside the lace curtains and to open the window. Air rushed in like a surprised gasp. It caressed her thick tresses of hair, brushing them away from her face. Her hands planted on the wide sill, she stretched her lithe body toward the window, hungrily drinking in the crisp scents of the night.

Though uncomfortable, I stood there mesmerized by the sultry scene, only to regain my senses when she chose to move away from the window. What was she after? Was it me? Was it my presence at Raven Manor the cause of her ill will?

"It's a lovely night, isn't it, miss?" she asked,

slowly turning down the quilts on the bed. "A night for lovers, wouldn't you say?"

I felt my cheeks grow warm as she smoothed the sheets with an open hand. "Evangeline, it's been an exhausting day and I'm very tired. Perhaps we can talk another time." My words were said only to appease her.

But she continued as if I hadn't spoken. "Can it be true that a beautiful woman like yourself knows nothing about love?" Her jeering voice ridiculed me and her penetrating gaze cut through me like the sharp blade of a knife.

"Evangeline, really, I must—"

"You know nothing about tempting a man so that he will do anything for you? A look, a touch, maybe a kiss to tease him, to make him desire more?"

A whisper of terror ran through me. She had seen Colin and me this evening! My blood turned to ice at the thought of her spying on our very private moment. I stood there frozen, unable to utter as much as a gasp.

"I know all about what happened. About you and the baby." Her eyelids narrowed to tiny slits. "You would be foolish to rely on what you did to get you what you want."

She picked up the pillow from the bed and held it against her. With her fingers spread, she stroked it with a deliberate gesture of control.

Something snapped in my mind. What was it? What was I supposed to see? To remember?

Slowly, she put the pillow back in its place. Her supple body moved toward me in measured steps. Every nerve in me leaped and shuddered. My mind was spinning but nothing made sense. I struggled to breathe as she came closer to me. Her eyes radiated hatred and I cringed.

I clenched my fists as panic rose in my throat. "What do you want from me, Evangeline?" I cried.

She sidestepped me then, her arm brushing up against mine. I recoiled at her deliberate touch, but did not turn to look at her. I heard her breathe deeply.

"I want you to leave him alone."

The quiet force of her words crushed me from all sides. I gasped for air but found myself suffocating. When I finally amassed the courage to face her, Evangeline was gone.

Chapter Thirteen

"Wear this one, child. It will look so pretty with your hair and bring out the color of your eyes."

In silence, I watched Margaret choose my green faille dress trimmed in black velvet ribbon from the armoire, and hold it up against her own stout figure. I tried to appear agreeable with her selection but my smile was weak and vanished quickly.

Margaret laid the dress on the bed, taking care not to wrinkle the fine silk material. By the way she was behaving, I knew that she was more excited than I was about Colin's invitation to dinner. Truthfully, after all that had happened, I did not even recall him asking until he reminded me of it during breakfast. He had already assumed that I had accepted, and, in my heart, though apprehensive, I already had.

"We'll leave early this afternoon, Britanny," he had said. "On Saturday the shops close at five o'clock and I thought you would like to browse through some before they do."

It was thoughtful of him to consider what I might enjoy and his eager smile had so lightened my otherwise weary heart, yet I had almost been afraid to look at him. Part of my nervousness had been the memory of his touch and all the sensations we had shared. But it was Evangeline's warning that truly had me frightened.

"I want you to stay away from him."

Even now I could hear the hatefulness in her voice. Smell the jealousy oozing from her lithe form. Could the attraction between Colin and Evangeline be just a fantasy driven by a sick mind? Or was it possible that he and this wisp of a girl were engaged in a passion of their own? I shuddered, staring at my pale, drawn face in the mirror on the dressing table. Was their clandestine love the reason Sorcha had died? Or, more likely, the reason she was murdered?

In any case, I had to find out for certain.

So shaken by Evangeline's visit last night, I did not have the strength to read through Sorcha's journal. I had planned to this morning, but with Margaret calling me for breakfast and now all her fussing over me, I hadn't had a spare moment to myself. I did have the good sense, though, to hide the book in my trunk. If I left it under the dresser, it might be discovered by Margaret as she went about her cleaning chores. Or, I swallowed the lump in my throat, by Evangeline.

"We should do something about this," Margaret said, combing her fingers through the length of my hair. "I'll curl it for you if you'd like."

I reached behind me, placing my hand on top of hers.

"Margaret, you've been so kind to me since I've come to Raven Manor."

She smiled. "You're part of this family, Britanny. You always will be. You and Sorcha are just like my own daughters."

It was strange hearing Sorcha's name placed in the present as if she were alive. An uneasiness crept into my heart. Had Margaret also seen the "ghost" of Sorcha roaming Raven Manor? Was she too frightened to let anyone know? Or did she really believe Sorcha had returned?

Oh, how I wished this day was over.

With Margaret helping me, I was ready quickly. She stood back, studying and admiring her work.

"Maybe this is not the time for me to say what I'm going to say, Britanny, but since you've been here, there's been a change in Mr.

197

Rutledge." Her eyes shone with gratefulness. "Oh, he still takes some getting used to, but something is different about him. He's happy again."

"You said the same thing about him and Sorcha," I reminded her. "Or don't you remember?"

"Oh, I remember," she said, reaching for my hand. "I know you're attracted to Mr. Rutledge, Britanny. I can see it every time you're with him. And I know he feels the same way about you. And I also know that this attraction is bothering you. Am I right?"

I sighed heavily, thinking it would relieve the guilt that had been rearing its ugly head since Colin and I had shared our first kiss. Though nothing had changed within me, for Margaret's sake I pretended it had. "You're remarkable," I said, hugging her. "Oh, Margaret, I'm so confused. Sorcha's only been gone for such a short time."

"Yes, I know. But the truth, no matter how difficult to face, is that she *is* gone. And life is for the living, Britanny." She smiled. "Posh on all that mourning. I'm sure that wherever Sorcha is, she approves."

We embraced again. Her words, though spoken from her heart, brought me little comfort. There were so many other facets to the mystery of Sorcha's death. So many secrets that needed unraveling. And there seemed to be so little time.

Colin was waiting for me in his study, a small room beyond the parlor. Though I remembered it to be Mr. Blackwell's office when he was alive, the room looked different somehow.

Gone were the dark, cumbersome furnishings and in their place was a more elegant French styling. The walls were painted in soft buttery shades, and the windows, their glass panels etched with beautiful designs, were undraped, allowing the clear afternoon light to enter. A bountiful fire blazed in the hearth, bringing a welcoming warmth to the room.

Colin sat at a finely polished desk busily writing with a thick quill flanked by a grand white plume. I stood there quietly, not wishing to disturb him, but it did not take him long to notice that I was in the room.

He smiled and replaced the quill in the silver inkstand in front of him. "Britanny, why didn't you tell me you were here?" He rose from his seat and walked toward me. He looked so handsome in his gray waistcoat and matching flannel trousers. His hair had been trimmed but not too short and the delightful aroma of bay rum filled my senses.

"You seemed so busy. I didn't want to take you away from your work."

He glanced over his shoulder and then back to me. "My work can wait. It's you I can't get enough of." He took my hand in his, brought it to his lips, and kissed it tenderly. "You are

199

so beautiful, Britanny. I am a lucky man."

I blushed and sighed at his sweet words, but an emptiness lingered inside me. Could I trust my heart with him?

Though not wishing to change the subject, I found myself asking about his study. "Everything looks so different. Nothing like I remember. When did Mr. Blackwell change it?"

The hatred in his eyes, though brief, was unmistakable. Not only was it was the same cruel, hard look he had had for Douglas, but also when I had first mentioned Sorcha's father upon my arrival a week ago. I blinked, shocked at his appearance, but said nothing.

"Kingsley Blackwell had nothing to do with what you see here," he said in a tone reserved for distasteful things. Then a softer expression seemed to melt away his overt malevolence. "It was Sorcha who had the room redecorated." He grinned. "A . . . a wedding present, she called it. Something of my very own."

He drifted away from me. Amusement still lurked in his dark eyes and he looked as though he was making a fool of everyone connected with the Blackwell name.

I felt a small spark of fury take hold of me. Did he intend on being so mean? Or was I just overreacting to everything I had been through?

When my thoughts finally ebbed into a sea of calmness, I glanced up and found that he was staring at me. A bright look of eagerness had replaced the arrogance and his eyebrows rose in obvious pleasure. He offered his arm to me.

"Shall we go?" he asked, the amber flames of the fire dancing in his eyes.

I smiled warily and reached for his arm. With a surge of immediacy about him, Colin led me from the room.

I was not surprised to see that the town of Hudson had grown considerably in the two years I had been away. I had often read about the developing of places such as this in the newspapers and marveled at their progress. Though far from rivaling New York City, the buildings, hotels, and shops were quite impressive.

As Colin steered the open gig down the cobblestone street, I noticed that there was more of a city flavor than the small-town atmosphere I had grown used to as a child. Sorcha and I had eagerly looked forward to Saturday outings with the family. Our eyes wide, our hearts hopeful, we would browse through the different shops, wondering what it would be like to wear a pretty plumed hat to a party or own a beautiful fancy dress that came all the way from Paris. But by the end of the day, all wishing aside, we had always been satisfied with a sack of bonbons or peppermint sticks.

With horses and carriage settled at a hitching post, Colin caught me at the waist with both hands and swept me out of the gig. Our bodies brushed lightly, and we stood close for a moment. He smiled at me and then we parted, almost reluctantly.

The air was invigorating and shafts of warm sunlight dropped through the marvelous swanlike clouds swimming across the sky. The bustle of the townspeople, the laughter of children, and the rattle of carriages completed the city scene.

Arm in arm, we walked down the promenade, looking like any other couple out for a stroll. But no one, not even Colin, could sense the emotions churning within my breast. My apprehension grew steadily as he nodded to passersby along the walkway. What were they thinking seeing Colin and me together? A man who had lost his dear wife only a little more than a month ago flaunting his friendship with another woman? Scandalous! Certainly, they disapproved in spite of their flashing eyes and pleasant smiles.

I glanced up at Colin a few times, perhaps looking for some sort of assurance that I need not be embarrassed or that I had concocted the scenario in my head. But he seemed unbothered, treating our time together as if it was meant to be. His relaxed attitude made me more at ease and after a time I was glad I had come.

The shops along the promenade boasted everything from a blacksmith to a book shop. I felt an ache inside me when we came upon a fruit stand similar to the one my parents had owned.

"Britanny, this is such a happy day and yet you seem so sad. Why?" Colin asked, pulling me nearer to him.

I told him of my reminiscing, finding it easy to confide in him.

"I understand. Being part of a family means a lot to you."

He knew my parents and I were not as close as I would have liked. I had been coerced by Douglas into telling my life story that evening when he and his mother were dinner guests at Raven Manor, and I was sure that Colin remembered. It was Sorcha's family he was alluding to. Something in my heart told me so.

I cocked my head. "Isn't family important to you, Colin?"

He stared straight ahead as the afternoon sun shone on his face like a gold veil. "No," he said dryly. "Family means nothing to me."

He voiced his feelings with such conviction that I paused for a moment. I had been curious about his background for so long and now it seemed a perfect opportunity to pursue my interest.

"You must have family somewhere, Colin. Someone who cares about you."

"No, Britanny," he answered flatly.

"Your mother? Father?"

He turned to me, his eyes flashing darkly. I

drew back from the hatred and torment that I saw there.

"My parents are dead. Sorcha was my only family, and now she's gone, too." His expression was hard and cruel as if daring me to continue my questioning.

"You have Melinda," I said quietly.

His face softened at the mention of the baby's name. He looked away from me. "Yes, I have Melinda."

Nothing more was said on the subject of family. Though disappointed at Colin's vague answers, I hoped that Sorcha's journal could provide me with the information I needed. If not, I would have to approach Colin once again. But no matter who or what would be my source, I was determined to learn all I could about the elusive Colin Rutledge.

The myriad of sights and sounds dazzled my senses, and when I glanced at the shingle of Madame Rousse's Dress Shoppe, a twinge of nostalgia wrenched my heart. A small, but elegant, establishment, this was the place where Sorcha and I had pressed our noses against the window to watch the beautiful women of the town choose the loveliest dress or latest accessories.

I felt Colin pull away from my side, but I was so mesmerized with one of the dresses on display, I wasn't even curious as to where he was going.

Made of the finest royal blue silk, the gown

caught my eye because of its simplicity. The sleeves were short and puffy and the embroidered neckline dipped below the shoulders. The only flounce was a ruffle that graced the skirt. Truly, it was elegant.

My musing was interrupted, though nicely, by Colin's sudden reflection in the window.

"For you," he whispered in my ear and held in front of me a tiny nosegay of orange blossoms.

"Oh, Colin," I said, reaching for the flowers and drinking in their sweetness. "They're lovely. Where did you—"

He moved aside and a flower cart bursting with colorful posies came into view. The proprietor, a pale, white-haired woman, smiled warmly.

"Enjoy them, dearie," she said, then winked at Colin.

His eyes, dark and inquisitive, locked with mine when I turned back to him. He bent toward me and I knew he was going to kiss me. It was what I wanted, too, even though I was aware that such a display of affection in public would be frowned upon.

The faint sound of someone calling Colin's name drew our attention to the other side of the street. There I saw a short, stocky fellow dodge the hubbub of carriages and horses, and I shut my eyes, horrified, when he nearly collided with a rushing carriage.

His eyes were red from the dust of the streets,

and he tipped his flannel cap to me, but was anxious to speak with Colin.

"Didn't know you'd be in town today, Mr. Rutledge, but I'm sure glad to see you," he said. "I was on my way to get Doc Barrens."

Colin looked concerned and placed his hand upon the man's shoulder. "What's wrong, Thatcher?"

From what I could gather despite Thatcher's noisy wheezing, there seemed to be a problem at the docks, more specifically with Colin's shipping firm.

He turned to me, his expression brimming with worry. "Britanny, one of the crates broke loose from the cables. Some of my men might be hurt."

I gasped. "May I be of some help?"

He took my hand, his eyes filled with gratitude. "No. It could be dangerous. I want you to stay here."

"Go, then," I urged, acutely aware of his anxiety. "Do not give another thought to me. I will find you there later. I remember the way."

He brushed my cheek with a kiss, then telling Thatcher to fetch the doctor, hurried down the street in the direction of the docks.

My heart was racing as I watched him disappear through an opening between two shops. Silently, I hoped that no serious mishap had occurred to any of Colin's men, and with all my heart I prayed for his safety.

My pulse started to slow and I took a deep

breath. Realizing I should keep myself occupied, I turned my attention back to the shops along the promenade.

I found the candle shop that Margaret had spoken of and purchased some wonderfully scented ones of jasmine and gardenia, the latter being a surprise gift for her. But as the pretty young shopkeeper assisted me in my purchases, I too had a surprise.

The tiny bell above the door tinkled lightly, announcing the arrival of Eleanor Garwood. She looked rather splendid in her sapphire-blue toilette and matching bonnet. Interested in the large selection of candles and holders, she did not look my way and I wondered if I should try to leave the store unnoticed.

I thanked the shopkeeper and was about to leave when I heard my name. I turned and came face to face with Eleanor. She wore a forced smile and her eyes were dark and empty.

I grinned back, embarrassingly so, hoping to hide the fact that I had planned to leave the shop without acknowledging her presence.

"Britanny, how nice to see you again," she said.

Her voice sounded strained, which made me wonder if she had finally recognized the Britanny St. James from ten years ago. But as she continued to speak, she gave no indication that she remembered me.

"I see you've decided to stay at Raven

Manor," she said with a questioning look in her eyes. "The last time we spoke you seemed indecisive about your plans."

I detected a slight frustration in her voice. Did the fact that I was still at Raven Manor bother her that much? Or was it an interest in Colin's and my connection that puzzled her?

"Yes. I'll be staying as long as Mr. Rutledge will have me." I sounded aloof and arrogant, though I didn't mean to be.

Eleanor grinned weakly, then reached up to touch the beautiful ivory-carved brooch that graced the high-necked collar of her walking suit. For some reason, her nervous gesture made me think back to the day she had come to Raven Manor to ask about Colin's whereabouts. She had seemed quite agitated then, too, though she had tried to hide it. But what struck me odd now was the similar way she had uneasily fingered another brooch she had worn that afternoon. I shrugged inwardly, believing her behavior to be overly anxious.

She tilted her head. "Are you here alone, Britanny?"

"No. Colin and I are in town to have dinner—"

"Well, where is the dear man?" Her gaze was exaggerated as it swept through the shop and she craned her neck to see past the window to the outside. She looked back at me with a wry smile. "Don't tell me he's deserted you? But then Colin Rutledge is a rascal with the ladies." Her discreet chuckle sounded more like the hiss of a snake.

I clenched my fists. "There was a problem on the docks, Mrs. Garwood, and Colin needed to take care of it."

She pressed her lips together in a sign of pique. "Oh, I see."

The brief lull seemed perfectly timed with my plan to escape. "I really must be going, Mrs. Garwood. Colin is expecting me. Good day."

I turned to leave but she caught me by the arm. My body became rigid.

"Before you go, Britanny, I wanted to make sure that you'll be coming to my social gathering next week. Douglas is so looking forward to seeing you there." She drew her lips into a tight smile. "He's quite smitten with you, my dear."

I felt heat rush to my cheeks. "Douglas is my friend, Mrs. Garwood. Nothing more."

"Well, he certainly doesn't see it that way. Why, he intends to pursue you until this friendship you speak of is something much more." Her words ran together in vapid chatter. "Douglas is quite wealthy, you know, and he has had many young girls chasing him. The shameless hussies have tried anything they could to trap him into marriage."

"What are you trying to say, Mrs. Garwood?" I asked. The hairs on the back of my neck began to tingle.

A dark flame of defiance glowed in her eyes and her hold on my arm tightened. "We watch out for our own, Britanny. I will not have my stepson tricked by the wiles of opportunistic women."

I stiffened again, not so much with what Eleanor said, but the way she had said it. I had the strange feeling, ever so brief, that what had happened at that moment was something else entirely. What was Eleanor Garwood really trying to tell me?

Finally, she let go of my arm. The dark veil of warning that had clouded her face was gone, but I did not relax with its disappearance.

"Well, do have a good day, Britanny, and give Colin my best." She turned away from me and busied herself once again with the wares in the shop.

Holding my small package close to my breast, I scurried from the place, the tiny bell signaling my hasty departure.

Attempting to remove the wrath of Eleanor Garwood from my mind was no easy task. She had made quite a disturbing impression, so much so that I could swear I still felt her gaze following me.

As I hurried along the walk, weaving in and out of the other strollers and sightseers, all I could think about was being with Colin.

It did not surprise me at how quickly I had found my way to the docks. Kingsley Blackwell had brought Sorcha and me here often, especially during the summer, when we would marvel at the huge ships sailing in and out of the harbor.

Once Sorcha and I had even made a secret pact to stow away on one of the freights.

"Just think of the places we'd see, Britanny. The wonderful, exotic lands. Oh, the things we could do," she would say, her eyes alight like a fire, drawing me into their silver-blue blaze.

Amazingly, we had gotten as far as the carriage house one night, determined in our search for adventure and riches. But the howl of a wild animal had sent us scurrying back to the safety of Raven Manor. It was just as well. The punishment we would have received if we had tried such a daring endeavor would have been swift and just. And so our madcap fantasies never did materialize.

Breathing in the crisp sea air now, I chortled out loud, thinking about that time with Sorcha. It felt good to remember, good to laugh, and as I did, the harsh, biting words of Eleanor Garwood became a fleeting memory.

Save for the regular noisy bustle of the longshoremen loading and unloading cargo from the stately clipper ships, the docks were free of the confusion of a mishap. It was a good sign. Perhaps nothing serious had happened to any of Colin's men.

My eyes drank in the colorful, romantic atmosphere. I looked around for Colin, but he was not on the pier.

The sign painted above the square, uninteresting building at the end of the wharf seemed smaller than I remembered. Only the words had changed. The name "RUTLEDGE" in bold, black lettering had been added to the beginning of BLACKWELL SHIPPING COMPANY.

It was strange seeing Colin's name alongside the Blackwell moniker. Aware, but not privy to the way he felt about Sorcha's father, I wouldn't have been surprised if he had done away with the Blackwell name completely. But then it was probably because of Sorcha that he had kept it.

The door to the office was ajar. My heart quickened at the thought of seeing Colin, though I wondered if I should disturb him.

But what I saw froze me to the spot and made my heart beat even faster. Colin was behind a massive wooden desk, flipping through papers and muttering to himself. I saw him throw a ledger aside, with a curse, and run his hand through his already-mussed hair.

I swallowed, telling myself that I had caught him at a bad moment. Perhaps something serious had happened to one of his men. Realizing how passionate a man Colin was, I was worried.

As I was about to enter the small, dimly lit room, I saw him move his lips and snort in disgust. A feral gleam poured from his eyes, giving him the look of a wild animal ready for the kill.

"Damn you, Kingsley Blackwell!" he hissed. His arm swung across the desk, knocking stacks of papers and a kerosene lamp crashing to the stone floor. "Damn you and your kind. Damn you all to hell!"

The burning hatred in his words ran through me, turning my blood to ice. I leaned against the cool brick of the building, not wanting to believe what I had just heard. I felt my insides turn to jelly and warm tears fill my eyes. My shoulders shook and I pressed my hands to my face.

Why? Why did Colin so detest Sorcha's father? What had Kingsley done to him? Or—I held my breath—was he truly a madman? Someone so unstable that my loving concern would not be enough to soothe his troubled mind? There were matters here that were far beyond me, and though I wanted with all my heart to believe that his abhorrence was tangled within a nightmare I had created, I could not.

And then, as I stood there, wiping the tears from my eyes, one sudden and cold thought crossed my mind. Certainly anyone who harbored as much hatred for Kingsley Blackwell, would be absolutely set against being a part of his family. Why, then, had Colin married Sorcha?

Unless....

I deeply inhaled the salty air and readied myself to plunge into the cold, dark waters of my own perceptions.

I thought back to the day that Sorcha had left for Europe. Was there more to her going away than just attending a boarding school to please her parents? Something she was too ashamed to confide—even to me?

A sudden chill wind slashed through me. I looked up toward the sky, my eyes swimming once again in tears I could no longer control. The lovely white clouds had turned steely-gray and heavy with rain. The darkness above seemed to press down on me and I caught my breath in a sharp sob.

It was Melinda who captured my thoughts now. That sweet, precious baby. Was she the reason Sorcha stopped writing to me? Why she never answered my letters, my pleas to come to Raven Manor?

My spine tingled. Had I been wrong all this time? Wrong about Colin? About everything? Could it be that Colin really was Melinda's father? Had he been forced by Kingsley Blackwell to marry Sorcha in order to give the baby his name and save the family from the disgrace of a child born out of wedlock?

But indeed there was more. What if my growing love for this man had clouded the truth? The deadly truth? The truth I had become afraid to face?

Raven Manor. The Blackwell money. All of

Kingsley Blackwell's profitable business hold-ings. Were they all part of the deal? And was Sorcha only an unsuspecting pawn in Colin's game? The words swirled around in my mind, bringing with them whispers of terror.

Colin owned everything now. Was he truly the last piece of this puzzle in Sorcha's death? My mouth went dry. I tried desperately to fight back the dreaded thought that was swirling inside me, as it had before. Though I had sus-pected him, I feared now that I believed he was guilty. It was no use. The feelings I had were too strong, too powerful for me to contain any longer.

Colin Rutledge, the man I loved, was Sor-cha's murderer.

Chapter Fourteen

How can this be? My mind screamed over and over until I thought my head would burst. My breath came in short spurts. I had to calm myself, I had to think.

Lost in my own turmoil, I was unaware of a presence beside me until I felt a hand grab my upper arm. A sudden chill invaded my body as I drew back in fear from the touch.

"Britanny, it's only me. There's no need to be afraid." His voice was like steel wrapped in silk. When I met his gaze, I was riveted by the knowing look deep within his dark, bold stare. He stared at me with deadly concentration and I shuddered, certain that he was probing my thoughts.

I tried to speak but my throat seemed to

constrict, allowing not the smallest of syllables to escape.

Colin's brows knitted into a frown. "Britanny, what has happened? You look terrified."

My mind in a swirl of dark emotions, I realized too late that he had pulled me into his arms, holding me with the tightest of embraces.

"No, Colin. Let go of me!" I shouted as tears threatened to dissolve the brave front I was fighting to keep between us. As I struggled to get free, I found myself caught achingly between the desire to remain in his arms and the desire to run.

What is wrong with you? my brain screamed. *This man . . . No, this monster could very well be Sorcha's murderer. And yet you have these feelings of love for him.*

"Britanny, what is the matter? You look so pale." Colin's features were etched with worry.

Suddenly, I felt a big cold drop on my cheek. I glanced up. A cloud, black and threatening, hovered over us.

Colin wrapped his arm about my waist. "Come inside. It's beginning to rain. Quickly now."

But I stood frozen to the spot. Several drops of rain splattered onto his cheeks and he wiped them away impatiently.

"Please, Britanny, you're frightening me."

I saw the odd, twisted look on his face and

217

I choked on the horrid irony that shrouded us.

"*I* am frightening *you!*" I heard myself shout with an edge of desperation in my voice. "I saw you, Colin. Just minutes ago, I saw how brutish you really are."

Something came into his dark, piercing eyes. The realization of my words began to take hold.

The rain fell faster now, harder, too. The sharp drops felt like needles against my face and hands. I shuddered as I stared into his unyielding expression.

"I'm sorry, you had to see me that way, Britanny. I . . . I was angry—"

"So angry that you found it necessary to curse Kingsley Blackwell's name? The dear man is dead, Colin. Why do you hate his memory so?"

"The dear man?" His voice was strange, almost evil. "That *dear* man had a heart of stone. He never cared about anyone but himself—and that included his daughter."

I was shocked at his insinuation. How dare he accuse Kingsley Blackwell of not loving Sorcha!

"I don't believe you," I said, shifting my eyes from his face. "I won't believe you."

Grasping my chin, he forced me to look at him. My breathing was shallow. My heart pounded wildly. I was getting soaked. My clothes clung to me and water ran into my mouth.

But the rain had no affect on Colin. Through the drops, I saw madness lurking in his eyes. He let go of me, but his penetrating gaze fixed me to the spot.

"Because of Blackwell's selfishness, because of his greed, Seth Dorsey could have lost his life today. A man with a wife and five children to support." His face twisted with disgust. "When I took over this company, I was told that the ships and everything on them were in excellent condition. All of them. Even the cables that snapped and sent a ton of crates hurtling just inches away from Seth."

"Sometimes things like that happen. It's unfortunate, but it's no one's fault—"

His angry expression cut off my words like a sharp blade. "Today I found out that your 'wonderful' Mr. Blackwell paid a sizable amount of money to an inspector so that he would turn his head to the fact that the cables were in very poor condition. It seems it would have been too expensive to replace them all."

"Stop! Stop it, Colin!" I shouted at him. "You're the owner of this company now. Perhaps it's you who should feel guilty about taking another's word for what you should have done yourself."

His eyes shone with a black veil of defiance. "Yes, you're right. I am to blame. I know that. But don't you see, Britanny? Kingsley Blackwell was an arrogant son of a—" He swallowed, wincing at the bitter taste of the unspoken curse. "He bought off everyone." His gaze dropped to the wet cobblestone beneath our feet. "Even me."

My mind reeled with the confusion of his words. "You're lying, Colin. The Blackwells were the most loving, generous people I knew. How dare you tarnish their good name."

Gone was the compassionate man I had fallen in love with. There was no tenderness or kindness evident in his eyes, only malice in his face and a low, menacing laugh that frightened me even more.

"I see you've been taken in by their kind, too," he said.

I flinched, uncertain of how to answer him. But fearful or not, I had to know, had to find out why he hated the Blackwells so.

"If this is how you feel, Colin, then why did you marry Sorcha? Did you really love her or was it everything else she had to offer you?"

He drew back as if I had slapped him hard across the face. He grabbed my shoulders tightly and a tiny cry of fright escaped my lips.

"I deserve all this wealth and power. I deserve everything—and more!" Madness glazed his eyes and a cruel smile twisted his mouth. "Sorcha understood why. She understood everything about me."

He released me and I struggled to breathe. "Did she understand when you grew tired of her? When the money and power wasn't yours to have while she was still alive?"

His fingers clamped around my wrist, squeezing my flesh to the bone. "What are you saying, Britanny?"

I pinned him with my stare. "Did Sorcha understand when you pushed her to her death?"

Everything inside me quieted. The only sound I could hear was the steady beating of the rain.

Colin blinked, a blank animal expression dulling his eyes. Then the realization of what I had said struck him, distorting his features. I began to tremble.

Without warning, he pulled me along the now empty docks, bringing us both back into town. I gulped in the rain and air and tried to scream, but the cries lodged in my throat. The streets were deserted. The downpour had seen to that. There was no one to help me.

Strands of my wet hair covered my face and eyes, and several times I stumbled over the hem of my dress.

"Colin, please!" I begged, heavy sobs mixing with my words. "Where are you taking me?"

He did not answer, but turned his head briefly to look at me. I cowered from the hatred that emanated from him. The wrapped package of candles and bouquet of orange blossoms slipped from my trembling fingers.

Colin dragged me toward the carriage, lifted me by the waist, and pushed me roughly into the seat. My clothing molded with the wet, shiny leather. My shoes sloshed in the shallow puddle that had formed in the bottom of the gig.

With one quick motion, Colin unhitched the restless horses and jumped into the driver's seat. He shouted and snapped the reins making the horses whinny and take off at a full gallop.

I was jolted back against the seat as the wind and strangling rain held me there with invisible hands. All I could see was Colin hunched over his knees, bouncing freely with each bump of the carriage.

"Colin!" I screamed, but he ignored my terrified shouting, leaving me to wonder what was to become of me.

"Whooaa!" Colin shouted, commanding the horses to stop.

Instinctively, I flung my arms out in front of me and braced myself against the inside of the carriage as I lurched forward in the seat.

Like a premonition of doom, Colin appeared. His hatred, still evident, had turned his features to granite. I recoiled as he reached for me, but once again his iron fingers encircled my wrist, holding me motionless.

Smothering a curse, he pulled me from the carriage. I stumbled against him. Every muscle in my body tensed and cried out in pain.

Where was I? Where had he brought me? As I pushed myself away from his rigid form, my eyes darted nervously. We were in an open area surrounded by a thick wall of trees. My heart sank. Any screams for help would be useless.

The rain had slowed, but the wind swept down on us with a cold fury. As my head cleared a bit, I now realized it was not just the wind I heard. The relentless rush of water roared in my ears.

Panic-stricken, I felt my heart lurch. I now knew where Colin had taken me.

"No!" I finally screamed and clawed at his hand locked around my wrist.

My plea fell on deaf ears. With inhuman strength, he dragged me along the rocky terrain until we reached the edge of a cliff.

Colin pulled me closer to him. "Look!" he yelled, and pointed to the raging St. Lawrence River so far below us. "This is where Sorcha died! This was where her battered body was found!"

"No!" I shouted again, more frightened at the sight than I had been the first time. It was then that a terrifying thought crossed my mind. Was Colin planning the same end for me as he had for Sorcha? My God! Was he going to murder me, too?

I struggled like a wildcat against his hold. If he did mean to kill me, I was not going to be a willing victim. I would fight with all the strength and courage I had in me.

But as I raised my free hand ready to scratch at his face, Colin suddenly let me go. I stumbled back, the weight of my wet clothes pulling me down to the ground. Stunned, I sat there, frightened and confused.

Colin turned to me, his eyes still dark and ominous. But now, even through my tears, I saw a flicker of sadness begin to melt the hatred that had burned there.

He reached for me, this time with a tender touch. Surprisingly, I welcomed his help, somehow knowing that he meant me no harm. For now, he was free of the torment that had twisted his mind.

"Britanny, forgive me. I did not mean to frighten you." His stone-cold features began to soften. "Every time I think about Sorcha—" He choked back a sob and turned his face from me.

Gently, I ran my hand down his smooth cheek, coaxing him to look back at me. The cold, hard mask he had worn was gone and a clear, but pained, expression had taken its place.

The rain had stopped and the wind had calmed somewhat. I should have been shivering, the clatter of my chattering teeth filling the air, but a warm blanket of tender passion surrounded me and I did not feel the cold.

Colin's dark eyes blazed across my face. "I had nothing to do with Sorcha's death, Britanny. You must believe me."

He was telling the truth. I was certain of that now. "I do, Colin. I do believe you."

"I loved her. I was trying to protect her."

I frowned. "Protect her? From what? From whom?"

His face was clear, almost bloodless. "I'm not certain, Britanny. That's what makes it all the more frustrating. All I know was from the moment we returned from England—"

"England?" I repeated, waiting expectantly, but Colin remained silent. I continued, "Sorcha was sent away to school in Switzerland. What was she doing in England? Is that where you met?"

He looked at me with pain in his eyes as though my questioning had wounded him in some way. "Yes," he finally admitted. "We met in England. We lived there for a while."

"After you were married," I said matter-of-factly, yet deep inside I knew there was more than what he was telling me.

He nodded. "When we returned to Raven Manor, Sorcha changed."

"Changed?" I could feel my face tightening. "How?"

"She became extremely nervous. Even fearful at times." He turned away from me and covered his face with clenched fists. "Dear God! If only we had stayed away, Sorcha would still be alive."

My insides wrenched with a sadness that only Colin and I could share. Yet, something more touched my emotions as I studied his tormented stance. His love and loyalty were still with Sorcha. I realized that now and though it pained me to know his true feelings, my heart ached for him.

I caressed his arm and the touch brought him back to me. "If indeed Sorcha was as fearful as you say, why then did she come back to Raven Manor?"

Grief, fear, and anger mingled on his face. "Out of a sense of obligation, I suppose. When her parents died in that carriage accident, she felt it was her duty as their daughter to return and care for Raven Manor." His dark eyes blurred and softened. "I could not refuse her anything, Britanny. I loved her."

My spirit was heavy, as sodden as the ground I stood on. I stared straight ahead, past the massive black cliffs and churning sea to the gray, moody sky.

"Margaret told me you were the one who found her here."

He was silent for a moment, deep in thought. "I had been away on business that day. When I returned home, Margaret was very worried. Sorcha had not come back from town. I went out to look for her." His voice seemed to fade into the cold swell of the wind. "I found the wagon and horses here. And then I discovered her—her body sprawled at the bottom of the cliffs."

I shuddered. "Oh, Colin," I said, looking back at him. "How horrible for you. I still can't believe that Sorcha's been taken from us."

Colin's features began to harden once again,

his eyes glowing like two flames. "Sorcha was murdered, Britanny. She did not kill herself as everyone believes. She was lured to this place by someone, the very person she feared, and then was pushed to her death."

My tears flowed freely now. "Oh, Colin. That is what I believe. Sorcha could never have taken her own life. And I know she believed that her life was in danger, too."

His brow rose and he gazed at me curiously.

"Some days ago I received a letter asking me to return to Raven Manor. There was no name, no clue as to who may have written it. I assumed it was Margaret, but she denied sending such a message. I even considered it might have been your doing."

The beginnings of a knowing smile graced his mouth. I found his expression curious indeed, yet I continued, now voicing my belief. "I think the letter might have come from Sorcha herself."

"Yes, Britanny," he said without hesitation. "Sorcha did write you that letter. I know because she told me that she wanted you here. She wrote it a few days before her death."

I blinked in astonished silence. In the dark recesses of my mind, I had thought such a thing possible, especially since I had found Sorcha's journal and the message she'd left there for me. The handwriting was the same. But having my assumptions confirmed heightened my interest.

"She wanted to explain about why she was sent away, about the baby..." He paused. "About me. I encouraged her, hoping that having you here might be good for her. Surely, she was not opening up to me about what was troubling her. Knowing how close you were, maybe she would confide in you." His eyes lowered and his shoulders drooped. "If only her letter had been delivered sooner."

"Why didn't you tell me all of this when I first arrived?" I asked.

His dark eyes bored into mine. "Sorcha's death made me so damned suspicious, Britanny, of everything and everybody. I had to know for sure that you were truly her friend." His face had a withered look to it, like that of a dying flower. "Please forgive my mistrust in you."

"Of course, Colin," I said, smiling. "I too distrusted you when we first met."

He laughed, a good solid laugh, and a glow came back into his face. "Then we will forgive each other." His hands caressed my cheeks as his thumbs gently wiped away any trace of my tears. He pulled me toward him.

I did not resist and I nestled against him. We clung to each other as the wind mounted again. Colin held me tightly and I could hear his heart beating furiously where my ear was pressed to his broad hard chest. There was no question as to why we sought comfort in each other.

His fingers tangled in my hair, still wet as it splayed behind me in the wind. He brought my face toward his.

"I love you, Britanny." His voice was deep and powerful. I saw the tiny light in his eyes as his mouth found mine.

I responded willingly, shamelessly, my soul leaping, my body a vessel for the outpouring of tension between us. He molded his body into mine and I arched against him, eager for more of his embrace. Our kiss deepened and a great sigh escaped from my throat when he lifted his lips to kiss my cheeks, jaw, and the length of my neck.

I entwined my fingers in his dark hair, unconsciously pressing his head against my breast.

"I want you, Britanny," he moaned, raising his head to kiss my neck and cheek.

"Colin. Oh, dearest Colin. I want to be a part of you." The words came so freely that saying them made me tremble. The howling of the wind seemed to carry me into a further frenzy.

His mouth came down on mine again, and his tongue probed deeply, tasting me. But in some dark part of my mind, I knew that what we were doing was wrong, even though I wanted this with all my heart.

He lifted his mouth from mine and his hands followed the curve of my hips, bringing me even closer to him. "Tell me you love me, Britanny. Tell me you'll be mine forever," he whispered hoarsely.

Once again I felt hot tears searing my cheeks. Summoning what was left of my strength, I pulled away from his passionate embrace. "No, Colin. This is wrong. We mustn't give in to these feelings no matter how much we both want to." I turned away from him and wrapped my trembling arms about my waist.

"Britanny, what's wrong? Why are you doing this?" He sounded surprised, angry.

"We can't feel this way about each other. It's wrong. So very wrong."

He grabbed me by my shoulders and forced me to face him. "Look at me," he demanded.

Slowly, I raised my eyes to his probing, puzzled stare.

"I love you, Britanny. I know you love me, too. I can see it in your eyes, your beautiful face. I can feel it when we hold each other, when our lips touch. It's like an unstoppable fire spreading through us." His breathing was unsteady, his body unyielding. "I want you, Britanny. What is so wrong about a man wanting the woman he loves?"

"Don't you see, Colin? It's not me you truly and completely want. It's Sorcha. You're still in love with her. She is your wife, even in death. She was my dearest friend." I could feel my heart breaking. "I cannot fall in love with you. I dare not, for it will only cause us more pain."

His mouth tightened. His eyes narrowed questioningly. "You believe that we're betraying Sorcha's memory? Listen to me, Britanny—"

I tried to break free from his grip, but the more I struggled, the tighter he held me.

"No!" I cried. "No more!"

"By God, you will listen to me!" He gritted his teeth and brutally dragged me closer. The heat from him singed my body. I felt vulnerable, defenseless against his savage behavior, yet all the time shamelessly burning with desire.

"We are not betraying Sorcha. We are not defiling her memory. Sorcha was not my wife, Britanny. We were never married."

I almost choked on a quick breath of utter astonishment. I stared at Colin, unable to react to his shocking words. Yet my mind was reeling.

"I am not Sorcha's husband," he continued, his voice lowering to a whisper. "I am Colin Rutledge Blackwell. Sorcha's brother."

Chapter Fifteen

"Kingsley Blackwell's bastard son!" Colin yelled over the howl of the wind. He threw back his head and all his pent-up emotions were released in a laugh that was distinctively cruel. It sent a shiver through me.

I struggled to breathe. The chilled air felt like a fire in my chest. "Sorcha's half brother?" I said, not hiding my surprise. "But she never—"

"Never told you about me?" Colin exhaled deeply and the tension seemed to drain from his body. He smiled as if to himself. "She never told you because she never knew about me. No one did. No one except that cur Blackwell."

"Oh, Colin." A sob escaped my lips as I saw the hurt in his eyes that he was trying to hide from me. "I'm so sorry."

"I want your love, Britanny, not your pity."

We clung to one another, almost afraid to let go. As our hearts and souls entwined, I knew that our silent vow of love would bind us together forever.

Though there was so much to share, we rode home to Raven Manor in silence. My mind was still reeling with all that had happened, but my body was racked with exhaustion and I almost didn't care about the scandals and secrets I was soon to hear. Just being with Colin was all that I wanted. All that I would ever want.

Margaret must have seen us approach, for as the carriage neared the house, she was already halfway down the front steps.

"My stars, what's happened to the two of you?" she asked, reaching for me with great concern etched on her face.

With the horses steadied, Colin jumped from the gig, then helped me down. "I'm afraid our plans were thwarted by the rainstorm, Margaret."

His eyes played across my face, sending me a gentle warning that Margaret was unaware of his true parentage. I nodded slightly, understanding his silent message.

"Margaret, please tell Thomas that the horses need tending immediately. I'll not lose two fine animals because of this blasted rain."

His hand at my waist, Colin led me up the porch stairs.

Margaret followed us through the door. "Never mind the horses, it's you two I'm worried about. Why, you'll catch your death if you don't get out of those wet clothes."

Colin turned to me, wearing a sly grin. He leaned closer, his lips pressed lightly against my ear. "I dare say Margaret is right, bless her heart. We should discard these damp, uncomfortable wrappings."

I blushed at his bold words, yet the thought of our bare skin molding together in passionate desire made me tingle inside.

"You'll both need hot baths and I'll hear no argument about that."

Colin agreed willingly and I caught the mischievous twinkle in his eye. "Let's do as Margaret says, Britanny. After all, she knows best."

"Stop your teasing, Mr. Rutledge," she said, and her lips tightened in a disapproving grin. "Now, have you had anything to eat?"

"No," I said, quickly realizing suddenly how famished I was.

"Say no more. Now, off with you. Hurry." She waved the back of her hands toward us, shooing us up the stairs, mumbling laments as we went. Colin and I laughed quietly so as not to insult her. Indeed, we were thankful that she cared so much.

I was also grateful that Colin had been teasing about our clothing and the bath that he proposed we indulge in together.

"We will talk, Brittany," he said as we stood in front of my bedroom door. "There is so much I need to tell you. But, go now. Relax. Let the hot water melt your fears, for there's nothing to be frightened of any longer." He reached for my hand, brought it to his lips, and kissed it. "I shall do the same, wishing with all my heart that you could be with me."

Once again my senses began to flutter with his touch. I wanted to throw myself into his arms, every inch of my body pressed against his. A vision of us submerged in a tub of hot fragrant water flashed in my mind. I saw my hands caress his smooth skin, stroking every muscle, hearing him groan with delight. I could almost feel his mouth moving over my lips, my neck, my breasts, with exquisite tenderness until my own whispers became uncontrollable cries of ecstasy.

Heat continued to surge through my body even as the vision disappeared, leaving me weak and vulnerable. I dared not look at him, for not only were my cheeks reddened with embarrassment, but my lips were slowly forming a secret smile that would surely have given my immodest thoughts away.

"Go now, Britanny. I will meet you downstairs in the parlor."

He strode down the hall, stopping at the door to his own room. He turned and our eyes locked once more. His possessive gaze made my body respond in ways that were new to me. Frightening, desirous ways. When he was no longer in my sight, I began to count the minutes until I'd be with Colin again.

The bath I had drawn for myself warmed my ice-cold skin. Being with Colin, surrendering to his touch, had so heated my body that I had been unaware of how chilled to the marrow I really was.

I opened the doors to the armoire and scoured through my clothing. Not wanting nor feeling the need to dress in a suitable outfit, I quickly donned my white cambric chemise and drawers, and slipped into a ruffled white dressing sacque tied at the neck with a blue satin bow. I spun around like a dancer, and the soft material billowed out from my legs and hips. I laughed, enjoying the freedom and comfort. But I stopped my impromptu elation when I caught my reflection in the mirror on the vanity. I bit my lower lip thoughtfully.

Was this the proper way for a lady to dress when with a man? Wearing nothing but undergarments? A secret smile graced my lips as I thought of Colin.

"Proper be damned!" I said with a toss of my head. My eyes wide, I quickly covered my mouth with my hand at the sound of my swearing. Laughter filtered through my fingers, an almost wicked laughter.

"How utterly shameless of you, Britanny." I

shook my finger at the face in the mirror. Colin's dark eyes flashed in my mind. "How wonderfully shameless."

Before closing the doors of the armoire, my eyes were drawn to my worn leather trunk, Sorcha's journal!

Kneeling now, I snapped the latches and opened the lid. I found the book quickly, scooping it up from the bottom of the trunk where I had hidden it. I ran my fingers along its ragged edge, then pressed it to my chest.

My heartbeat quickened. Between the pages of this journal could be the answers I had been searching for since I returned to Raven Manor. Now, I wanted Colin to share in this discovery, too. Sorcha was his sister, and he loved her, and like me wanted to avenge her murder. A wave of determination rushed through me. I would show him the journal when the time was right.

"How would you like to go on a picnic?"

Colin's question caught me by surprise. He was leaning against the hearth in a casual pose. The glow from the fire played upon his royal blue silk wrap. The top partially covered his muscular chest and I could see a hint of dark curly hair through the opening.

I swallowed. I had never seen a man's naked chest before. Even half-naked. I knew I was staring, yet I couldn't help myself.

"A picnic?" I asked. Even though a brief

237

laugh escaped my lips, I was curious. Standing in the entranceway to the parlor, I shuddered as he started to walk toward me. "Colin, it's still raining," I began to babble as if trying to keep up with the quickened pace of my pulse. "And we're obviously not properly attired—"

He placed a finger against my lips. His dark eyes glinted with mischief and a trembling thrill raced through me. Taking me by the hand, he led me past the piano and leather chairs.

I followed him willingly, puzzled and certainly not prepared for the surprise I was soon to encounter.

A large blanket was spread upon the floor. My eyes widened with delight, seeing a bowl filled with ruby apples and dark purple grapes. Near the luscious-looking fruit, a wedge of cheese and loaf of bread begging to be savored sat stately on a small marble slab. China, crystal glasses, and a bottle of wine glittered in the glow of the fire.

"Oh, Colin, this is wonderful," I said, sounding as giddy as a child on Christmas morning.

"I must confess it was all Margaret's doing." His hand stroked the length of my hair and I fought the temptation to nestle against his broad, muscular body. "Your hair is still damp. Come. Sit by the fire. We have much to talk about."

I settled myself on the blanket close to the hearth, the heat from the flames caressing my back. Colin knelt down next to me and poured the wine into the long-stemmed goblets. With eyes as clear as the sparkling liquid, he handed me a glass. Our fingers touched lightly and a pleasing smile came to his lips.

"To us, Britanny," he said, raising his own glass to meet mine.

I looked directly at him, seeing nothing else, and I suddenly felt very fragile. What was I going to learn from Colin tonight? Would I be shocked? Relieved? I lowered my gaze and sipped the wine, tasting its cold sweetness with my trembling lips.

"Margaret doesn't know who you are, does she?" I finally asked, ending my own uncomfortable silence.

"No. And I prefer she doesn't, at least for now." His expression was pensive, yet troubled. "I will tell her. I just hope she can forgive me."

"Forgive us," I corrected.

He smiled, grateful for my loyalty. A sudden burst of laughter escaped his lips. "It's so strange," he said, shaking his head.

"What is?" I asked, curious at his lightheartedness.

"For so very long now I've been aching to tell someone who I really am, and what I believe happened the night Sorcha died."

I tilted my head. "And now?"

"I look at you, at your beautiful face, and I don't know how or where to begin." He took

239

my hand tenderly in his own.

A wave of compassion welled inside me. Boldly, I brought his hand to my face and pressed it against my cheek. He seemed to relax.

"I'm afraid that some of what I say might disturb you, knowing how close you were to the Blackwells."

I drew his hand to my lips and kissed his fingers. I looked at him then, my eyes narrowing. "If they hurt you, I shall never forgive them."

He shook his head and his brow wrinkled into a frown. "No, Britanny. I don't want to make a sham of your memories. I just want you to realize that sometimes the people we love are not as perfect as we might believe them to be."

I saw the remorse in his eyes and some of my anger drifted away.

The sound of a log falling through the grate in the fireplace startled me. I took a generous sip of my wine this time and readied myself for what was to come.

Colin stared past me and into the flames. Their dazzling red-gold heat appeared to consume his thoughts and I wondered if I would ever learn the truth that he now seemed reluctant to tell.

"My mother was Anne Rutledge," Colin began, his voice intense yet distant. "She was an exquisite, gentle woman, with skin the texture of cream and the color of honey." He looked back at me and smiled. "You remind me of her, Britanny. Her hair was darker, but she had your eyes. Vivid green, as though chips of emeralds were embedded within them."

"Your description of her is truly lovely," I said quietly.

"I do not do her justice." His expression was one of regret. Yet it was mixed with the light of hope. "Yes, she was beautiful, but also too naive, too trusting." The darkness in his eyes had returned. "She met Kingsley Blackwell at a social gathering given by a friend. She was so young, barely fifteen when she fell in love with him, and that blackhearted bastard took advantage of her love."

I winced at his heartless words. I had always known Kingsley Blackwell to be nothing less than a gentleman—kind and caring, having great love for his family. Colin must have read my expression and the confused thoughts that were racing through my mind, for he covered my hand with his own in a protective way.

"He courted my mother, promising her marriage, a home, and family. When he finally charmed her into bedding with him, he left her alone and destitute." His words were raw and angry.

"And carrying his child," I finished.

His gaze dropped to our entwined hands. "Yes."

I felt his grip tighten. "Perhaps he was unaware of your mother's dilemma. Perhaps—"

The hard look upon his face stopped me cold. "Kingsley Blackwell knew and it was his denial of me that caused my mother's parents to throw her out of their home!"

I suddenly felt a deep and powerful urge to protect Colin. I desperately wanted to wipe away all the cruel memories that had tormented him then and now.

"How did your mother survive?" I asked, blinking back the tears that were forming in my eyes.

"A kind, older woman found my mother begging in the streets and took her home with her." A warm smile melted his cold expression. "Mrs. Nanette Pilgrim was her name. A widow and living alone in a splendid house outside of London. She was looking for a companion— an *au pair*. Fate smiled down on us that day. She hired my mother, and they became fast friends."

Colin was happier now in his reminiscing, and my own heart lightened from the sadness that surrounded it.

"After I was born, she took care of my mother and me," he continued. "I loved Nanette Pilgrim. Besides my mother, she was the only family I knew."

"What happened to Nanette?" I questioned.

"I was twenty years old when she died. She was old and frail and at times I think she welcomed death. It was very sad at the end and my heart broke when I said good-bye to her for the last time.

"My mother had saved a considerable amount of money from the salary that she received from Nanette, so we were not worried about being thrown out into the streets again." Colin took a breath. "But imagine our surprise when a few days after her death, Nanette's lawyers came to see my mother to tell her that Nanette had left her everything—the house, her money—everything. She had no children, no living relatives. My mother and I were her only family."

I smiled, happy that he had had a good life, a life he deserved. Still, I was puzzled. "Then how did Kingsley Blackwell—"

"Find me?" he finished.

I nodded.

"The newspapers printed the story of the wealthy widow Pilgrim and the two people who inherited all her worldly belongings. I suppose that's how the cur discovered my mother was still alive." Once again his eyes glinted with rage. "He had contacted my mother several times, though I found that out later. I was away at school in England."

"Perhaps he wanted to right the wrong he had done, Colin," I said quietly.

"I will never believe that!" he shouted. "Where was he from the moment I had been conceived? While I was growing up? He had already denied his son. He had another family—a daughter." His eyes narrowed to tiny slits and he stared past me and into his own thoughts. "No. Kingsley Blackwell was not heartsick over what he had done. He was afraid. Afraid that my mother, a suddenly wealthy and powerful woman, would expose him for the viper he really was!"

I shifted uneasily at his words. The storm outside was growing louder now, and I wished with all my being that the wind and rain could somehow take away his brooding hurt.

I reached toward him to touch his cheek. He caught my hand, brought it to his lips, and kissed it tenderly.

"Tell me about Sorcha," I said. "Tell me what happened."

There was a tinge of sadness in his eyes. "It's funny how things come full circle. Twenty-five years later, after denying me my birthright, Kingsley Blackwell needed my help because his daughter was in the same predicament as my mother had been."

Colin's raw, angry words did not shock me. Sorcha had been with child. That was why she had been sent away. Though furious over their cold, calculated treatment of her, I could understand the Blackwells' embarrassment, their secretiveness. But why hadn't Sorcha told me the truth?

"Mother had passed away when Blackwell wrote me of my half-sister and the situation. In his letter, he feigned feelings of regret for the dreadful way he had treated my mother and me. His apology was almost laughable." Colin's eyes blazed with hate. I should have been frightened, but instead I felt myself being drawn to him all the more. "What infuriated me most, though, was the subtle way he demanded that I look after Sorcha. I was *family*, after all."

I remained silent. The pain he'd tried to disguise with anger was evident now. My heart ached for him.

"Blackwell gave me his word that he would acknowledge my birthright if I cared for his daughter. I didn't believe all his empty promises. It was the scandal he feared should Sorcha's predicament be known. The *precious* Blackwell name would be disgraced."

I gazed deeply into his dark eyes. "Knowing how you felt, why did you agree to take care of Sorcha?"

"Because I would have finally had Blackwell in my control. The man was a fool." He threw his head back, shaking it from side to side. "So, I agreed to his terms, but planned to get even with the man who rejected my mother and robbed me of my legacy.

"I had schemed that once she arrived, I would set out to make Sorcha Blackwell's life miserable. I had even envisioned selling her to the local brothel or leaving her alone and destitute to beg in the streets for her meals and shelter, just as my mother had had to do." He looked directly at me, his eyes shining with satisfaction. "Does my cruelty appall you?"

I shook my head, saying nothing.

"You hardly know me, Britanny, and yet you seem so sure."

"You could never be cruel," I answered honestly. "I could never feel the way I feel about you if you were."

His face twisted with shame. Then it softened. "Dear Britanny. From the first moment my eyes saw you, I felt there was much more than your beauty that mesmerized me. It's your faith in me and your determination to learn the truth that hold me captive now."

He moved toward me and his lips brushed mine in a tantalizing invitation for more than just a kiss. We parted too soon, our eyes locking in a hungry gaze, yet both of us resisted the temptation to fulfill our desires.

My heart reacted immediately to Colin's passionate stare and my cheeks grew hot with the flame of needing him. Neither embarrassed nor distressed was I from my feelings. They only made me more eager to surrender myself to him with sweet abandon.

"Please go on, Colin," I said, suddenly breathless from his unyielding look.

"When Sorcha and I finally met in England, where I was living, all my feelings of revenge disappeared. It was indeed strange, for I had so craved to exact my retribution on Kingsley, and what better way then to punish his daughter." Troubled compassion graced his features. "But I could not bring myself to humiliate Sorcha. I saw my mother in her sweet face and loving disposition. And like my mother, she too had been a victim of cruel circumstances. She accepted me for who I was, sympathized with the way her father had treated me. I felt no animosity toward her—only love." His smile was strong and heated. "She was my sister and I loved her."

I smiled, too, remembering Sorcha's goodness and innocence. The way she changed people's lives the moment they met her was difficult to forget.

"After Melinda was born, I felt as though I had been blessed again with another family. I had already secured a position with a prominent bookkeeping firm and we were prepared to stay in England indefinitely. That is until—"

"Until the Blackwells' accident," I said.

He nodded. "Yes. Then everything changed."

"You said Sorcha had been afraid once the two of you returned to Raven Manor. Do you know why?" I asked.

"No. I asked her countless times, begged her to confide in me, but she would not." Tears filled Colin's eyes. "If only I had known, I might have been able to prevent her death." His face twisted with pain. "Her murder."

The darkness of Colin's words made my

whole body tense. "Colin," I began, my heart pounding, "do you know who Melinda's father is?"

"Douglas Garwood is Melinda's father," he said, his eyes glowing with hatred. "He was the one who took advantage of my sister's love. He was the one who wanted nothing to do with her after he learned she had conceived his child."

I was not surprised at his revelation. I had already voiced the suspicion of Melinda's parentage, even if it was only to myself. I shifted and felt a sharp poke against my hip. Reaching into the pocket of my wrap, I suddenly realized that I might very well possess the key to Sorcha's fear, possibly even her death. I held the journal out to him, like an offering.

"Colin," I whispered, "I have something to show you."

Chapter Sixteen

Wide-eyed, Colin studied every inch of the leather-bound book. "Where did you find this?"

I told him of Sorcha's and my secret hiding place beneath the floorboard in her room. He laughed at such a childhood fancy, but was grateful I now shared this discovery with him.

"Open it," I said, and he did. "Look there. Read her message. It was meant for me, Colin. Just like her letter. The handwriting is the same." I pointed to the hurriedly scrawled sentence.

"I knew you would come." He whispered the words as one would a prayer. A secret smile softened his lips as he looked up at me.

A pause ensued and for a brief moment I

thought he was going to kiss me again. But his expression alerted me to the fact that there was something more pressing on his mind. He gazed at the journal. "We must read this, Britanny. It could very well hold the clue to Sorcha's death." He held out his hand to me. "Come. Stay by me. If there's anything to discover within these pages, then we shall learn of it together."

I sat with my back nestled against Colin's chest, my head brushing the bottom of his sturdy jaw. His arms were wrapped around me, sheltering me from the unknown fear that was quickly consuming Raven Manor. I had never felt so safe in my life.

Being so close to him, I could feel the beat of his heart and the warm wave of his breath in my ear. The firmness of his body sent a fire through every part of body.

I scolded myself silently for getting caught up in the pleasure pulsing through me. We were together now because of our desire to a-venge Sorcha's death. Yet I couldn't help but wonder what would become of us. Our passion. Colin had proclaimed his love for me. But were we both only caught up in the moment? Would he still feel the same way toward me once the mystery was solved?

By the light of the fire, I held the journal open for the both of us to see while Colin read the dated passages aloud. Most of the earlier entries were of girlhood notions and fancies.

Sorcha wrote about her summers growing up at Raven Manor, of her family, and of me, and our friendship.

It was strange, but I did not feel as though I was prying into Sorcha's secret thoughts and feelings. In fact, I welcomed her words into my heart. It seemed as though she was in the room with Colin and me, talking and laughing with us.

Once in a while, I gazed up at Colin as he read. His longing, yet joyful expression revealed that he too felt the same.

It was when we reached the middle of the journal that the accounts began to take on a dark side, something I had never expected could come from Sorcha.

"July 29, 1875

I know now that coming back to Raven Manor was indeed a mistake. There are too many dangers here. I fear for Melinda and Colin, but mostly, I fear for my own life as well.

I saw him again today. He was spying on me from the carriage house. His look sent shivers through me. I know he means me harm."

"Sorcha was afraid of a man," Colin whispered hoarsely.

I looked up at him, frowning. "You sound as though you know who this man might be."

He said nothing, but the rage lurking on his face caused me to turn away. I shifted in his arm. "Tell me, Colin. Do you know who he is?"

"Douglas Garwood." He viciously spat out the name.

My head started to spin, my mind reeling with denial. His protective embrace had become an obsessive grip, engulfing me in his sudden fury.

I turned to him and tried to wedge myself between him and his anger. "Surely, you're mistaken, Colin. Sorcha would never be afraid of Douglas."

Colin's eyes were ablaze with hate. "You do not know him the way I do, Britanny. A man like that is capable of anything—even murder."

I shivered, but calmed myself enough to remember the conversation I had had with Douglas only a few days before. He said he had loved Sorcha, loved her with all his heart. Why would he want to see her dead?

"No, Colin. You're wrong about this. Douglas is not the man Sorcha feared. Douglas loved her. He has told me that. Why would he want to harm her? She was the mother of his child."

"His illegitimate, unwanted child," he added firmly.

No. My mind could not accept Colin's unfounded accusation. A memory closed around me suddenly, so vivid, so close that it startled me.

"Britanny, you're trembling."

I heard Colin's concerned voice, but it seemed distant, far away from what was whirling through my brain.

"I wonder . . ." I heard myself say quietly.

"Wonder what?" Colin asked, gripping me by my shoulders. "What is it, Britanny?"

I looked at him now with deadly concentration, my eyes narrowing, my jaw tightening with the vision I could still see in my mind.

"I saw a man, Colin, out by the carriage house. A horrible old man. He was drunk and he frightened me terribly."

"Who was he?" Colin asked, frowning. "What did he want?"

"I don't know who he was. But he threatened me. He told me I should leave Raven Manor while I was still alive." I shuddered openly, reliving the scene.

"Why did you keep this from me?" He stared at me aghast.

I looked at him sheepishly. "There are other things I must tell you." Fretful now, I pinched my lower lip with my teeth. "Someone else is trying to frighten me away from here. Someone who might have played a part in Sorcha's death."

My heart quickened as I told Colin about seeing Sorcha's ghost several times, once at the cemetery and twice in the house. There was doubt in his eyes, quick, denying glances, though he tried to hide it. I couldn't blame

253

him. The story sounded preposterous, and I might have reacted the same way on hearing it.

I told him of Evangeline's threats then. The jealousy I felt exuding from her when she dropped the apple cobbler in my lap. The night she came to my room to warn me to stay away from Colin.

He looked at me incredulously. "Are you sure it's me she has this infatuation with?"

I shrugged. "It is a feeling I have," I said simply.

It was when I told him about the night I was almost murdered in my bed that I saw his handsome face twist with alarm.

My own nerves were strained as I relived the horror, and when I was finished, I felt a sudden chill overtake my body.

Pale and breathless, he drew me close to him. "Oh, Britanny, if I ever lost you ..." he murmured, stroking my hair.

Nestled against his supple strength, I began to cry softly. I felt his body ripple with the tension I was expelling through my tears.

"We'll put an end to Evangeline's infantile tricks," he said softly. "And we'll find this maniac." His gentle rocking motion was a soothing elixir for my fears. "No one will ever harm you again. I promise you that."

I believed him. With all my heart and soul, I trusted that he would take care of me and because of that trust I found myself surrendering to the feelings that drew us together.

"You'll stay with me tonight, Britanny. There is nothing to fear. I will keep you safe."

Colin drew my face up to his and I did not stop his mouth from pressing down on mine in a warm and gentle kiss. His lips moved against my cheek, then wandered down my neck.

An urgent moan escaped my lips as I reached for him. My hands skimmed his robe, finding their way past the silkiness of the material until his heated flesh was beneath them.

"Britanny," he murmured against the hollow of my neck. "Britanny, you must stop me. We should not be doing this." He gasped. "Surely, I cannot stop myself."

With that, his mouth came down on mine again and wild pleasure surged through me as I parted my lips, allowing his tongue to entwine with mine.

We were on fire. Strong and vivid cravings coursed through me. With a tearing reluctance, I slid my lips to one side to get a breath. Colin's skilled fingers began to untie the ribbon of my wrap. His dark eyes burned with a silent hunger. He must have felt as I did, for we seemed lost in each other's desires.

He slipped the robe from my shoulders, freeing my arms and letting it fall to the floor in a white lacy pool. His eyes drank in the sight of me, and my skin flushed hotly from his stare.

"You are so beautiful, Britanny. I want you so much that I ache inside."

I too was aching, painfully, longingly. And though I was inexperienced about the intimacies a man and woman shared during lovemaking, I knew now that I would not rest until the passion I tasted with Colin was satisfied.

I did not push him away as he undid the buttons of my chemise. It gave way easily, making me feel defenseless and vulnerable.

I gasped when he cupped my breast with his hand. Then he placed his mouth over my nipple, and I thought I would lose my mind from the tremor of ecstasy that spread through my body. My stomach twisted with the hard knot of needing him. All I wanted to do was enjoy this moment as greedily as possible.

Colin moaned and pressed his head against me. My hands tangled in his hair as I drew him closer.

"I want you, Britanny. I want you now." His demanding words sent shivers of excitement through me. "I need you to be a part of me. We need to be a part of each other."

He kissed me again and I clung to him, breathless with these new sensations. Yes. Yes, my body cried out. I wanted to be a part of Colin. I wanted it more than life itself.

But then, something within my mind snapped. A spark. A feeling of danger. I pushed Colin away from me in a faltering yet firm gesture.

He stared at me, probing into my soul. I found my chemise and quickly covered my trembling body with the flimsy material.

"Colin, I—"

"Hush," he said. His hands covered mine and he took over the task of fastening the chemise across my breasts. "I was wrong, Britanny. I should not have expected so much of you. Not after what I told you about Sorcha and my mother."

I gazed up at him, my eyes brimming with tears. He had read my thoughts, felt my deepest fears that even I hadn't realized until now.

Dark, but caring, eyes met mine. I could still feel a reckless passion flowing through me, tightening my nerves and muscles. I was neither embarrassed nor ashamed at the way Colin had touched me. I could not explain it, but I knew what we had just experienced was natural for the both of us.

"I love you, Britanny. I want you," he said. He took my hand and kissed my fingers. "But it is not time for us yet."

My lower lip quivered with disappointment. "Will there ever be a time for us, Colin?"

Smiling, he gathered me in his arms. "Do not worry, my love. We will be together soon." He brushed back some damp strands of hair from my face and looked into my eyes. "And when that time comes, we will belong to each other—forever."

Though my heartbeat slowed somewhat,

Suzanne Hoos

Colin's words of commitment brought a warmth to my soul. Moving closer to me, he sealed his promise with a soft, moist kiss.

We lay down upon the blanket then, and I cuddled against the lean, supple strength of his chest.

"I love you, Colin," I whispered.

As the fire dimmed with a dying flame, Colin's steady heartbeat lulled me into the soft darkness of sleep.

Chapter Seventeen

The warmth of the sun cradled me like an invisible hand. With my eyes closed, I savored the feeling, keeping the outside world at bay. I tried to ease myself back to sleep, eager to return to the lovely dreams I had been having all night. But my eyelids began to flutter open making sleep impossible.

I stretched slightly, arching my back. My muscles ached and everything around me was blurred. Where was I? Blinking away the sleep from my eyes, I heard the murmur of my name against my cheek. I turned my head toward the low sound.

Colin's sweet face was close to mine, bathed in fingers of sunlight that seeped in through the slats of shuttered windows. I was aware of the weight of his arm across me. I smiled, remembering now how special the night had been for the two of us. How much we had shared and the difference we had made in each other's lives.

I managed to sit up, propping myself on my elbows. His arm slid down and draped itself across my hips sending my senses aflutter.

I gazed down at Colin. The sleep had not yet left him. Aroused by his tranquil features, I touched my hand to his cheek. The night's growth of beard on his face bristled against my palm, and I smiled.

Many thoughts crossed my mind, least of all were those of shame. Was this what it felt like waking up with a man? Though the night had been quite innocent, pleasure surged through me.

After wiggling out from under his embrace, I found my wrap and put it on. I noticed the remains of last night's "picnic" and a wave of panic rippled inside me. I thought of Margaret. Surely she knew that Colin and I were together all night. What would she think of me?

Envisioning Margaret's scolding, I walked slowly across the room, opened the window, and threw back the shutters. A sweet, crisp wind caressed me, and the air was pungent with an earthy smell. The gentle sloping lawn and plants glistened from last night's rain. I stretched toward the sun, its bright, crystal warmth washing away all my doubts and fears.

Strong arms slipped around my waist from behind. Sighing from the gentle embrace, I drew myself against Colin until I was aware of his entire length.

"Good morning, love," he whispered in my ear. He kissed my hair, then moved his sweet mouth to my neck in a feather-like touch.

I smiled dreamily as my body throbbed excitedly from the strength, and scent, and feel of him.

"Good morning," I answered. "Did you sleep well?"

He nuzzled my ear and a giggle escaped my lips. "What do you think?" he said, and his own wicked-sounding chuckle vibrated against my cheek. He hugged me tighter. "Mmmm. You feel wonderful."

Though still not learned in the ways of intimacy between a man and woman, I nevertheless felt close to Colin. In my wildest dreams, I could only imagine what it would be like once we did succumb to our deepest passions.

A wave of grayness seemed to pass over me then. My shoulders drooped and moistness gathered in my eyes. "I disappointed you last night, didn't I?"

With his hands on my hips, Colin turned me toward him. His eyes, mirror-brilliant, swept over me, making me blush. "You did not disappoint me, Britanny." His full, liquid voice covered me in a cloak of velvet. His hand reached behind my neck and he took my lips in a soft, captivating kiss.

I clung to him, wanting the kiss to go on forever. Colin pulled away, leaving me breathless.

"Oh, Britanny, if only you knew how deep my feelings are for you," he said.

Sighing, I relaxed against him, leaning into the safe cove of his muscular arms and broad chest. Feelings and common sense warred with each other. I felt so weak. It was almost impossible to stop myself from wanting him.

But I did control myself, even though a gamut of emotions were still churning inside me. There were other things to consider and I knew I had to keep my mind clear.

Reluctantly, I pulled away from him. "Colin, what about Margaret?" I asked grimly. "I'm sure she knows that we were together all night."

He smiled, his eyes sparkling in the light of the sun. "Don't worry about Margaret. She's not going to say anything, and that's not your concern."

"Then what is my concern?" I asked quite honestly.

"To make me happy," he answered. Taking me by the hand, he led me to the parlor doors. "Do what you need to do now and I will meet you by the stables in an hour. Wear something comfortable. It's a beautiful day to take the horses out for a run." He tilted his head, his expression questioning. "You do ride, don't you?"

"Of course," I said, pretending to be insulted at his candid remark. "Like the wind."

He opened one of the doors. The light from the parlor splayed out into the foyer. "Do I hear a challenge arising, Miss St. James?"

I slipped past him, but turned before mounting the stairs. "Quite possibly, Mr. Rutledge. Perhaps you would like to wager a bet on who will be the best horseman today."

Colin's eyebrows raised. "Why, Miss St. James, you sound confident as to who would win such a title. Could it be you have a secret that you haven't shared with me?"

I climbed three steps, then faced him again. "That's something you'll have to find out for yourself."

With a flip of my head, I headed for my room. I could still feel Colin's penetrating gaze following me, making me shiver with delight.

The hour away from Colin was like a lifetime. As I pinned my hair into a soft topknot, my mind wandered with thoughts of him. The excitement of his touch. The hunger in his kisses. It frightened me to know that I wanted someone so much. But the love that I had for Colin overpowered my concern.

I caught my dreamy smile in the mirror's

reflection. Even though danger was all around us, I would only concentrate on being happy with Colin. Today was our day, this was our time. I was determined not to let anything ruin it. For now I knew he was not involved in Sorcha's death.

I stood and fussed a bit with my tan faille skirt and short-waisted jacket. The collar and front of the jacket were emphasized with a sable embroidered design. I liked the way the neutral color brought out the golden highlights in my hair and the peach glow on my cheeks. Sweeping my skirt back, I looked down at my shiny brown leather boots. I liked the way they hugged my ankles with a butter softness.

The boots, as well as the ensemble, were presents from my Aunt Elizabeth, just before I left for the Academy. Riding lessons were also a gift.

"A young lady should be instructed in the ways of an equestrian," she used to say. "It is a sign of good breeding and accomplishment."

Aunt Elizabeth herself was an expert horsewoman and had often accompanied me on my rides. Sorcha and I too would run the horses for her father. It was great fun pretending to be Knights of the Round Table, jousting for the fair princess's hand in marriage, or to be rugged cowboys whom we had read so much about in the expanding states out West. Whatever the fantasy, Sorcha and I would play it without ladylike reserve and often return to

Raven Manor covered in dirt and grinning with well-deserved fatigue.

I not only smiled because of my reminiscing, but for my thoughts of today as well. Though I considered myself far from an expert horsewoman, I knew I could hold my own with the best. And today, that included Colin.

For the second time in the last hour or so, I found the hallway empty. Leaving Colin and hurrying to my room before, I had almost been certain that I would run smack into Margaret flitting about the house, tending to her daily chores. Or worse, she would have been waiting in my room, her face twisted in an odd blend of happiness and disapproval.

But I had seen no one, not even Evangeline, and though curious, I was nevertheless grateful. Especially where the young servant was concerned. Her harsh warning came back to me as I slipped from my room and hurried down the stairs. What dreadful remonstrations would she hurl at me now if she knew that Colin and I had spent the night together and had proclaimed our love for one another?

A darker thought pressed down on me as I reached the bottom stair. What could I do to convince Colin that Evangeline's threats were more than "infantile tricks?" Fear pricked at me as I half-expected her to jump out of the shadows and attack me with a catlike swiftness.

I shuddered with relief as I made it safely to

the front door. With a heavy sigh, I closed it behind me, my heart shuddering with anticipation.

Colin was waiting for me outside the stables.

"I missed you," he said, gazing down at me with clear black eyes. He held me and drew me close to him.

I wrapped my arms around his waist and skimmed my palms over the hard muscles of his back. He lowered his head and his mouth met mine in a light, but lingering, kiss. I sighed against his lips before we parted.

"I've saddled the horses," he informed me. The twinkle in his eye made me smile.

"Where's Thomas?" I asked.

"He and Margaret always have Sunday to themselves. Right now, they're probably in church"—he winked—"praying for our souls."

"Colin!" I said, shocked at his incessant teasing.

He threw his head back and filled the crisp autumn hair with honest laughter.

"What about Melinda?" I asked, remembering Margaret's strong opposition to allowing Evangeline to care for the baby.

"Margaret takes Melinda with her. The rest of the day she visits with a friend in the next town. There's a brood of children for Melinda to play with. She has a wonderful time." He took my hand and we walked behind the stables. "She takes Thomas with her, too. He has no family here in the States and she doesn't want him to spend his time alone."

I smiled. It was just like Margaret to share the good fortune of friendship with others.

Waiting for us were two handsome steeds. One was a shiny black velvet; the other a soft, golden color.

My heart leapt in my chest. "Butternut?" I said. Picking up my skirt, I hurried over to the gorgeous animal, eager to satisfy my curiosity.

I stared into the brown, soulful eyes and stroked the white muzzle. The horse's ears pricked and then wiggled.

"Oh, Butternut, is it really you?"

Colin was at my side. He patted the horse's cheek in a loving gesture. "Sorcha once mentioned that Butternut was the horse you used to ride. I thought I'd surprise you."

"When Margaret told me about the fire, I thought that Butternut—" I paused, biting my lower lip. "I was afraid to ask her if he had survived."

"He's a fighter. As I hear tell, at the first sign of danger, he broke down his stall, then the stable doors, and hightailed it to safety."

"This is a wonderful surprise." I grabbed the fine leather rein and turned to Colin. "You're wonderful."

Colin broke the short silence between us. "Enough talk. I'm curious to see what sort of challenge you pose."

I watched as he made his way to the restless black stallion. Without any more hesitation, I mounted Butternut in a flash. He responded positively to my command as if no time had passed between horse and rider. We tore up the gravelled path, leaving an unprepared Colin behind.

My hair became undone in the wind and splayed out behind me as Butternut and I headed for the trails. The ride was exhilarating and it was easy to forget the dark secrets that had cast their shadows over Colin and me.

Pulling back on the reins, I slowed Butternut's pace to a easy gait when we came to the wooded trail. Some of the trees that arched the path had already lost their leaves, but most of the foliage was still alive with color. Dazzling sunlight danced through the openings above, bringing a magic aura to the place.

Pictures of my rides with Sorcha flashed through my mind. I was so involved with my memories that I didn't hear the sound of hooves coming up quickly behind me.

"I would never accuse you of such guileful tactics if I hadn't seen them with my own eyes."

Hearing Colin's voice, I smiled to myself but kept my eyes straight ahead.

"After all, you look so sweet, so innocent. Who would guess you could be so devious as to speed off before I had a chance to mount?"

"I didn't realize this was a race," I said. "Are

we involved in some sort of competition?"

Colin maneuvered his steed alongside mine. "I believe it was your idea to wager as to who was the better horseman."

"Horsewoman," I corrected him. "And, yes, it was my idea. I just didn't realize you would be so slow in starting."

"Well, I must say you are an expert rider. But the day is still young, and I intend on winning this little bet."

My chin high, I looked over at him now. His disheveled hair and wind-kissed face held me spellbound for a brief moment. Then his bright look of eagerness blended with a strong stamp of arrogance, and I knew he was serious.

"We shall see about that," I said with an air of confidence.

Colin ducked, missing a low branch. "By the way, what is the prize?"

"That, sir," I began with a flip of my head, "is up to you."

The mischievous sparkle in his eyes grew stronger. I laughed and dug my heels into Butternut's flanks. The horse took off again, heading for the open field just beyond the trees. But this time Colin was ready, and I could hear his stallion's hooves pounding the earth behind me.

We galloped through the meadow at an incredible pace. A strange tingling filled my entire being. Not only was it the thrill of competition, but also my own hinting at the exciting prospects to come.

Butternut held his own against Colin's magnificent horse. Though concentrating on the ride, every so often I caught the stallion's muzzle inching its way past us. But Butternut always seemed to pull ahead as if he knew what was at stake.

The scenery blurred around me. The chill in the air only heightened the feeling of my own arousal. It was a primitive sensation, immediate and staggering.

Suddenly, I was conscious only of Colin's nearness. That, coupled with the stimulating rhythm of the ride, sent wildfire through every nerve in my body.

I felt an explosion race through me, shooting upward and outward with a powerful force. It was then I heard the frightened braying of Colin's horse.

With a swift and controlled tug of the reins, I forced Butternut to a quick halt. I lurched forward, grasped his mane, and braced myself against tumbling from the saddle and onto the ground.

Blood pounded in my ears as I turned Butternut around to see what the commotion was all about. A few yards back was Colin's stallion, pawing the ground in a worrisome gesture.

My eyes grew wide with fright. Where was Colin?

I threw my leg over the saddle and slid down

from the steed. My legs nearly buckled beneath me as I started to run toward Colin's horse.

I saw Colin then, a crumpled heap on the ground. A thunderbolt of fear jagged through me and a scream caught in my throat. I ran to him, stumbling over the uneven terrain. Kneeling down beside him, I stifled a gasp. He was lying face up, his arms and legs sprawled out in an unnatural pose. His face was ashen and there were some surface scratches on his forehead and chin. I placed my hand against his cheek, feeling the clamminess of his skin.

"Colin," I whispered, suddenly paralyzed with fear.

"Ohhh," he groaned, moving his head slightly. "Britanny? Britanny, is that you?" His eyes opened slightly.

Thankful he was conscious, I ordered him to lie still, not knowing how badly he had been hurt. He felt for my hand, clutched it. I held it tightly.

"Night Wind bolted," he managed. "Threw me."

"Shhh, don't talk," I told him, stroking his forehead.

"Rein—snapped."

He tried to rise but I caught him by the shoulders and forced him back down. "Don't move. I've got to get you to a doctor."

"No," he protested. "I'm all right. Really. Just shaken a bit."

Tears of joy and worry glittered in my eyes.

"Oh, Colin, I thought you were . . ." My voice trailed off and I swallowed.

"You thought I was dead," he finished. He started to smile, then winced with pain. "You'd go to any lengths to win this bet, wouldn't you?"

His unfeeling quip made me furious. "Colin Rutledge, that's not funny!"

He groaned as he tried to sit up again.

"Serves you right," I said, sounding like a mother scolding her child.

Without warning, Colin flung his arms around my waist and pulled me on top of him. I struggled, but he held me fast.

"Colin! Stop!" I shouted, but to no avail. Obviously, he was not as badly injured as I thought.

His mouth claimed mine in a soft, moist kiss. I moved against him in an urgent response, parting my lips, drinking him in as if he were my last breath. Wild pleasure surged through me when his tongue caressed mine.

"Oh, Colin," I murmured, our lips apart now. "I was so frightened."

His fingers lingered on my mouth, and he moved his own lips as if wanting to say something. Instead, he gazed up into my face. I felt like I was drowning, staring down into those dark eyes.

"Hush, now. That's enough fretting." Gently, he moved me off him, and wrestled to an upright position.

As he struggled to his feet, I winced with a sympathetic pang. "Colin, where are you going? You should be resting."

He didn't answer but staggered over to Night Wind. The poor horse looked just as frightened as I felt. He patted the animal, calming him. "That's all right, boy. Easy, easy."

Holding the rein in his hand, Colin studied the leather strap from all angles. Curious, I stood and went to him. A worried expression formed on his face.

"Britanny, this bridle and bit belonged to Butternut. I put the new one on him that Thomas purchased a few days ago."

I frowned, puzzled. "If it was damaged, why did you put it on your horse?"

"But it wasn't damaged. It may have been old and slightly worn but it was usable." He shifted uneasily and his hard-pinched expression filled me with dread. "There's something else. Look at these reins. They just didn't snap." His hands were shaking as he showed me both of the straps. "See these clean lines? These reins were deliberately cut, Britanny."

Something cold seized my heart. "What are you saying?"

"Someone knew there might be a chance you would ride Butternut while you were here. Thomas would have dressed the horse with this bridle."

I hid a thick lump in my throat. "This accident wasn't meant for you," I said in a flat, inflectionless voice. The sudden realization of my words left me numb and chilled to the marrow.

Terror glazed his eyes and he gathered me into his arms. I could feel his body trembling against mine.

My mind reeled as I tried to take a breath. *No*, I thought, clinging to him with all my strength, *this accident was meant for me.*

Chapter Eighteen

For a long while we stood there, wrapped in each other's arms, in each other's fears.

Who could have done such a thing? How had I become a target for some madman's pleasure? Was it because I came looking for answers to Sorcha's death? Or was it something else that compelled this person. Jealousy, perhaps?

Evangeline's face appeared in my mind. Was she behind everything that had happened to me since I arrived at Raven Manor? Was she Sorcha's "ghost"? Had she tried to smother me that night? My God! Could it be?

"Britanny, let's rest. You're still shaking." Colin released his hold on me and tried to steer me to a tree we could sit under.

I stopped walking. "No," I said firmly. "I want to go back. Now."

Butternut had already ambled over to where we were. There was a quiet confusion in his eyes as I took his reins.

"Are you sure you want to go back?" Colin asked, brushing some strands of hair away from my face.

I nodded.

Without argument, he took hold of Night Wind's bridle and the four of us walked across the field toward the wooded trail.

As the stables finally came into view, I turned to Colin. He looked distracted. What thoughts was he harboring?

"Colin, what are you thinking?" I asked, suddenly having a deep desire to know.

The sun reflected in his eyes, causing a glow that seemed to come from behind his pupils. "About how much I love you," he answered without hesitation. "And how close we came to losing each other."

I tried to smile, but with all that had happened, it was difficult. I reached for him, taking comfort in just holding his hand.

We fed, watered, and brushed down the horses. The work, though strenuous, kept my mind closed to the horrors that had befallen me, if only for a short time. Being with Colin also helped. It was only when we finished and headed back to the house that the two of us seemed lost in our own thoughts once again.

The house was quiet. Ravenous, we made a dash for the kitchen, in hopes of finding something to eat. Leftover slices of a roast and cold chicken were more than we could ask for.

After gorging ourselves, Colin suggested we relax in the parlor where we could talk. Though hardly in the mood for a conversation, I nevertheless needed to be with Colin.

As he started a fire, I immediately noticed that the room looked different. The food and blanket from last night was gone. There was something more, though I could not place my finger on it. I mentioned my discovery to Colin.

"Perhaps Margaret tidied up before she left this morning," he answered, unconcerned.

The flames in the hearth came alive as Colin stoked the fire with the iron. I gazed at the brilliant colors and felt their heat surging through the room.

It was possible that Margaret had indeed picked up after us, though I had my doubts.

"What about Evangeline? Do you give her Sundays off, too? Where does she go? Who does she see?"

Satisfied with the strength of the fire, Colin took my hand and led me over to the setee. "Why so many questions about Evangeline, my love?" he asked, sitting close to me.

The worried expression on my face caused Colin concern. "If you're intent on knowing the young girl's whereabouts, then I cannot help you. She's a strange, quiet thing. She was in need of work and I thought Margaret could use the extra help so I hired her. She started her duties shortly before Sorcha's death."

"Then Evangeline knew Sorcha—or at least knew of her," I said thoughtfully.

"I suppose." Colin stared straight ahead and the sorrow etched on his face made me wish I wasn't so inquisitive. "But Sorcha wasn't herself during that time. I'm not sure any of us really knew her anymore." His eyes met mine. "Why so curious?"

Restless, I stood and went to the hearth. I gazed long and hard into the fire as if searching for something. Its warmth left me cold.

"Suppose someone is trying to scare me away from Raven Manor," I said.

Colin's sharp laugh died away quickly. "From what you've already told me, I'd say that was certain."

I turned to face him. "But what if the reasons are different?"

Colin frowned. "I don't understand."

"What if my finding the truth about Sorcha's death is only a pretense to get rid of me? What if the true reasons are personal?"

"Britanny, what are you—" He stopped and I saw a light in his eyes. "You suspect Evangeline, don't you?"

"A woman scorned is a dangerous animal," I said, trying to be nonchalant.

"Yes, but Evangeline? You're accusing her because you think she is enamored with me."

"It is what I believe," I said quietly.

Colin shook his head doubtfully. I saw his gesture as patronizing, and it annoyed me. Common sense battled with my emotions, making me even more confused. I wondered now if all my suspicions about the young maid were unfounded. Still, she had warned me to stay away from Colin. I had not fantasized such a stern admonition.

Realizing I was upset, Colin frowned and patted the place next to him. "Come. Sit by me. I want to hold you in my arms. Let's forget about all of this talk for a while."

And so we sat, staring into the fire, just being content in each other's arms.

The time went too quickly. Margaret, holding a giggling Melinda, and Thomas soon returned. We greeted them and exchanged details about our day. Neither Colin nor I said anything about the riding accident lest we worry Margaret or Thomas.

I took note that the housekeeper was her usual jovial self. If she suspected Colin's and my tryst, innocent as it was, it was not evident in her behavior. I was glad, not relishing the idea of fumbling through an explanation.

We kept Melinda with us for the rest of the afternoon and early evening. Margaret gathered some of the baby's favorite playthings and Colin and I spent hours on the floor, entertaining Melinda with a wooden top, colorful bouncing balls, and a rag doll named Bo-Bo.

Colin was remarkable with her. I could see by his patience and love that he truly cared for his niece. As I watched him delighting Melinda with funny faces and songs, I couldn't help thinking of Douglas.

Though Colin loved the child, it was Douglas who should have been with her. A daughter needed to be with her real father. If anyone could attest to that, it was I. And though my love for Colin knew no bounds. I just wouldn't believe the accusation he had made against Douglas. I was certain that Douglas Garwood was not responsible for Sorcha's death.

"Come, Britanny, play fair. Give us the ball." Colin's childlike order snapped me out of my reverie. He was sitting, cross-legged, in front of me with Melinda perched on his lap. We had been rolling a large blue ball back and forth until I had become lost in my thoughts.

"Sorry," I said, and tossed the ball toward Colin. In a flash, he caught it before it sailed over his head. Melinda giggled heartily, her deep blue eyes wide with surprise. But Colin's brows creased in a frown.

"Is something wrong, Britanny? You don't seem yourself." He gave the ball to Melinda, who immediately put her tiny mouth on the smooth rubber toy.

Before I had a chance to answer, a voice as cold as the eyes I gazed up at spoke from the doorway of the parlor.

"Perhaps Miss St. James would like some

tea. I could fetch you both some if you like."

It was Evangeline.

The planes of her bronzed, angular face were like the sharp edges of a knife. The tiny hairs on the back of my neck prickled when I saw the hatred in her vivid blue eyes. Her lips drooped cruelly and the point of her tongue slowly moistened her bottom lip. She looked as though she could eat me alive.

Gathering my courage. I swallowed and forced myself to look at her hard, pitiless features. I was not about to let her horrid tactics get the better of me.

Colin glanced over his shoulder. "That would be fine, Evangeline. Thank you." He turned back to me with a look that asked for my approval.

"Y . . . yes," I stammered. "Tea would be much to my liking."

"Very well," she answered. "I'll tell Mrs. Tuttle."

After she was gone, Colin's brows lifted in surprise. "I do believe that is the most I've ever heard her say." His eyes narrowed in a playful expression. "It must be that magic spell you've cast on everyone here."

I blushed and shook my head. "I'm doing no such thing."

"Oh, no?" he said with a sly grin. "Then why is my heart totally at your mercy? It must be magic."

"Ma—ah," Melinda sputtered. Her chubby

arms reached out for me.

Colin laughed. "See? Melinda thinks so."

"I don't think Evangeline would agree with you," I murmured. I hadn't intended for him to hear me, but when I looked at Colin, he was frowning.

"Brittany, I know you distrust Evangeline, but until there is some evidence implicating her in the strange goings-on at Raven Manor, then I'm afraid there's not much we can do."

I didn't answer. It was obvious that Colin would not believe me until I could somehow prove that Evangeline was behind all the peculiar events.

Melinda was becoming restless. The ball had slipped from her tiny hands and rolled across the floor. She was trying to squirm from Colin's hold, intent on retrieving her plaything. Pulling back my skirt, I crawled to where the ball was and rolled it back to her, then returned to my place on the thick woolen rug.

Colin's mouth was pursed. "Now what's troubling you?" he asked, aware of my silence. "Is it still Evangeline?"

"No," I lied, though grateful for his concern. "It's that fall you took today. I can't get it out of my mind." I paused for a moment, suddenly aware of what I was about to say. "Or the fact that the 'accident' was really meant for me."

A serious and troubled expression distorted Colin's face. He unwrapped his legs from around Melinda and slid over to me. The feel of his arms embracing me brought me comfort.

"You mustn't think about such things," he said, drawing me close to him. "After all, we can't be sure that you were the target. It could very well have been me. Being in the shipping business, I do have some enemies."

I rested my head on his shoulder. "There are other reasons why people act strangely, Colin."

I felt him take a breath, ready to speak, but the words never came. Instead, it was Margaret who began to chatter as she came into the parlor, carrying a tray. She set it on the table, then bent down and scooped Melinda up in her arms.

"This little missy had a busy day and now it's time for bed," she said, gently bouncing the baby in her arms.

Melinda looked at me, her eyes wide, ready to protest in her baby talk. But Margaret would have none of it.

"Say good night, Melinda." With the baby's hand in hers, she pretended Melinda was throwing a kiss.

"Pleasant dreams, little love," Colin said, throwing a kiss back to her. He got to his feet and then helped me to mine.

Alone now, Colin and I enjoyed the tea and sweet cakes that Margaret had left for us. Our conversation was light and pleasant, centering mostly on Melinda. No further mention of the accident or Evangeline came to light. After a while, however, the effects of the difficult day were wearing heavy on my mind and body.

"I'm afraid that Melinda isn't the only one who needs her rest," I said. "I think I shall retire, too."

The weariness I felt must have been evident on my face. With his hands on my shoulders, Colin leaned forward and kissed me tenderly on the forehead. "You do look tired, love. Perhaps a good night's sleep is what you need."

He tucked my arm through his and walked into the foyer.

"Good night, Colin," I said, reluctant to let go of him.

His smile reached clear to my heart and kept me warm even after I was gone from his sight.

If it hadn't been for the singing that was drifting through the upstairs hallway, I would have already been in my room and tucked beneath the bed covers. The haunting sound caused a shiver to race up my spine. I shook myself, berating my imagination for running wild. It was probably Margaret singing Melinda to sleep.

Curious, I tiptoed to the nursery and found that the door was ajar. I peeked inside, and as my eyes grew accustomed to the dark, my heart began to hammer in my chest at what I saw. It was not Margaret whose lullaby floated lazily through the room. It was Evangeline who held the sleeping Melinda.

My throat went dry, my muscles tensed.

Though the tranquil scene looked innocent enough, I couldn't help feel a whisper of terror rushing through me.

What was she doing in the baby's room? My mind reeled with all sorts of horrible thoughts. First and foremost, Melinda's safety.

Not concerned with my own welfare, I was about to enter the room when Evangeline stopped singing. Instead, I silently moved back into the shadows of the hall, hoping she would put the baby back in her cradle and just leave.

Still holding Melinda, she began to talk, her voice like steel wrapped in silk.

"Oh, precious baby. Sweet baby," she cooed. "You could have been my baby." Her voice grew louder, as if she didn't care who heard her. "You should have been mine. Mine and Douglas's."

I gasped and clamped my hand over my mouth. My mind was spinning with this new revelation. It was not Colin she wanted me to stay away from but Douglas!

Evangeline's hatred for me began to make sense now. I thought back to Douglas's visits, to the way he fussed over me, flirted with me. Everything that had happened between Evangeline and me was because of Douglas Garwood. She was in love with him!

"Have you lost your way, Miss St. James?"

The cold, threatening tone made me jump. Startled, I spun around. In the sickly yellow light of the sconces, Evangeline's dark, angular face appeared in the shadows. Her large eyes burned with a blue flame of malice. They stunned me, and for a moment, I could not speak.

"Perhaps I can help you." She thrust her hand toward me and I recoiled in fear. Her maddening grin jumped out at me and there was a certain thrill of alarm in her quiet laughter. It seemed strange. She was obviously more concerned with frightening me than whether I had been privy to her demented ravings. "My, my. You ladies of the manor are certainly a nervous lot."

"I don't understand," I said, finally finding my voice.

"Mrs. Rutledge acted the same way. Fretting all the time. Trembling like a frightened kitten. And look where it got her." She let out another rumble of thick laughter.

My feeling of dread reached a fever pitch. Everything seemed to be closing in on me.

The eerie sound emitting from her lips stopped abruptly. she moved closer to me. Her dark eyebrows arched over her piercing eyes. Every nerve in my body was taut.

"But then, I'm sure you know all about Mrs. Rutledge's horrible fate. And we mustn't speak ill of the dead." She tilted her head. "Isn't that right, Miss St. James?"

I drew a much-needed breath. "If you'll excuse me, I want to check on Melinda." I sidestepped her and whisked myself into the nursery, my feverish head pounding.

Surprisingly, she did not stop me, not even with words. As I looked down at Melinda's sweet, sleeping face, all I could hear was the echo of Evangeline's evil laughter trailing down the hallway.

Chapter Nineteen

I swallowed slowly and began to breathe normally once again. My pulse was slowing and the tears of anger which had been threatening to spill from my eyes had dissipated.

Satisfied that Melinda was all right, I slipped from the nursery and headed back to my own room.

I undressed quickly, took care of personal matters, and donned a simple nightgown. Though ready for bed, I could not sleep, not now.

I gazed out the window and watched the clouds scurry across the half-moon. Its silver light brought a magic aura to the gardens below.

There was already a chill in the autumn air.

Soon snow would cover the ground, and I wondered if I'd still be at Raven Manor come winter—and all the seasons after that. All my fears and insecurities came flooding back to me.

I thought of Colin, his handsome face, the way he made me feel safe whenever I was with him. But could he protect me from Evangeline? Was anyone safe from her wrath?

I shuddered as her words came back to me. She had all but insinuated her part in Sorcha's death. My throat turned dry. How far would she go in her obsessive plan to win Douglas? Could she have murdered the woman he loved?

I had to find proof. If I could not incriminate her in Sorcha's death, then at least I could uncover that she was the one trying to frighten me away from Raven Manor. Then, hopefully, everything else would fall into place.

I slipped beneath the covers and closed my eyes. I wanted to see justice done. I wanted Sorcha's murder to be avenged. And now, feeling as I did, I knew nothing would stop me. Not even Evangeline.

It was the middle of the week when I finally had the opportunity to prove my theory. That day, morning came with foul winds and strangling rain. Though I had not slept well, a strange feeling of vigor and determination surrounded me.

I rose and attired myself in a practical dress and went downstairs to the kitchen to find

Margaret in her usual busy state. She dished up a plate of sausages and oatmeal for me, while I poured fresh milk from the pitcher and tore a piece of the hot bread that had come straight out of the oven.

We talked about the horrid weather and what my plans were for the day. I confessed that I had none, but would probably be content curling up in front of the fire and reading.

I found myself instead keeping busy by helping Margaret with her household tasks. Though she protested, if only for a matter of seconds, she was nevertheless happy for my assistance.

The house was quiet. Melinda was napping and Colin was at the shipping company. A shipment of rare teas and spices was on its way from India and he had practically spent his days and nights at the docks, waiting for the freight to arrive.

I missed him but being alone had its advantages, too. It gave me time to think and plan a way to catch Evangeline at her own game, dangerous though it was.

I went into the parlor to find Margaret standing by the window, watching the rain beat on the glass. Her face was etched with heartfelt sorrow. She didn't wait for me to speak.

"It was a day like this when Sorcha left us." Her voice faltered with the painful memory.

I went to her and put my arm around her shoulders. "We all miss her, Margaret."

The two of us stood there, dealing silently with our own grief.

"Where's Evangeline?" I asked, suddenly needing to know.

Margaret groaned with exasperation. "Went off into town. Said she had to take care of something. And in this weather. Lordy, she's a stubborn one. I hope she's all right." She went back to her dusting.

My ears perked up at Margaret's words. "Oh, I'm sure she can take care of herself," I said casually. But inside, a confusing rush of anticipation and dread held me fast.

Evangeline was gone from the house! Undoubtedly, the powers that be were certainly smiling down at me through the dark gray clouds. This was my chance to do some snooping.

I quickly made up some excuse which I was sure Margaret never heard. She was still thinking about Sorcha and that fateful day. It was just as well. Lost in her memories, she would be oblivious to what I was about to do.

The servants' quarters had always been a cluster of rooms off the kitchen. As I made my way down the dark corridor, I somehow sensed some unseen danger. I shivered and wondered if I should forgo this idea.

No. I had to go on. I had to discover the truth for myself. But what if I was wrong? I had no idea of what I would find—or worse, what I wouldn't find. Suppose there was nothing. No evidence that Evangeline was the one responsible for my fears and suspicions. What then?

I recognized Margaret's room right away. The door was partially unlatched, and I took the liberty of opening it the rest of the way. The familiar green print wallpaper caught my eye. The bed's wooden headboard, the armoire, and the marble-topped dresser, adorned with bric-a-brac, spoke of Margaret's preference for simplicity. It was a happy room, one in which Sorcha and I spent many rainy afternoons such as this reading to each other.

The next door was locked. Frustration settled in the pit of my stomach. Was this Evangeline's room?

In all my planning, I did not once realize that she could very well have bolted the door against uninvited guests—such as me. I gave the handle one more good push, but it was useless. The door held fast.

But the door across the hall was unlatched, and though it was not a bedroom, it was indeed interesting. The room was used as a catchall, a kind of storage place. I eyed the furniture, rolled rugs, and crates that were strewn about in an orderly fashion.

I entered the room, careful not to trip over the myriad of articles. The air was stuffy and damp and chilled me to the bone. When my eyes grew accustomed to the dim light coming from the only window, I noticed the massive standing closet along the far wall.

Quickly, I hurried to it and in my haste threw open the double doors. A worn hatbox tumbled from the top shelf, barely missing my head. I muttered an unladylike curse and shoved it aside with my foot.

The closet was a miniature version of the room. Boxes of material scraps, old books, and clothing lined the bottom. Above, there was just more of the same.

Disappointed in my search, I stooped down to retrieve the hatbox, wanting to keep everything just the way I had found it. But as I picked up the round container, I noticed the top had come off in the fall. My eyes widened and my heart skipped a beat. Inside the hatbox was a wig! With a shaking hand, I put the box down, lifted the long raven hairpiece, and held it up in front of me. I stroked its soft strands and studied it from every angle. It was expensive-looking. Something that would take half a lifetime to save for.

A dark thought crept across my mind. Was this the disguise that someone was using to dress up like Sorcha? Someone like Evangeline? The wig certainly looked like Sorcha's long, luxurious tresses. The evidence was far from conclusive, yet some part of me knew instinctively that I had found what I was searching for.

One thing bothered me, though. Unless the wig had been hidden away here by the Blackwells, it seemed unlikely that Evangeline could have purchased it with her meager wages.

The rain rattled against the window, startling me, but I was grateful for the nudge. Time was fleeting and I knew I had to leave this room. Should Evangeline come back and find me here, there was no telling how she would react.

I scooped up the hatbox from the floor. Something made a scraping noise along the bottom. Curious, I drew out the item and held it toward the light.

My whole body tightened. It was Sorcha's journal!

A barrage of questions battered my brain, especially the obvious question of how the journal had gotten here. My mind flipped back to a few days ago, to the night that Colin and I pledged our love to one another. It was then that I proved my trust in him by showing him the book. Wasn't it he who kept it that night? My mind was a blur.

Nervously, I leafed through the journal, by no means ready for the next shock I was about to encounter. Every page had been slashed completely through with an x. They were angry cuts, filled with fury and resentment.

And then I knew. It was Evangeline who had tidied up after Colin and me that morning. She had found Sorcha's journal. There was no doubting it any longer. Only a sick, crazed mind could have done something so brutal. Blood roared in my ears. We were all in danger.

I heard footsteps coming down the hallway.

My heart pumped furiously, as I threw the journal and wig back in the hatbox and placed it back on the closet shelf. Ready to dash for the door, I gasped, realizing that I hadn't closed it behind me. Whoever was tramping toward the rooms was sure to wonder about the open door.

I pulled myself into the shadows and hid behind a large crate next to the closet. The footsteps were becoming louder.

"Please let it be Margaret," I whispered.

But it wasn't Margaret. Peering through the wooden slats, I saw Evangeline's slight figure outlined in the doorway. She looked disheveled. Her eyes glowed hauntingly. Her jaw was clenched.

She moved with ease amid the furniture and crates and headed directly for the closet. I held my breath. She was so close to me that I could reach out and grab her. I stifled a nervous twitter, and envisioning her startled expression should I choose to pop out and frighten her.

Tiny raindrops glistened in her thick hair, and her clothing looked as damp and dreary as the weather. She pulled open the doors of the closet. Her gaze flew to the shelf. She reached for the hatbox and hugged it to her. I saw her mouth twist in an arrogant grin.

Beads of perspiration broke out above my upper lip and trickled from my temples down to my cheeks. The thumping of my heart seemed so loud that I was sure Evangeline could hear it, too.

I watched as she opened the top of the hatbox and studied the contents. Moving the wig aside, she drew out the journal. I thought I saw her eyes narrow suspiciously. I held my breath. Did she suddenly realize that someone had tampered with the contents? Or worse, that I was hiding just a few feet away?

A smile of confidence lit up her face, while a tiny grin of relief eased onto my lips. Thank goodness I had read the signals incorrectly.

Evangeline replaced the cover of the hatbox but did not return it to the shelf. Instead, she closed the closet doors, turned, and hurried from the room.

I waited for what seemed an eternity before I was sure it was safe to venture out of my hiding place. During that time, my mind replayed what my eyes had seen. Evangeline had taken the wig and journal with her. Was she going to disguise herself as Sorcha again? Would it be tonight? Tomorrow? My stomach tightened into a hard knot. No matter when she decided to play her nasty little game, I was going to be ready.

My muscles cramped and my legs felt like jelly as I shakily stood up. I grasped onto the crate that had served as my fortress and took a much-needed breath.

The room was dark and quiet. The only sound was the splatter of rain against the window. Wilted and drained from the harrowing ordeal, I stumbled to the door and peeked out into the hallway. It was empty. Still feeling the slight foreboding of being discovered, I slipped quickly through the opening and made my way back to the main house.

No sooner had I closed the door to the servants' quarters behind me than Margaret burst into the kitchen. When she saw me, her brow raised in surprise and then fell to a frown.

"Where have you been, child?" she asked. Her hand clutched her heart and she gasped for breath. "I've been all over this house looking for you."

I played innocent. "What's wrong, Margaret?"

"A package came for you a few minutes ago."

"A package? Who is it from?"

"The man who brought it didn't know. Only that he was to deliver it here."

My curiosity was aroused. No one save a scant few friends from the Academy knew where I was. I brightened. Perhaps Mrs. Hemsley had sent me some of my books so that I could keep up with my studies, bless her practical heart.

"Where is it?" I asked.

Margaret smiled, joining in my excitement. "In the foyer. You can't miss it. It's as big as a house."

I found it just as Margaret had said. It was on the floor, leaning against the table. Though she exaggerated the size somewhat, the package was rather large.

I picked it up. It was too light to contain books, and when I shook it, I heard the rustle of paper. I brought it into the parlor, sank down into the settee, and balanced it on my lap.

My heart skipped a beat as I slid the cord from around the rectangular shape. Carefully, I undid the plain brown wrapping paper, while fighting the incredible urge to tear into it with a wild enthusiasm.

I lifted the lid, threw it aside, and grappled with an abundance of tissue paper. My eyes grew wide with utter astonishment.

"How can this be?" I muttered aloud.

A gown. A beautiful gown of sapphire-blue. My senses reeled. It was the exact same one I had seen in the window of Madame Rousse's Dress Shoppe the day Colin and I were in town.

With one movement, I took the dress from the box and stood up. The box fell to the floor at my feet.

"Where did you come from?" I asked the gown, wishing for a moment that it could answer me. It looked even more wonderful now that I held it in my shaking hands.

Draping it across my arm, I bent down to retrieve the box and searched ardently through the mounds of tissue paper for a card, anything that might identify the sender. There was nothing.

I held the dress against me now, admiring the color and delicate flounces that made it so appealing. It was easily the most gorgeous gown I had ever seen.

"Beautiful as it is, it cannot surpass your beauty." The deep voice made the room shudder around me.

In my excitement, I had not noticed that someone had come into the parlor. I looked up and my spirit soared.

."Oh, Colin," I said, gazing into his clear black eyes. "Was it you? Was it you who bought me this dress?"

He didn't answer but I could tell by the way a smile of delight broke across his handsome face that he, indeed, was the one.

I carefully draped the gown across the settee and ran to him. His waiting arms gathered me, pressing me close against the rigid muscles of his body. His clothes were damp and smelled of the rain. My fingers weaved through his wet hair. Shamelessly, I drew his face to mine. I kissed him, my mouth moving over his in wild abandonment. I thought I felt him shudder in my arms. I pulled away then and planted tiny taunting kisses along his cheek.

"If this is the way you show your gratitude, then next time I shall buy you *two* dresses," he said, grinning slyly. "Or maybe enough to fill a room as big as this!"

I laughed and hugged him tightly. "What made you do such a wonderful thing?"

"I saw you admiring that gown in the dress shop window. I wanted you to have it."

"I love you," I said, my heart bursting with joy. I broke free from his hold and returned to the settee. Gathering the silky material in my arms, I placed the gown against me, letting it cover my full length. I looked to Colin for his approval. He caressed me with his eyes, and a strange, exhilarating tremor rushed through my body.

Colin's gaze traveled over me. "You'll be the object of every man's desire at the party Friday, Britanny. And won't they all be jealous when they learn you belong only to me."

"Party?" I said, hearing nothing else.

I watched him walk to the table and pour himself a glass of sherry. He offered me some but I declined.

"The Garwood party," he said. His expression twisted as if there was a bitter taste in his mouth. He took a large swallow of the burnished liquid, then put down the glass. "Don't tell me you've forgotten. You did promise to be Douglas's escort, after all."

I blushed with the memory. "You have forgiven me for that, haven't you?"

"Should I?"

"Oh, Colin, stop teasing. Things are different now."

His eyebrows raised. "Are they?"

I ran my tongue over my bottom lip. "You know they are."

I watched his gaze focus on me. I could almost feel his thoughts. My heart thudded like a drum.

"Come here." His voice was breathy and urgent.

For a moment I was numb, paralyzed with the fear of wanting him so much. I didn't move. I couldn't. The gown slipped from my fingers and settled into a silky blue pool at my feet.

Before I could utter so much as a breath, Colin seized me and pulled me into his arms. His mouth came down hard on mine, searching, demanding, as though he was desperately seeking something from me. I was conscious of the pressure of his hands, his taut, muscular body. His heart pounded furiously against my breast, and I felt crushed by his strength.

His mouth scorched a trail across my jaw and down to the pulse beating wildly in my throat. I clung to him, trembling, my skin on fire.

His fingers raked through my hair, loosening it from the silver combs. He tilted my head back, and his dark, heavy-lidded eyes burned into mine.

"Say it, Britanny," he snarled. "Say you love me. Say it!"

"I—I love you, Colin." I could hardly breathe.

"I want you to be a part of me, Britanny. I want it always to be so."

Ragged whimpers of sheer need escaped my

lips. Yes, I wanted to belong to him. I could not explain the urgency I felt, but I knew it was right. I knew I loved him and could love no other man in this way. Whatever he would do with me, show me, I wanted with all my heart.

Swiftly, he scooped me up in his arms. His cheek against my hair, his hands gripping where he held me, Colin carried me up the stairs to his bedroom and closed the door behind us.

He laid me on the bed, and I reached for him, my body aching and ready. I was beyond stopping him, beyond embarrassment or shame. He stretched out on top of me, and a mutual shudder ran along our lengths.

"Colin, Colin," I moaned in his hair. The pressure of his body fanned my sparks of arousal into a leaping flame. I caressed the back of his neck with my fingers. His lips devoured mine. I arched against him, wanting to cry out my love for him, but his tongue moved inside my mouth with strong impelling strokes.

He unfastened the buttons of my dress until he was able to slip it off my shoulders and wrench it down. I began to shiver in the cool air in the room, but soon the feel of his fingertips against my skin began to warm me.

"Britanny," he said, his breathing ragged yet filled with excitement. His hand stroked my breast, moving magically, kneading its smooth roundness. "I've wanted so long to have you like this. From the first time I saw you, I've wanted you."

"I've wanted this, too, Colin," I whispered. I wrapped my arms around him and gloried in the length of him. "I am yours. But I don't know what to do. I've never ..."

"Do not worry, my love. I will show you. I will be gentle. Let me love you as we are meant to love each other."

My heart soared at his words. I kissed him, feeling my body come alive, yearning for a conqueror.

His mouth closed softly over my nipple and I gasped, never before experiencing such a force of passion. His hand moved over the curve of my hip and thigh.

He moaned and pressed his head against my breasts. "I want you, Britanny."

"Then take me, Colin," I said, aware of our burning impatience. "Show me how to love you."

He raised himself up, and with his eyes gazing into mine, removed his shirt and trousers. He covered my trembling nakedness with his own.

I reached eagerly down his strong, smooth torso, and when I hesitated, he guided me further until I felt the steely hardness of his desire. I caressed him and delighted in the pleasure it brought to him.

He groaned, and I sensed that he could wait no longer. His muscled legs pushed between mine, parting my thighs. I shuddered openly as fire bolts of desire and fear raced through me.

"It will hurt the first time, my love," he whispered hoarsely. "I will try to be gentle."

My fingers clawed at his back as I felt the raw urgency of his manhood entering me. I gasped at the tightness and the searing pain filling my trembling body. I tried to relax, thinking of nothing else but Colin's love for me. Soon, my body seemed to take on a movement of its own, meeting each of his movements with my own, though my insides ached.

His mouth came down on mine, drinking in my moans and sighs. Finally, my pain numbed and his steady thrusts of possession became a hunger in me that was nearly satisfied.

There was no dividing us now. I could not tell where Colin began and I ended. We had become one and my body was just as much his as my own.

He sensed my readiness, and his movements suddenly became deeper and more demanding. My body opened to him, understanding the rhythms of his passion. I thrilled as his raw, fevered thrusts seemed to go higher and higher in me. I pulled him closer, wanting all of him.

"Britanny," he cried out, and his powerful spasms melded with mine in an explosion of ecstasy. My response was shameless, instant and total. The earth opened beneath me, hurling me into a world of wondrous sensations.

Finally, he trembled and moaned and lay against me, with his cheek resting on my breast. My body shook with sighs of satisfaction and glowed warmly in the aftermath of learning the joy of finally being a woman.

I held him to me, knowing now that no matter what would befall us, we would never be parted. So deep was the love I felt for Colin that an uncontrollable tremor seized me.

Gradually, our heartbeats quieted, our breathing slowed and deepened. As we lay there in silence, I could hear the gentle tapping of the rain against the window. Soaked in Colin's warmth, I closed my eyes and slept.

When I finally awoke, the shadows in the room were long and spindly. My eyes darted about, glimpsing dark furniture and heavy green drapes. The heavy scent of lemon polish permeated my senses. I shuddered, feeling the chill in the room. Immediately, the memory of our lovemaking rushed over me, and I blushed in embarrassment.

I looked down at Colin, still asleep in my arms. The side of his face rested peacefully against one of my breasts, and every curve of his body seemed molded to mine.

I smiled as I thought about the incredible intimacy that Colin and I had shared. Had I really given myself to him with such wanton abandonment? Was I so swept away with my desires that I had given no thought to the consequences?

What would we say to each other? How would we act? React? Here, in this very room, we had created our own world. But what would it be like when we had to face other people?

A thousand thoughts were swirling through my head. None of which were sensible or reserved. One, though, persisted, working its way through all the rest. Would what we had done affect my relationship with Colin?

I lifted the hand he had draped over me and kissed his fingers. he stirred, moaning quietly, then opened his eyes and looked up at me.

"My love," he said hoarsely. "How wonderful you were. How much I love you."

His words brought me warmth, but not solace. "Colin," I began, hesitating. My mouth had gone dry, and there was a tightness in my heart.

He smiled and stretched himself along my body, reaching my face and brushing my lips with a kiss. "You are so beautiful," he said, stroking my other breast tenderly.

Waves of delight began to flow through me again. I heard a moan escape my lips, as I tried to control these new and compelling sensations. I stopped his touch, slowly pulling his hand from my breast and caressing it in mine.

His eyes questioned me. "I'm sorry if I hurt you, Britanny. I tried to be as gentle as I could.

But you were so lovely, so desirous. I'm afraid I might have been too anxious to love you."

I smiled warmly at his concern. Brushing his hair back with my fingers, I looked into his worried eyes, seeing nothing else. "Oh, Colin. It's more than the pain I felt. You are a tender, sensitive lover, and you've made me feel like a woman should feel."

"Then why do you seem so distant, so uneasy?"

I sighed. "It's Margaret and Melinda—it's you and me. Doing what we did, how can we face anyone?"

"Oh, my dear, dear Britanny," he said with a glimmer in his eyes. "There is no shame in loving someone. In wanting to give of yourself body and soul."

"I want to believe you, Colin. Truly, I do. But—" I faltered.

He put a finger to my lips. "Then believe this, Britanny. I love you, and nothing has changed between us. Nothing. Raven Manor can tumble down around us and I will still love you."

"Oh, Colin. I love you, too." Though I spoke the words from my heart, my mind was still troubled.

"Perhaps what I am about to say will ease your disquieting burden."

I frowned, puzzled, yet eager to take in his words.

"Marry me, Britanny. Be my wife and I shall be your husband. Together there is nothing that can harm us ever again."

I thought my heart would burst from my chest and soar heavenward. "Oh, Colin, yes. Yes, I will marry you and be your wife."

We clung to each other, our lips sealing our promise with a sweet, throbbing kiss. Suddenly, the world had disappeared once again as Colin reached for me.

Chapter Twenty

Even though Colin had tried to put my mind at rest, I knew that facing Margaret would be difficult. It was already early evening when Colin and I ventured downstairs to face what he had laughingly called "our inevitable judgment." I did not find his humor funny.

The aromas of supper tingled my senses when we walked hand in hand into the kitchen. Margaret was there, feeding Melinda mashed carrots from a small bowl. She did not look up when we entered.

She knows! my mind kept telling my heart. *She knows Colin and I are lovers!*

"Something smells delicious, Margaret," Colin said. He walked to the stove and lifted the lid on one of the pots.

Her eyes slid to him now. "Poached chicken, Mr. Rutledge," she said matter-of-factly.

I could not detect her mood from the tone of her voice, but knowing Margaret was never one to mince words or hold back her feelings, I braced myself for the worst.

"Your daughter was crying, sir," she said, holding a spoonful of the orange mash to Melinda's mouth. The baby gobbled it hungrily. "I knew you were home so I went looking for you." Margaret's cheeks now began to glow a crimson color. Embarrassment? Anger? My heart pounded. "I thought you might've enjoyed spending some time with her before dinner."

Colin offered nothing and I shifted uneasily. Her eyes found mine and raked them with silent scrutiny. She didn't need to speak another word. She had heard our lovemaking! I was sure of it!

"Margaret . . ." I began, swallowing hard.

To my utter amazement, a smile as big as the sky and bright as the sun graced her lips. Her eyes shone with tears of joy. She rose from the chair, leaving poor Melinda confused as to where her next spoonful was coming from.

I too was wary, and at first I drew back from Margaret's open arms. Before I knew it, I was being held tightly in her embrace.

"Oh, Britanny," she whispered in my ear. "I'm so happy for the two of you."

She released her hold and I stared at her,

dumbfounded. "Margaret, Colin and I—that is, we didn't plan—"

"Plan to fall in love?" she asked, a twinkle in her eye. "For heaven's sake, child, don't apologize. It is I who should be doing that. What goes on between a man and woman is private." She blushed.

"You overheard, didn't you, Margaret?" Colin asked, amused.

Margaret nodded and avoided his gaze. "I'm so embarrassed."

Colin gently cradled Margaret's face in his hands. "I'm glad you know. Britanny and I are in love. I want the whole world to know." He suddenly seemed subdued. "You're not angry at us because of Sorcha, are you?"

"Sorcha is dead, Mr. Rutledge. She'll never come back no matter how much we wish it to be so." Margaret blinked back the tears moistening her eyes. "I knew Sorcha well. She would have wanted this for the two of you." Her smile returned. "Just as I do."

I sighed easier now. Margaret's words were comforting and true. It was almost as if Sorcha had given Colin and me her blessing. A feeling of joy overwhelmed me.

Colin guided Margaret back to a chair, motioned for me to sit down, and then did the same. Melinda rocked restlessly in her high chair, her mouth puckering, searching for the rest of her food. Colin stroked the baby's hair, her dark curls peeking through his fingers. She quieted somewhat at his touch.

Once again I held my breath, only guessing what Colin was up to. As his elated features turned somber, I knew I was right. Margaret was about to hear the whole fantastic story. She was about to hear the truth.

"Margaret, I want you to listen to me." Colin's voice commanded the kitchen. Even I sat straighter in my chair.

She looked worried. I wanted to comfort her, to tell her that everything was going to be all right, but I kept silent.

"Margaret..." Colin took a deep breath. "Sorcha and I were never married."

She gazed at him for what seemed a long time. "What are you saying?"

"Sorcha and I were never husband and wife," he said. "I'm her half brother."

I watched as her eyes grew wide with a fragile, lost look. My heart ached for her, for the way she had been deceived. I could only hope that Colin could ease her pain.

Slowly and clearly, he told her the entire story he had told me about his mother, Kingsley Blackwell, and that Douglas was Melinda's real father. He told her also of the "ghost," the cut reins, and my brush with death.

I could see she was stunned by the whole explanation and I wondered what her reaction would be when Colin was finished.

"And that's why Britanny is here, Margaret. Sorcha sent her that letter to come to Raven

Manor. She feared for her life. Though she had my help, she wanted Britanny's, too." He leaned in closer to the teary-eyed housekeeper. "We're going to find Sorcha's murderer, Margaret. We promise you that."

The tears that were swimming in her eyes now spilled onto her soft cheeks. "Oh, my poor dear," she gasped. "You've been in such danger all this time." She covered her mouth with her trembling hands. "Oh, my poor Sorcha."

Colin and I comforted her the best we could. Soon, her sobbing stopped and she regarded us gratefully.

Colin stood, took me by the hand, and pulled me close to him. "I've asked Britanny to be my wife, Margaret. She said yes. She's going to marry me." Colin glowed with the news.

Margaret cried out with joy. "How wonderful! I'm so happy for you both." She jumped out of her seat and gave us a mutual hug.

"So you see, Margaret. Everything is going to be all right," I said, thrilled that she approved.

Melinda's sudden sharp cry let us know that she wasn't happy at being ignored. But when the three of us looked her way, we gasped in surprised. Her face and frock were covered in mashed carrots. Seeing our reaction, she smiled through the orange mess.

"Well, almost everything is all right," I piped up.

The howl of laughter filled the kitchen with Melinda the loudest howler of all.

I was relieved that Margaret knew the truth. Well, a good portion of it, anyway. Colin had kept back my suspicions about Evangeline and his own about Douglas. He explained to me later that Margaret's weakness at hiding her feelings could put her in danger having to be around the servant girl or by chance meeting Douglas. I agreed.

That same evening I told Colin about seeing Evangeline in the storage room, about the wig, and Sorcha's journal that she had obviously taken from the parlor. He scolded me for placing myself in such a precarious position. Still, with all I had revealed, he would not give up on the idea of Douglas being Sorcha's murderer. Men. They are so stubborn when they think they are right. Even when they're wrong.

The one thing I had not told Colin was about my spying on Evangeline in Melinda's room. I was afraid he might dismiss her from her position at the manor. I needed her there. I needed to keep a watchful eye on her.

The next two days passed quickly. Margaret became more of a guardian to me than a friend. She was worried about my safety, and it was difficult to convince her that I did not need someone trailing behind me everywhere I went. She meant well and for that I was thankful.

I saw Evangeline often. She was usually serving the meals or turning down my bed for the evening. I kept calm and tried not to show my fear whenever she was around me. Once I learned how to relax in her presence, I began the task of studying her every move. There was no doubt in my mind. She had a petite frame like Sorcha's. Put that together with the long, black wig and I had my "ghost," though no sightings of it came to pass during those days.

The day of the Garwood party finally arrived. That afternoon I felt almost decadent as I soaked in a hot bath for almost an hour. A sweet vanilla aroma wafted up with the spirals of steam. I breathed deeply, enjoying the scent which reminded me of Margaret's sugar cookies.

As I dried myself with a fluffy white toweling cloth, other thoughts entered my mind. Dark ones. Ones that I was not eager to face.

Though the idea of going to a party in a big, beautiful mansion with Colin excited me, I was also fearful that serious trouble could rear its ugly head. Having Colin and Douglas in the same room, even amid wealthy, important guests, might prove volatile. I suddenly felt helpless. I could only pray that somehow a confrontation would be thwarted.

Margaret helped me dress. Gushing over the sapphire-blue gown, and the fact that Colin had bought it for me, she slipped the silky material over my head. The puffy sleeves settled on my shoulders and tightened at my wrists. The rounded neck was cut low, exposing my pale skin and amplifying my bustline. The waist fit snugly, then billowed out from my hips. A gathering of ruffles finished the hem, hiding my simple black leather dress shoes.

Margaret twisted and coiled my hair on top of my head, securing it with pearl-studded combs. She wet a few tendrils and curled them around her chubby finger so that they fell in soft spirals against my face.

She stood back and studied me. "You look beautiful, Britanny. The gown was made for you."

As I paraded in front of the long, standing mirror that Margaret had Thomas drag down from the attic, I had to agree with her. The dress was beautiful and it made me feel the same way.

When I turned, I saw Margaret slip something out of the pocket of her pearl-gray dress. It was a black velvet box and she handed it to me.

"This is for you to wear tonight, Britanny," she said.

Puzzled, I took it from her, opened it, and gasped. Nestled inside a drape of more black velvet were the most elegant earbobs and necklace I have ever seen. The strand of the necklace was laden with tiny diamonds, joined in the middle by a dark blue sapphire. Outlining the perfect square gem were more brilliant diamonds. The earbobs echoed the necklace.

"Oh, Margaret. Thank you." I went to embrace her for her thoughtfulness, but she stopped me.

"They're not from me. They belonged to Mr. Rutledge's mother. He wanted you to have them."

An odd feeling came over me. I put the necklace on, but my hands were shaking so that Margaret had to help me with the catch. The earrings dangled daintily from my earlobes.

I stared at my reflection, admiring the sparkling pieces of jewelry but admiring more the woman to whom they'd belonged. Knowing the story of Ann Rutledge's struggle, I couldn't help feeling sad. Yet there was happiness within me, too. She had overcome her lot in life and raised a fine son. I was proud to be wearing the finery of such a strong, gentle woman.

Colin's powerful gaze met me at the bottom of the stairs. He was pleased by the way I looked and his seductive smile brought a tingle of delight.

"You take my breath away, Britanny. You are a vision. An angel. My angel."

Gingerly, I touched the sapphire around my neck. "Thank you, Colin," I said, suddenly shy.

"My mother would have insisted that my bride-to-be wear her favorite jewelry," he said. "They look exquisite."

I gazed up at him. He too looked extremely

317

handsome in his splendid evening jacket, silk vest, and matching trousers. A soft black cravat was tied in a fashionable bow around the high stiff collar of his white silk shirt. In his hand was a black top hat.

"Shall we go, Miss St. James?" he asked, extending his arm to me.

I took hold of it and we walked to the front door. He helped me on with my cloak that I had draped across my arm. I turned, feeling Margaret's gaze from behind. She was there at the bottom of the stairs, wearing her best motherly expression. I blew her a kiss and then allowed Colin to take my arm.

The night air was filled with the earthy scents of autumn. Stars sparkled in a black velvet sky and a sliver of a white-gold moon brought a magic aura to Raven Manor.

The carriage was waiting for us with Thomas as our driver. He looked particularly dashing in his tweed waistcoat and dark trousers. With a hearty "good evening" and a special nod of approval for me, he opened the carriage door and assisted me inside.

In the darkness of the carriage, Colin and I held hands. I sighed, feeling like a princess with her handsome prince at her side.

"I expect you to be on your best behavior, Miss St. James," Colin said sternly. There was a twinkle in his eye that he failed to hide.

The shadows veiled my smirk. "The same warning I am issuing to you, dear sir, or I shall be forced to take measures."

"And what measures are those?" he asked, leaning into my hair. His masculine scent was intoxicating and my heart skipped a beat.

I tilted my head and brushed his lips lightly with a kiss. "And that, Mr. Rutledge, is only the beginning."

"Pray then, dear lady. If that is my punishment, then expect me to swing from Eleanor Garwood's chandelier!"

We laughed wickedly at the wild thought, but soon, our lighthearted nature began to dwindle. I suspected that we were nearing the Garwood mansion when Colin's mood turned somber. I was sure that his suspicions of Douglas were weighing heavily on his mind. There was nothing I could say. Nothing that could ease his tension.

My own thoughts dwelled on Evangeline. I shuddered openly. Would we ever know who killed Sorcha?

Suddenly, I wished Colin and I were back in his bedroom, delighting in the wondrous discoveries of lovemaking. Holding each other. Touching and kissing. Each of us giving the other the fullness of our love.

But it was not to be. Not tonight at least. I stroked Colin's hand tenderly, knowingly. He smiled, but the smile did not reach his eyes.

Thomas stopped the horses, lining them up behind a slew of shiny black carriages. As Colin and I alighted, the immensity of the Garwood estate was quite overwhelming. I flinched and nervous gyrations began to spiral in my stomach. I had never before seen a place so grand. Not even Raven Manor, as special as it was, could come close to this gracious residence.

What struck me first was the starkness in color. Even in the pale moonlight, I could tell that the entire structure was a pristine white. Arched windows graced the several levels and behind each one a light shone warmly.

My gasp was noticed.

"Is something wrong, Britanny?" Colin asked, stopping in front of the four Grecian columns that stood like sentries outside the entrance door.

"It's quite lovely," I whispered hoarsely.

"Vulgar," he said as though he was correcting me.

Just before his foot settled on the first step of the veranda, I pulled him back. "What's that?" I asked, tilting my head toward a curious sound.

"What's what?"

"That noise. That rushing sound."

"The Garwood estate overlooks the St. Lawrence River," he said matter-of-factly. "That's the sound of the water beating against the cliffs."

My heart jumped. "The cliffs? Do you mean where—"

"Yes. Where Sorcha died," he finished. His tone was troubled. His gaze had a faraway look. "Though not here, but where I showed you. That blasted spot is about a mile away." His face softened when he looked at me. "Shall we go in now?"

I smiled and let him lead the way.

We were greeted at the door by a Negro manservant, who promptly took my cloak and Colin's hat. I stood mesmerized in a huge entrance hall. Slowly, my eyes traveled up. My jaw dropped at the sight of an oval rotunda that opened to three more stories above us.

The manservant indicated the doorway to our left. As we entered the beautiful ballroom, I couldn't believe my eyes. There were people everywhere. As near as I could guess, possibly a hundred guests had been invited to the Garwood party. Across the expanse of the room, a small orchestra was playing softly. There were tables set up around a polished dance floor, and servants, balancing trays of food or drinks, scurried among them. Some of the guests were dancing, some sat at the tables, deep in conversation, while others, champagne glasses in hand, mingled with other clusters of people.

My knees buckled and I leaned against Colin. "This is the small party that Eleanor spoke of?" I asked, my heart racing as I surveyed the crowded ballroom.

Colin smiled down at me and patted my hand, sensing my apprehension.

The men looked dashing in their evening attire. The women's gowns were of the latest designs. I was suddenly relieved that Colin had bought me this elegant gown. I had nothing in my wardrobe that could even begin to compare to the loveliness of the fashions that surrounded me.

"Darling boy!" The screech of Eleanor's voice from across the room set my teeth on edge. Some of the people closest to us turned to see who she was calling. I lowered my gaze, feeling intimidated by their stares.

As she pushed her way through the crowd, I detected a satisfied glow about her. Perhaps she enjoyed playing hostess, showing off her home, her money. I smirked. She certainly had come a long way since her servant days back at Raven Manor.

I eyed her pink evening toilette of velvet and lace and trimmed at the sides with silk cabbage roses. The bodice was cut so low that a teasing glimpse of her breasts showed above the lacy inset. Her white gloves reached to her sturdy upper arms and she carried a white clipped ostrich fan. Around her neck was a three-strand pearl choker that captured the pink hue of her gown.

Brazenly, she threw her arms about Colin and kissed him on his cheek. "Oh, Colin. I'm so glad you're here." She slipped her arm through his. "Come. I want you to meet some people. Tycoons. They have so much money, they don't know what to do with all of it. I've told them all about you. They're interested in investing in your shipping business."

I was amazed that she had lasted so long without a breath. Colin didn't budge. Eleanor's eyes flew to me. She looked surprised, as though she had just noticed that I had come to the party with Colin.

"Why, Britanny. Hello, my dear," she said, studying me. "My, my, don't we look lovely."

I smiled out of courtesy. Inside, my blood was beginning to boil.

Eleanor pursed her lips. "That gown is rather expensive, isn't it? How does a school-girl such as yourself afford such a luxury?"

My body went rigid and I knew my green eyes were sparking with anger. I curled my fingers into tightly clenched fists. I wanted to tell her. I wanted to scream that the gown was Colin's doing but mostly that he had asked me to be his wife. I wanted to take pleasure in seeing the arrogant look on her face wither away.

Blast this ladylike composure, I said to myself, gritting my teeth into some semblance of a smile.

Colin must have read my thoughts. Other than telling Margaret, we had promised to keep our engagement a secret until Sorcha's murderer was found. By the way I looked, I imagine he thought I was about to blurt out the news just for the satisfaction of it.

"Britanny, you won't mind if I borrow Colin

for a bit, will you, dear?" Eleanor said, stroking his arm.

Before I had the chance to answer, she was already dragging Colin into the crowd. He flashed a helpless side glance, and I stood there alone, trying my best to look inconspicuous.

I took several deep breaths to calm myself from the encounter with Eleanor and to build up my courage. Except for Colin, Douglas, and Eleanor, I knew no one.

As I walked among the guests, I resisted the impulse to touch my hair or tug at my gown. I didn't want to appear nervous, although I felt as if Melinda's wooden top was spinning inside of me, out of control.

A roving waiter offered me a goblet of champagne, and I accepted. I did not take a sip, but it made me look as though I belonged here. The strategy seemed to work. Men nodded to me. Women smiled. I felt a little more comfortable than I had when I first arrived.

The orchestra began to play a lovely melody, and for a moment all I wanted to do was stand and listen. Two hands grabbed me by the waist and spun me around. I gasped, clutching the goblet to keep it from slipping from my hand.

"I knew it was you," Douglas said. "I knew it was you from across the room." His practiced masculine eye took in every detail of my appearance, as if I was on display for no one but him.

"Douglas, you startled me," I said, breaking away from his hold.

"You look beautiful, Britanny."

"Thank you."

He took the glass from my hand and placed it on the tray of one of the waiters that passed us.

"May I have this dance?" he asked.

Before I could say anything, Douglas's arm was about my waist. He whisked me out on to the dance floor and into his arms. We danced the waltz and I found him to be exceptionally light on his feet. We didn't speak but concentrated instead on our steps. Soon, the last strains of the music ended. Douglas's sweeping bow took me by surprise. I curtsied, and he led me off the dance floor.

"Thank you, Douglas. You're a wonderful dancer."

He smiled warmly. "Then we must do this again before the evening is over."

I agreed.

"Where's Colin?" he asked, surveying the room. "Certainly, you did not come along."

"I'm afraid your mother has whisked him away to talk about business."

He nodded, looking rather satisfied. "Well, good for Mother. Now I have you all to myself." Douglas raised my chin with two of his fingers. "Why so shy, Britanny?"

I looked up into soft blue eyes that missed nothing. Sensitive, liquid eyes. Eyes of a lover.

Not a killer. No matter what suspicions Colin harbored against Douglas Garwood, I knew he would have never harmed Sorcha. I smiled, relaxing.

The pleasant moment was shattered by chiding laughter. "There you two are. See, Colin, I told you Douglas would take good care of Britanny." Eleanor, wearing a satisfied expression, still clutched Colin's arm.

An annoyed look dominated Colin's face. It was difficult to tell whether he was angry because I was with Douglas, or if he had had enough of Eleanor. But, as our eyes locked, his granite-hard face began to soften.

"Come. Dinner is going to be served," Eleanor announced. "Douglas, have Britanny sit at our table." She gazed up at Colin, fluttering her thick, sooty eyelashes. "Excuse me for a moment, won't you, dear boy? I must gather my guests." And she was off, leaving the three of us alone and uneasy.

I felt Colin's hand slip into mine, his thumb lightly playing on the fullness of my palm. The sensation was warm and intimate.

"I don't think Britanny and I will be staying for dinner, Garwood," he said. "You mother's connections have served me well. I need nothing further from your family."

I felt my body begin to tense. I squeezed Colin's hand, hoping to stop an argument before it began.

"Since you no longer feel any obligation,

then you would be foolish not to stay. The desserts alone are worth a king's ransom," Douglas said cordially, the perfect host.

For a moment I wondered if he was trying to mend some fences with Colin. Or was he just being polite because I was standing between them?

My smile wavered uncertainly. "Colin, I would like to stay."

He looked at me and sighed, but he did not refuse my wish. Douglas showed us to the table, and soon a bubbling Eleanor joined us.

Douglas was right. The meal was fit for a king. We dined on clear soup, jellied macédoine of fruit, cold salmon, an anchovy savory cream cheese, tomato salad, and roast lamb and peas. The fresh fruit tarts, creamy cakes, and floating islands with citron preserves were a delight to the eye as well as to the palate.

The conversation was civil enough. Eleanor dominated most of it, anyway, with her talk about the inevitable financial boom that Colin's shipping company was sure to benefit from now that he had the proper backers.

Colin was rather tight-lipped when it came to Eleanor's predictions. I knew how important wealth and power were to him because of his past, but tonight he seemed somewhat ashamed of his monetary ambitions.

"That is quite a lovely necklace, Britanny," Eleanor said when the talk of business had died down.

Suzanne Hoos

Instinctively, I touched the smooth sapphire and smiled. "Thank you. It belonged to Colin's mother." I didn't think that Colin would mind if I revealed the source. By the pleasing glow that illuminated his face, I knew that I was right.

Eleanor's eyebrows raised with my disclosure.

Douglas laughed. "Mother certainly knows her jewelry. Don't you, Mother? And is very fond of it, too. Why I remember just some months ago when she lost this topaz-and-gold brooch. How she carried on. One would have thought that the damn piece was worth millions of dollars!"

I smiled politely as Douglas told the story, but it was Eleanor who caught my attention. Her sturdy face was clear, almost bloodless. Her jaw was clenched, making her cheeks stand out like tiny puffs. I noticed the vein throbbing in her short, stocky neck. Her brown eyes widened and protruded slightly, and her smile had jelled into an expression of repressed fear. At that moment, if I had reached across the table and gently touched her hand, she would have screamed in terror. I was sure of it.

"Now, now, Douglas," she said, having trouble keeping her high-pitched voice under control. The edge of desperation was clearly evident, at least to me.

I sneaked a sideways glance to Colin, needing to see if he had any reaction to Eleanor's strange behavior. But he was staring straight ahead, as though blocking out everything around him.

"The brooch had sentimental value, after all," Eleanor continued. The redness was beginning to leave her cheeks. "Your father had given it to me on our first wedding anniversary."

Douglas patted her hand as a silent apology, and she seemed to be much more relaxed with the gesture.

My mind reeled with a bevy of thoughts. None of which seemed to make any sense. But one thing was certain. There was something more to this story than just being a humorous family anecdote. Eleanor was completely terrified at the mention of her lost brooch. But why? Was there a connection between the jewelry and something horrible that might have happened to her? To someone else? I struggled to control my curiosity.

The orchestra, which had been entertaining the crowd with softer, quieter melodies during the meal, now picked up its pace with a lovely waltz.

Colin stood, towering over the rest of us. Gently, he lifted my chin and delved into my eyes. "Dance with me, Britanny." He reached down for my hand, and more than willingly, I slipped mine into his palm.

My spirits soared as Colin spun me around

the dance floor. Except for the music, all the noise and chatter seemed to fade away. I was conscious only of his nearness and the way my body shaped itself to his. His fingers splayed firmly across my back. I was aware of his firm chest and the long graceful span of his thighs as we moved together. I felt my heart skip again and again. I loved being in his arms, knowing the pleasure of feeling him.

The music stopped too soon. Glancing around, I noticed that many of the guests were staring at us, some nodding their approval. As Colin led me off the dance floor, I smiled secretly, enjoying the attention.

After the last dance, the guests began to depart. I nodded pleasantly to Eleanor and thanked her for her invitation. Like any other hostess, she accepted my appreciation graciously, but now there was something different about her, something that was making her as skittish as a frightened kitten. It seemed as though she could not move me out of her house fast enough.

"When are you leaving Raven Manor, Britanny? Surely, you have to get back to your studies," she said. We were alone in the entry hall. Most of the guests had already left. Some were still milling about the ballroom.

"I'm not certain when I'll be leaving, Eleanor. I've become very comfortable there. Very used to things," I told her.

The corner of her left eye twitched.

"In fact, I'm quite taken ..." I paused briefly but carefully, baiting her, "... with Melinda. She's such a precious child."

By her stark expression, I knew she had expected me to say Colin's name. It was shameful for me to tease her that way, but oh, so satisfying.

Still, was it my imagination or had she drawn back from me at the mention of Melinda? My insides fluttered. Did she know? Did Eleanor know that Melinda was Douglas's child?

Eleanor's forced smile made me uneasy and I was glad when Douglas helped me with my cloak and ushered me outside. Colin had gone to find Thomas.

"It was wonderful seeing you again," he said.

Suddenly, I felt compelled to say something to him about my feelings for Colin. I did not want to hurt him, but I had to turn his attentions away from me.

We walked between two carriages that seemed to blend in with the surrounding darkness. Several gaslamps lit the stone path, emitting a spectral blue shimmer that left me cold and restless. Colin was nowhere in sight.

"Douglas..." I hesitated. Something distracted me. Someone ...

Standing by one of the waiting carriages was the shadowy outline of a man. Douglas was unaware of the figure, or he just chose to ignore the man. In any case, I was suddenly aware of an unknown dread.

"Yes, Britanny?" Douglas asked.

But I did not answer. I could not. I choked back a gasp, fear closing my throat. Craggy, sallow features, now visible in the eerie light, peered out at me from the darkness. Eyes, wide and hateful, locked with mine. Every nerve within me leaped and shuddered. This was the man I had seen by the carriage house the morning I had visited the cemetery! The man who had warned me to leave Raven Manor. I was sure of it!

We had already passed by the stranger, yet my heart throbbed. I glanced over my shoulder. He was still staring at me, his features twisted in a repulsive leer.

"Britanny, is anything wrong?" Douglas asked.

"That man. Standing by the carriage. Who is he?"

Douglas looked, then with a low laugh, glanced back at me. "Did he scare you?"

I nodded. *If you only knew*, I added to myself.

"Roger Winfield has that effect on people."

My mind raced, curiosity quickly replacing my fear. "A Roger Winfield used to work at Raven Manor some years ago."

"The same. Mother hired him about a year or so ago as our caretaker. She says he's a good worker, though I haven't seen evidence of it as yet." He grunted. "Scruffy, disgusting man, if you ask me."

"Quite interesting," I murmured.

"More of a coincidence in some respects," he said thoughtfully.

"Meaning?"

"The servant girl who works for Rutledge—"

My heart started to pound. "Evangeline?"

He brightened. "Yes, that's her. Roger Winfield is her father."

Chapter
Twenty-One

Douglas's news had stunned me so that I could not say anything during the drive home from the Garwood party. It wasn't until Colin and I were back at Raven Manor, sitting in the parlor, that I told him about Roger Winfield.

"Winfield," he muttered. "The name sounds familiar—"

"He took care of the stables here," I cut in. "Kingsley Blackwell fired him."

Colin's brow furrowed. "The man who was accused of setting fire to the stables?"

"Yes. And I'm sure he was the man I saw the morning I visited the cemetery."

He looked worried. "Sorcha told me about him once."

I grasped his arm as a thought suddenly evolved. "The man Sorcha wrote about in her journal. The man she said she feared. Could he be Roger Winfield?" A wave of excitement fluttered inside me.

The amber light from the fire flickered in his dark, troubled eyes. "Britanny, what threat could a simpleminded stable hand pose?" he asked. "Why would he have killed Sorcha?"

I shrugged. "Revenge?" The word left a bitter taste in my mouth.

He pursed his lips. "A possibility. And you say he's Evangeline's father?"

"Yes. My 'ghost's' father. It fits, Colin. Don't you see? Evangeline wants to scare me away to protect Winfield."

His hand closed protectively around mine and the warmth of his touch riveted my senses. He said nothing but held my gaze as if trying to read my thoughts. His eyes darkened.

"I don't want you anywhere near the Garwood estate, Britanny. We have enough trouble at Raven Manor. At least here I can protect you."

"But, Colin—" I started to protest.

"No, Britanny," he said more lovingly than firmly. "It's too dangerous. Now that you've come into my life, I'll be damned if I'll lose you. This is a matter for the police."

I jumped from my chair. "The police? What can they do? We have no real evidence that Winfield murdered Sorcha. Evangeline's threats and pranks will mean nothing to them. So who can we accuse?"

"We will tell them what we know, what we believe to be fact, and they can start an investigation."

"By that time it will be too late. I've had this terrible feeling that something horrible is going to happen soon if we don't take matters into our own hands."

Colin rose from the chair. The glow from the fireplace sharpened his features considerably. "Britanny..." he began, smiling wryly.

"Why are you looking at me that way?" I asked, fury building beneath my somewhat civilized demeanor.

"I like the way your eyes flash when you're angry. It's as if all the emeralds in the world gave up their brilliant color just for you."

I sighed deeply. "We have Sorcha's murderer almost in our reach and all you can think about is the color of my eyes."

"I'm thinking about more than just the color of your eyes," he said with a sly smile.

Heat stung my cheeks and my heart quivered expectantly.

Colin caressed my shoulders and drew me against him. "Have I told you how beautiful you looked tonight? How inviting?" His dark eyes smoldered with passion. He bent his head and seized my lips in a warm, moist kiss.

I felt myself melt against his powerful form. "Colin," I whispered as he kissed my cheek. There was nothing else I wanted more than to be in his arms, holding him, loving him. Experiencing all the joys of our love for one another. But now, my heart was heavy. My senses blurred. My emotions too tightly woven.

He pulled back from me with a look that was troubled yet compassionate.

I was puzzled by his expression. "Have I done something to displease you, Colin?" I searched his dark, serious eyes.

He uttered a soft laugh, then hugged me to him again. "My sweet Britanny. Don't you know by now that I'm a part of you? We're part of each other. I know when you are happy, when you are hurting. I can't explain all of it, but it's true."

"And now?" I asked, listening to the sound of his heartbeat.

"I know how troubled you are about all that has happened. I think it's better that you get some rest and we'll talk more tomorrow."

I looked up at him and smiled. "I love you, Colin." The words came easily.

"I love you, too, my sweet. Now go"—he leaned close to my ear—"before the temptation to have you becomes too great to resist."

A kiss soft but lingering sealed our love. I left him there, though reluctantly, and headed for my bedroom where a restless sleep awaited me.

I awoke early to the uncomfortable feeling of something tickling my nose. I bolted up in the bed, my childish fear of bugs far outweighing my need for sleep. But when I realized my mistake, I laughed, even though my heart was still pounding against my rib cage.

There, laying on my pillow, was a lovely red zinnia from the garden, its thin petals like a fire burst. I picked it up and held it to my cheek, enjoying its velvety softness.

My eyes then gravitated to the note. A small piece of paper that had been hiding under the flower. "Meet me by the cliffs this morning. Something important to show you. Colin."

My heart began to race again. I bounded out of bed, hurried to the bathroom, splashed cold water on my face, and readied myself. I dressed quickly, choosing a simple beige blouse and a plum-colored traveling suit. As I twirled my hair into a topknot, I could feel my curiosity rising. What had Colin discovered? Was it something about Sorcha's murder? Or murderer? It had to be. Otherwise, why would he ask me to meet him at the place where she died? He had something to show me. Perhaps he remembered some significant detail that he had until now overlooked.

The eighth chime of the clock in the foyer ended as my foot hit the last step.

"Margaret!" I called as I neared the kitchen.

She was busily cracking eggs into a bowl when I appeared at her side.

"Child, why all the fuss? You sound as though you're in an absolute tither. I thought you'd still be dreaming about the party."

"Margaret, did Mr. Rutledge leave the house?" I asked.

"Yes. Early, in fact. But—"

I hurried to the kitchen door. "Good. Then it's true. He left a message for me to meet him. I'm taking Butternut. I'll be back soon."

She stopped tending the eggs. "Meet him where? Where are you going in this weather? It's not safe."

I opened the door. Cold, damp air rushed over me and the forlorn gray light of the unpleasant morning filtered into the kitchen. Dark, thick clouds anchored to the sky threatened rain.

"I'll be all right, Margaret," I assured her. As I dashed out the door, the last thing I saw was her fretful face.

My feet ached by the time I reached the stables. Thomas was there, and catching my breath, I asked him to saddle and bridle Butternut. He did so without question, for which I was glad.

The damp air cut through my clothes and skin. My teeth chattered from a combination of the cold and Butternut's gait. A low-lying mist clung to the earth, barely making the

Suzanne Hoos

horse's hooves visible. In all this grayness, I silently prayed that I would find my way to the cliffs.

The rushing sound of angry water intensified as the trees thinned. The harsh smell of the sea air burned my nostrils and lungs. Butternut snorted. I pulled back on the reins, slowing his stride. The fog was thicker here, more like a blanket of snow than some aimlessly floating mist. A steady wind swirled around me and roared in my ears.

I urged Butternut onward until I sensed I was in a clearing. Consumed with a potent surge of energy and hope, I knew I had finally arrived at the place where Sorcha had been killed.

I brought Butternut to a halt and dismounted. Rounded stones buckled the soles of my soft leather shoes.

"Colin!" I called over the mighty torrents. "It's me! Britanny!"

I waited and listened. When there was no answer, I called again. Still nothing.

Perhaps something had delayed him. But what? A strange nervousness overcame me.

Stop it, Britanny, I scolded myself. *Colin will be here.*

I walked, rather I paced back and forth, squinting, trying to see past the fog that was now starting to lift. Minutes dragged on, making my waiting for Colin seem like an eternity. A terrible uneasiness settled in my stomach.

The wind was picking up. Should I return to the house? Was it possible that Colin and I had missed one another in our efforts to be together?

My decision made, I headed toward Butternut, now eager to get back to Raven Manor. I lurched forward suddenly, and my ankle wrenched beneath me. I grasped for Butternut's mane, but my reach fell short, and I tumbled to the uneven ground. Though the pain in my ankle was slight, I cried out. It was the unexpected fall that had frightened me.

I felt Butternut's soft, warm muzzle gently pushing against my shoulder, as if offering his assistance. I laughed heartily, even though hot, salty tears stung my cheeks.

"Always the gentleman," I quipped.

Using my hands as leverage, I started to get up when something pinched the fleshy underside of my right thumb.

"Oh!" I cried, pulling my hand back. A pin dot of blood stained my flesh. Instinctively, I drew the redness from the tiny wound by gently sucking my thumb. In a matter of seconds the stinging stopped. Carefully, I eyed the ground for whatever barb had inflicted the swift, but sharp, bite.

I drew a breath and frowned. I had expected a stiff pine needle or cocklebur to be the culprit, but when I had brushed away the smattering of gravel and dead leaves, I saw I was wrong. Very wrong indeed.

341

The brooch was upside down, the pin clasp unhooked and upright. Something else caught my eye. On the back was an inscription. "To *EG* Love *LG*." I turned it over. A lovely amber stone sparkled even in the dreary weather.

Like a dangerous, hidden current, Douglas's words flooded my thoughts. "Months ago . . . Topaz-and-gold brooch . . . lost . . . ."

Once again I studied the inscription: *EG*—Eleanor Garwood. *LG*—Lance Garwood.

Douglas had described his mother as frantic when she lost the piece of jewelry. And Eleanor's face was bloodless and frightened as she listened to her son innocently tell the story.

Suddenly, I couldn't breathe. My heart thumped wildly, and terror possessed me. I had to get back to Raven Manor. Colin had to know about this!

My hand wrapped tightly around the brooch, I once again wrestled to my feet.

"Bri–tan–eee."

The voice was low, almost inviting.

"Colin?" I whispered, my eyes darting. The mist had cleared considerably, yet I saw no one. Butternut whinnied and pawed the ground nervously.

"Easy, boy," I whispered, stroking the side of his face.

"Briii–tan–eee."

Every nerve in my body leaped and shuddered. "Who's there?" I shouted. "Show yourself!"

"I'm here, Britanny. I'm all around you. Please come with me. Don't leave me alone." The voice was louder now, closer.

"Stop it!" I cried, more angry than fearful.

And then I saw her. The slight form. The long, dark hair covering most of her face. She was standing behind me at the edge of the clearing.

"Who are you?" I shouted.

She did not answer but started to walk toward me. The wind blew the hair away from her face and I could see the eyes now, scornful and full of contempt.

"Evangeline!" I cried out suddenly, and the figure stopped in mid-step. There was fright in those ice-blue eyes now. "Evangeline, I know it's you. I know you've been disguising yourself as Sorcha to try to scare me away from Raven Manor. Away from Douglas."

My words seemed to paralyze her. She didn't move, but stared blankly at me, her face totally devoid of any sign of recognition.

This was my chance. I lunged for her and before she knew what was happening, I had grabbed her by the arm. She winced, yet I held on tightly. With my free hand, I took hold of the wig and yanked it from her head.

"Why, Evangeline?" I said in a strangled voice, throwing the hairpiece aside. "Why are you doing this? Why?"

She fought me, struggling to get free. But I

343

held on, determined to learn the truth from her.

"Let her go!" A voice behind me growled in a threatening tone.

Evangeline took advantage of my surprise and wrenched herself from my grasp. "Little fool!" she hissed.

I turned, trying to ignore the wild beating of my heart.

"Winfield," I whispered hoarsely. His maniacal grin sent a shiver through me. But it wasn't just his horrid presence that made my blood run cold. For standing beside him, her face a combination of smugness and contempt, was Eleanor Garwood.

Chapter
Twenty-Two

"Eleanor," I said calmly as if expecting her.

"Well, well, Britanny. I'm glad you could make it to our little gathering." She was poised, unwavering. Her face had taken on a watchful, determined look, like that of a cat about to pounce on a bird.

Seeing her here, like this, with her two cohorts, made me realize that I had been tricked. A hard knot of fear began to grow in my stomach.

"Colin isn't coming. He didn't write that message, did he?" I turned to Evangeline. "You wrote the note. You lured me here."

Her angular features sharpened with her complacent look.

"You're a very clever girl, Britanny," Eleanor said. "But see where that cleverness has gotten you?"

My pulse quickened. Blood coursed through my veins like a flash fire. "You used the same type of letter to lure Sorcha here. Only you used Douglas's name. You killed her, didn't you?"

"My, my. You're more than clever, Britanny. You're brilliant." Eleanor addressed her repulsive partners, "We have a veritable genius on our hands."

I had enough of her despicable comments. "I demand to know what you want from me!" I shouted.

"You're in no position to demand anything!" Her brown eyes sparked. Her nostrils flared. "How dare you even talk to me that way. Those days, my dear girl, are over."

I frowned but kept silent.

"Funny how birds of a feather ... Well, you know the rest. You're just like Sorcha. Two of a kind. Always giving orders."

"What are you babbling about?" I asked.

"Working for the Blackwells. You do remember me, don't you?"

"Yes. Your real name is Ellie McDonald."

She smiled. "And I remember you, Miss St. James. A poor, little waif who just happened to befriend the daughter of one of the wealthiest men in the country. How lucky you were."

"You're accusing me of something you know nothing about. Sorcha and I were true friends, and not because she came from a privileged family," I said, defending myself.

"But you so enjoyed that kind of life, didn't you? You and your precious friend. 'Ellie, fetch our lunch,' and 'Ellie, put away our things.' Oh, you two had a fine time telling me what to do."

"We were children. You can't blame us for that."

She snorted. "No, I can't blame you. But children do learn by what they see and hear. Diedre Blackwell was the real thorn in my side."

"Sorcha's mother?"

"She took great pleasure in ordering me around. She was jealous of me, you know. I was younger and prettier than her and she knew her husband took a fancy to me."

The water thundered below us, the clamorous sound echoing off the glossy gray-brown cliffs. I stared at Eleanor, watching her with macabre fascination. Her rather attractive features began to twist into a hideously cruel expression.

My eyes traveled up and down her expensive wine-colored traveling suit and plumed hat. "You seem to have done all right for yourself," I said.

"Oh, yes," she answered proudly. "I suppose, in a strange way, I have Diedre Blackwell to thank for what I have. After she fired me, I had to learn how to claw my way through the dirty little secrets of the rich to become just like them."

"Fire you? Margaret told me you left of your own accord."

"Margaret's getting senile," she scoffed. "Or maybe the poor wretched creature was never told the real story. Diedre caught Kingsley and me in my bed one afternoon. Seeing her husband's naked and flabby body rubbing against my taut, desirous flesh made her insane with jealousy. Oh, and the names she called me. Whore! Slut! She ordered me out of the house that very night. She even threatened to kill me."

I took a deep breath. I could not believe what she was saying. "And Kingsley?"

"The bastard," she shot back. "Dierdre forgave him after he told her some cock-and-bull story about me drugging him with laudanum. Called me a witch. Told her I was the one who seduced him!" Her eyes glittered with hate. "It was Kingsley Blackwell who forced his way into my room, tore my clothes, and defiled me!" She stared past me and out to the cliffs. "After I was thrown out of Raven Manor, I had nowhere to go, no one to turn to. It wasn't long ago that I stood here on the edge of these cliffs, contemplating my own death. If Lance Garwood had not ridden by when he did, and stopped me from taking my own life—" She looked at me now, the trancelike state gone from her face. "But that's not why I've brought you here, is it?"

My hands at my side, I clenched my fingers into fists. "Why, then? What do you want from me?"

"Why, your life, Britanny. You know too much. You know I was responsible for Sorcha's death. I even arranged the Blackwells' 'accident.'"

My eyes widened. "You killed Sorcha's parents?"

"Oh my! I thought you had that figured out. Maybe you're not as clever as I thought." She began to laugh, a sinister, hideous laugh that brought a chill to my entire being. "Actually, Winfield here did the real work. Loosened their carriage wheels. Worked charmingly, wouldn't you say?"

There was no doubt in my mind. Eleanor Garwood was a madwoman. "But why? Why did you do such horrible things? You had everything you've ever wanted."

"Revenge, my dear. Sweet, pure, and simple revenge." She smiled. "Even Winfield enjoyed himself with that plan."

He nodded and grinned, showing his jagged, broken teeth. "Had a score to settle with that blackhearted bastard. Had me fired from my stable-hand job. I didn't mean to start that fire.

He could've given me a second chance." He gave a low laugh. "Well, now he and his wife can burn in hell for what they did to me."

My heart thumped wildly. This was like a nightmare from which I could not awaken. "But why Sorcha? Why did you kill her?" Tears welled in my eyes, threatening to spill onto my numbed cheeks.

"I did it because of my son. When I married Lance Garwood, I owed him everything, even my life. And when he died, he asked me to look after Douglas always, as though he were my own. I was only fulfilling Lance's last wish."

"But Douglas loved Sorcha. They have a baby! How could you have taken her away from him?"

"That was the Blackwells' doing. They were the ones who sent Sorcha away. They were the ones who were so ashamed of having an illegitimate grandchild that they forced her to marry some man she didn't know."

I realized that Eleanor did not know the truth about Colin's and Sorcha's relationship. She was not aware that Colin was in fact Sorcha's half brother.

"I thought she'd stay away for good. Give Douglas a chance to forget about her. But that damned 'accident' brought her back to Raven Manor." She scowled. "Douglas was still in love with her, even though she was married. He was a fool. He pursued her relentlessly, especially when she told him about the baby. He told me he wasn't going to rest until he had convinced Sorcha to divorce Colin and marry him. I had to stop him. Think of the scandal that would have made! No, I would not allow such a thing to happen. I would not have the name of Garwood tarnished. Not for a Blackwell. Never!"

A single tear rolled down my face, searing my cheek. "So, you pushed her to her death."

"I only managed to get her to this place. In fact, it was the same way I got you here. Evangeline gave Sorcha a note, saying it was from Douglas and that he wanted to meet her by the cliffs. Evangeline was a stranger to Raven Manor then. A stranger to Sorcha. But Sorcha believed her. Of course, I had written the note. And when she rushed here to meet her lover, she found me instead. We argued. I told her to leave Raven Manor while she still had the chance. To go back to Europe with her husband and child and leave Douglas alone." Her lips curled back in a cruel smile. "I even had the pleasure of telling her about her 'wonderful' father whom she adored, and how he had raped me, and about her mother throwing me out of the house with nothing but the clothes on my back. She was quite stunned with that information. Still, she was stubborn. Said she loved Douglas more than anyone and that despite my feelings, they were going to be together. Little fool! Anyway, it was Winfield who pushed her."

351

Suzanne Hoos

"I told you I didn't want to do that, Mrs. Garwood." Winfield suddenly spoke up, his eyes as wide as saucers. "Miss Sorcha, she was good to me when I worked there. I liked her, I did. You forced me to kill her."

"It was either that or jail. After all, only I knew that you caused the Blackwells to have that carriage accident. No one would ever believe that I could be involved. Not Lance Garwood's widow."

Winfield hung his head, saying nothing.

I looked at Eleanor, my blood boiling. "You threatened Sorcha before you killed her, didn't you? Colin said she had been frightened over something—or someone. She never told him, though."

"Then she was smarter than I gave her credit for. Yes, I 'threatened her' as you say. I even had Winfield play along. I warned her that harm would come to Colin if she should cross me." Eleanor suddenly looked thoughtful. "Of course, I would never hurt such a handsome, virile man as Colin Rutledge. After Sorcha was out of the way, I was going to have him for myself." She glared at me. "And I almost did—until you came to Raven Manor."

"Is that why you want to kill me? Because Colin's in love with me?"

"Well, that, but mostly because you learned the truth about Sorcha's death. You're a headstrong, little miss, my dear Britanny. I knew you would never accept the fact that Sorcha

352

killed herself. You knew that someone murdered her. Now, I'm afraid your determination has placed you in a very dangerous position. For you see, now you must be dealt with in the same manner your dear friend was." Her features fell with a distorted look of sorrow. "You understand why this has to be done, don't you, Britanny? The Garwood name *has* to be protected at all costs." A glazed look veiled her eyes. "I promised my husband that I would do so. I promised him on his death bed."

No one noticed that I had taken a few steps back. If I could manage to get to Butternut, I would be able to escape. I kept talking, though, so as not to arouse suspicion.

"How is Evangeline involved?" I asked Eleanor.

"I believe you already know that, my dear. She is your 'ghost.' I knew that when you heard about Sorcha's death it would only be a matter of days before you arrived at Raven Manor. I had told Evangeline about you, told her to be on her guard against you. That you would try to steal Douglas away. She's in love with him, you know."

I looked at Evangeline, who confirmed Eleanor's words with a seductive smile.

"When she found out who you were, she tried to frighten you that very same night. Of course, the wig and having her pretend to be Sorcha was all my idea."

"Evangeline, don't you see she's been using

you. Your father, too. You two have just been pawns, doing her dirty work," I said, taking another small step backward. I could almost feel Butternut's hot breath on the back of my neck.

I saw something flash in Evangeline's ice-blue eyes, something that seemed to trigger a thought. "But Douglas is mine, now. You won't have him."

"I was never in love with Douglas. Evangeline. It's Colin I love."

"Is this true?" Evangeline asked Eleanor.

Eleanor frowned. "How can you believe her, after all I've done for you and your father? Of course she's in love with Douglas."

"Evangeline, listen to me," I cried. "Do you think that she's going to allow you, a mere servant girl, to marry her son?" I felt Butternut's muscular flank against my back. *Easy, boy. Don't move. Please, don't move*, I silently prayed.

"You promised me!" Evangeline shouted suddenly. "You said if I did everything you asked, Douglas would marry me."

"Enough of this foolishness!" Eleanor said. "Grab her, Winfield!"

He lunged for me and I sidestepped him, his body slamming into Butternut's solid form. Frightened, the horse reared, but Winfield managed to move out of the way before Butternut's hooves came down on him.

"Don't let her get away!" I heard Eleanor

354

yell above the squalling wind.

My throat was dry. I couldn't breathe. Instinctively, I thrust my hand into the pocket of my skirt and drew out the brooch I had found.

Winfield bolted for me again. With the pin clasp protruding through my clenched fist, I jabbed at his face and pulled downward, leaving a deep, nasty scratch along his cheekbone.

He recoiled in pain, wiping the area with his hand. When he saw the blood from the wound, he snarled like a wild animal. "You little—I'll get you for this!"

I tried once again to mount Butternut, but the horse was too skittish and kept moving back, so that I could not get a firm grip on the saddle. This time Winfield grabbed the back of my skirt. I heard a tearing sound. His one hand clamped around my waist. With the other, he wrenched the brooch free from my grip.

I kicked and screamed as he dragged me over to Eleanor.

"Well, lookey here, Mrs. Garwood. Ain't this what you been searching for all these months? It's that pin you lost." He tossed it to her.

"Seems you've done me a favor, Britanny. This is the only piece of evidence that can incriminate me in Sorcha's death. When Douglas told that story at the party. I saw something in your face. Something that made you suspicious of me. Something ever so slight, but it was there." She held the brooch at arm's length, then put it into her own skirt pocket. "Now, no one will be the wiser."

"Don't be a fool, Eleanor!" I yelled. "Colin knows. I've told him everything. He's always suspected that Sorcha didn't kill herself."

There was a vicious glint in her crazed eyes. She grabbed a clump of my hair and yanked it down hard. I stifled a cry as pain shot through my head.

"Don't lie to me. Colin has too much respect for me to think that I could do such a horrible thing. After you're gone, I'll have that handsome, virile man all to myself. Oh, he'll mourn your death. Probably, even blame himself. But I'll be there for him." She pulled my face closer to hers. I could almost smell her dementedness. "Comforting him. Loving him. And he'll be grateful. Then it will be just a matter of time before our lips touch, before his naked body moves slowly against mine."

"You're insane, Eleanor!" I screamed through gritted teeth. "You'll never get away with this! And you'll never have Colin! He knows I would never take my own life."

She released me then, pushing my head back roughly. She sighed. "Of course he wouldn't believe such a thing. That's why you're going to have an accident. It was foggy, you couldn't see where you were going, and you and your horse plunged to your deaths."

I drew back in horror, knowing what she had

planned. "No! Not Butternut! Leave him alone!" Tears flew down my cheeks like rain.

"My, my. Aren't we the noble one? Worried more about the life of a stupid animal than your own." She waved her hand. "This one bores me, Winfield. Get rid of her."

On Eleanor's command, Winfield began to drag me to the edge of the cliff. I screamed, but the churning waters below swallowed my cries for help. *Think. Britanny. Think...* I dug my heels into the earth, but my efforts were futile. Winfield was bigger and stronger. A wave of dizziness rushed over me as my foot slipped into nothingness. *Colin,* my mind cried. *Colin, I love you!*

"No, Papa! Don't do this! No more killing!"

At the sound of the pleading voice, Winfield turned, bringing me back onto solid ground. Evangeline was rushing toward us.

"Don't you see she's been using us all this time? Please, Papa!"

"Stay back, Evangeline. You don't know what you're saying!" Winfield shouted to his daughter.

"Hurry!" Eleanor snarled. "Do it! Kill her! Now!"

Evangeline did not heed her father's warning. Instead, she grabbed his arm that was wrapped tightly about my waist and pried it loose. A surge of damp air filled my lungs.

But Winfield jerked forward too quickly. Everything around me blurred. I let out a strangled scream as I felt my feet slide out from under me and then my body jolt to a dead stop. There was something solid under my feet. I pushed myself forward and leaned into cold, jagged stone. Each breath was short and agonizing, but nonetheless a reminder that miraculously, I was still alive!

I blinked and the hazy view before my eyes cleared. I looked down and saw that I was tottering on a long ledge of stone no wider than two of my feet. Far below me, the tumultuous St. Lawrence River surged. One misjudged move would cost me my life.

Screams of help reached my ears and at first, I thought they were coming from me. I turned my head. A few feet away from the ledge was Evangeline. She too had fallen with me and now she was clutching desperately to a tree limb that was jutting out from the wall.

"Evangeline!"

My cheek and nose grazed the rough stone as I looked straight up. Winfield was there, kneeling on the ground above us, his eyes locked on his daughter.

"Papa! Help me!" she cried.

Her panic-strickened movements were causing the limb to bend with her weight. Her hands slipped slightly. Even in my own dangerous situation, I knew I had to do something to help her. I feared that the limb would break at any moment.

Her dangling feet brushed over the ledge.

Though I saw that it was narrower than the section I stood on, I was sure that, carefully executed, she could drop herself down onto the overhang.

"Evangeline!" I shouted over the raging river. "Let go of the limb! There's a ledge below you."

When she looked over at me, her features displayed pure panic. I wasn't even sure if she had heard me.

"A ledge!" I said again. "Below you!"

"Do what she tells you, Evangeline!" Winfield yelled from above. "You'll be saved!"

But Evangeline only dangled helplessly, too afraid to listen to her father or me.

There was only one thing left to do if Evangeline's life was to be spared. Taking a deep breath, I began to inch my way to where she was. The jagged stone scraped against my face, arms, and body. Still, I continued, with a prayer on my lips, and my heart lodged in my throat. If I could just reach her, I might be able to hook my arm about her waist and pull her to safety.

The ledge was slick with the mist of the river. Once my foot slipped and I grabbed onto the edge of one of the larger boulders that protruded from the wall. I pulled myself into the wall and caught what was left of my breath.

Even over the raging tumult, I heard the sound of the limb cracking. Evangeline's face twisted in fear. She tried to hoist herself up, but the branch only began to bend downward.

"Don't move!" I shouted. As I fought for my life and Evangeline's, I didn't notice Eleanor standing above us until it was too late.

"Winfield, you fool," she said, her voice seething with anger. "You're of no use to me anymore."

My mind screamed. I knew what she planned to do, and before I could warn Winfield, she shoved him forward. He tumbled past me and I closed my eyes when I heard his screams.

"Papa!" Evangeline cried out in terror.

Everything happened so fast. She twisted and I watched her body wrench downward. I heard the final snap of the limb and Evangeline's high-pitched scream.

"Evangeline!" I yelled. But it was too late. She had already joined her father in death.

I gasped for breath. My throat was dry. I felt a heaving in the pit of my stomach, but I held back the bile. I looked up. Eleanor was peering down at me, her features distorted with an air of conquest.

"You're more trouble to me than you're worth, Miss St. James. But you can't hold on forever. Soon, you too will be gone. Then I will have Colin all to myself."

She was right. Already my legs and arms were numbed by the cold, my body weakened from the strain of my determination. But though the physical strain was becoming too much to bear, my mental capabilities were stronger than ever. I thought of Melinda, of Margaret, and especially of Colin. His face, his touch, our lovemaking, our future. All of those visions swirling inside my head kept my spirits high and strengthened my will to live.

"Britanny! Britanny!" Someone was shouting my name. It was then I heard Eleanor's muffled cries. She disappeared from my sight suddenly and in her place was Colin. Was I seeing things?

"Colin," I gasped. "Is it really you?"

"Yes, love," he said as he lay prone, his body halfway over the edge. His face was pale, his eyes reflected my fright. He stretched his arm down toward me, but his reach fell short and he edged further over the cliff. "Quickly, give me your hand!"

I was paralyzed with terror as I thought of Evangeline's gruesome end. "No. No, I can't. I'm afraid."

"Britanny, you can do it. You must. Just one hand. Reach up and I'll have you. Please, Britanny. You must do this. Britanny, *look at me!*"

"I'm frightened, Colin. I'm frightened to let go."

"I know you are, but you have to do this. You have to help me. I promise I won't let you fall, but I can't keep that promise unless you reach up to me."

Hearing the conviction in Colin's voice gave me the courage to pry my fingers away from the jagged rock. My eyes ravaged with tears, I looked up at him. His dark eyes pleaded with me. Slowly, carefully, I reached up to him. His powerful grasp crushed my wrist.

"I have you, Britanny," he shouted. "Now give me the other hand."

I felt Colin's love soar through me. I let go my other hand from the rock. His arm stretched down to mine and we clasped together like iron bands. My feet left the ledge as I dangled between life and death. I gasped with terror as Colin drew me upward and into his waiting arms. He crushed me to him.

"It's all right, Britanny. You're safe now," he murmured.

Sobbing with wild relief and remembered horror, I felt myself wavering as darkness overcame me.

Chapter
Twenty-Three

The low, booming chime of a clock echoed in the dark recesses of my mind. Something cold touched my forehead. It felt soothing, and I sighed. I heard voices. They were only disjointed sounds at first then pensive whisperings.

"She's coming around."

"I pray she's all right."

It was difficult to wake up, but I opened my eyes to blurred figures hovering over me.

I heard my name. Someone was calling me. Someone's hand was gently stroking my cheek. The shapes above me were slowly coming into focus. I groaned and tried to move.

Suzanne Hoos

"Lie still, Britanny. It's over. It's all over." Colin's calming voice wrapped around me like a warm blanket. "You're home, Britanny. Do you understand? Everything is all right."

Concerned dark eyes peered into mine. He clutched my hand, and I held on, finding comfort in his touch.

I felt a hand upon my forehead. "Margaret?" I sighed feebly.

"Shhh, child. Don't talk. Save your strength," she answered.

I managed a smiled as my gaze drifted to her worried face. My eyes darted about the room. I was back at Raven Manor, lying on the sofa in the parlor. Home with the people I loved.

I caught my breath, suddenly remembering. "Evangeline. Winfield." I said their names in a strangled cry.

Colin looked grim. "There was nothing any of us could have done, Britanny. I'm sorry."

I shuddered openly, reliving the horror of the servant girl and her father plunging toward the boulders below the cliff.

"Oh, Colin. It was Eleanor who had Sorcha killed. Evangeline and Roger were her accomplices, but she was behind all of it."

"I know, my love." He pressed my hand to his lips and kissed my fingers.

"How?"

"Douglas."

I stared at him. "Douglas?"

Another voice came from behind Colin. "I've always suspected my stepmother had a hand in Sorcha's death, Britanny. And last night I found the proof to confirm it."

I struggled to a half-sitting position, my elbows precariously balancing my aching body.

Douglas, his face pale and drawn, could hardly look me in the eye.

"What did you find, Douglas?" I asked.

He sank into one of the leather chairs and sighed deeply. "Notes that Eleanor wrote and some insignificant letter I had written. They were among some papers on her desk. All the notes read the same: 'Sorcha, meet me in the clearing by the bluff. I have something important to tell you. Love. Douglas.' She was duplicating my handwriting. One of those messages finally lured Sorcha to the cliffs."

Douglas's face was racked with pain. The type of pain that comes when someone you love and trust betrays you horribly. My heart ached for him.

"Do you have the letters?" I asked.

"No. The constable took them for evidence along with Eleanor's brooch. It too was found there."

"I know," I said. A sigh escaped my lips. "I was the one who found it."

"Did she tell you why she did such a horrible thing?" Douglas asked, sitting forward on the seat of the chair.

I nodded slowly. Feeling stronger, I told the

three of them the whole ugly story that led up to Eleanor's heinous crime. They all looked quite shocked after I was finished.

"How did you know where I was?" I asked, breaking into their somber moment.

"Douglas came down to the docks early this morning and told me about his discovery," Colin began. "We came back to the house to tell you. When Margaret said you had gone somewhere to meet me because of a message I had left you, I knew you were in terrible danger. Douglas rode back into town to get the police and I went to find you."

I reached for his hand, squeezed it tightly, and smiled gratefully. "Where's Eleanor now?"

"She's in custody at police headquarters," Douglas said, rising from his seat. "What she's done is inexcusable, I know, and I'm not sure I can ever forgive her, but she is my family and I must go to her now."

"Of course you must," I said.

He smiled slightly. "I'm sorry for all the pain and anguish my stepmother caused you and Colin."

"Oh, Douglas," I said, "none of this is your fault. She hurt you, too."

"Thank you, Britanny," he said, looking more at ease. "I only wish the best for the two of you now."

Colin stood and offered his hand in a gesture of friendship. Douglas accepted and the two of them shook hands. "I'm sorry, too, Douglas. There were times when I didn't trust you, but now I know you loved my sister."

So Colin had told Douglas that he was Sorcha's half brother. I was glad. A warm feeling of happiness rose wonderfully inside me.

Colin's gaze briefly met mine and then he turned back to Douglas. "Britanny and I want you to visit Melinda as often as you wish. She is your daughter, after all, and she will know you're her father when she is old enough to understand."

Sunshine seemed to break across Douglas's face. I felt Margaret's hand squeeze my shoulder, and a tear trickled down my cheek.

After Douglas had gone, Margaret hurried off to the kitchen to fix some hot tea and broth for me. Colin and I were finally alone.

He drew me to him, and I closed my eyes, thankful to be in his arms. I shuddered slightly, realizing how close I had come to never seeing him again. I shook the horrid memories from my mind. Colin was right. It was over. All of it. Over.

My gaze was drawn to the portrait above the mantle. Sorcha's silver-blue eyes no longer harbored the fear I had seen when I first came back to Raven Manor. They were as I remembered them—laughing, caring eyes. And now thankful.

When Colin lifted my chin, his black eyes delving into mine, I knew he was right about us, too. I was a part of him. What we had shared had made us a part of each other.

"You haven't changed your mind, have you, Britanny?" he asked. "You will marry me, won't you?"

Once more my eyes rested on Sorcha's face. She seemed to be smiling. I turned back to Colin. "Yes, oh, yes, Colin. I will marry you. I will be your wife."

He bent his head and his lips met mine in a deep, loving kiss.

"Colin," I sighed against his mouth. "I love you."

We parted ever so slightly.

"I love you, *Mrs.* Rutledge," he whispered. And when we kissed again, I knew then that all my desires, everything I'd ever want or need, was right here in my arms.